Christmas at the Chateau

Annabel French is a bestselling author of several contemporary romantic fiction stories for HarperCollins. Based in south-east England with her family, when she's not busy locked in her study writing, or daydreaming, she can be seen in the great outdoors, running after her two dogs, Wotsit and Skips. This is the second novel in the chateau series.

Also by Annabel French:

Summer at the Chateau

ANNABEL FRENCH

Christmas at the Chateau

avon.

Published by AVON
A division of HarperCollins*Publishers*
1 London Bridge Street
London SE1 9GF

www.harpercollins.co.uk

HarperCollins*Publishers*
Macken House, 39/40 Mayor Street Upper
Dublin 1
D01 C9W8

A Paperback Original 2023

1

First published in Great Britain by HarperCollins*Publishers* 2023

A catalogue copy of this book is available from the British Library.

ISBN: 978-0-00-855824-6

Typeset in Birka by Palimpsest Book Production Ltd, Falkirk, Stirlingshire

Printed and bound in the UK using
100% Renewable Electricity by CPI Group (UK) Ltd

*To all the wonderful romance
readers who love a happy ever after!*

Chapter 1

Naomi Winters pressed her fingernails into the palm of her hand, fighting the urge to glare at her soon-to-be ex-husband across the pale fake-wood table of the meeting room and call him something obscene. She was doing her best to be a grown-up about the whole divorce thing, but there was only so much a woman could take in one sitting.

The words of their respective solicitors drifted in the air as they finally came to an agreement of how their money, their possessions, their life together would be split, and Ollie's passive gaze made her want to throw something at him. His green eyes that she'd found so attractive when they'd first met were gazing down, and his mouth was fixed in what she'd always called his 'constipated accountant' face: an expression as devoid of emotion as a particularly emotionless robot.

Unfortunately, she hadn't brought anything to the meeting except for her handbag – the expensive one she'd treated to herself to – and she didn't want to fling that his way. She eyed up her solicitor's heavy-looking Filofax that was sitting on the desk between them. She didn't think people had those nowadays, but she was happy he'd bought it; it would be perfect to inflict a decent amount of damage if she put some power behind it. Without thinking she picked it up, weighing it up in her hand, earning confused glances from everyone at the table. She put it back down, pretending that what she'd just done was completely normal.

Ollie still hadn't looked at her.

What was he actually looking at? she wondered, knowing the solicitor had everything in hand. The table top was clearly some kind of veneer, which was surprising given he'd insisted on using one of the top divorce lawyers in London. She was using a contact of one of her colleagues and so far he was doing a pretty good job. She knew from her own legal experience, it was better to let the solicitor do their job than continue to interrupt them.

Rain pelted the window, drawing her attention away from the table. She stared out of the small window seeing nothing but the grey, blurry outline of office blocks and the enormous buildings that clustered London's skyline.

Ollie suddenly whispered something to his solicitor and then returned to staring at the table top. Naomi was tempted to wave her hand in front of his face or ask him what was so mesmerising about a layer of fake pine.

'And what about the futon?' Ollie's solicitor asked. She

was older than Naomi, her grey hair tied back into a severe bun with a decorative hairpin protruding from it. Could she use that to jab her ex-husband with?

'I'm sorry?' Naomi raised her eyes for the first time, sure she must have misheard.

'The futon. In the spare bedroom. My client would prefer for that to come with him to his new property.'

His new property. That he had a 'new property' – a little flat all of his own and they were now totally separate entities – made her burn with anger. She'd had no idea this was coming and even a year later, she still hadn't got used to it.

'Well, this isn't on Mr Epps's list that was submitted to us before the proceeding,' her solicitor began.

'No, but he has decided he'd like it, and as he purchased it . . . We have receipts if necessary.'

Of course he did. Ollie only ever threw his receipts out after seven financial years had passed. Her solicitor went to speak again to argue, but Naomi had to stop him. She leaned over and whispered in his ear. He whispered back.

'He can have it,' Naomi said, deliberately answering so Ollie would have to look at her.

He didn't. His eyes were still pinned down. Had he been hypnotised? She'd seen a video once where someone had done that to a chicken. Was that what had happened? How could it be that they'd been together for so many years, shared so much, and yet now, he couldn't, or wouldn't, even look at her?

3

'Are you sure?' Ollie's solicitor asked. 'I'm sorry it wasn't on the original list. We're just trying to get everything sorted out today and this came up at the last minute.'

In what circumstance did a futon come up at the last minute?

'Perfectly sure,' she replied, calmly. 'He can futon away.'

As quickly as the annoyance came, it was gone, and a wave of sadness rushed over Naomi. Without thinking, she did what she'd always done when an uncomfortable emotion hit her; she pushed a hand through her chin-length caramel-blonde hair, tucking it behind her ear and glanced at the ceiling. She'd always found drawing her attention to the floor, the ceiling, a corner of the room gave her a moment to compose herself.

Even though it was November, the freezing air-conditioning hit her face, cooling her flushed cheeks. Ollie still refused to look at her, but his eyes had now shifted from the laminate table top to the notepad he'd brought with him. He hadn't written a single word and the page was pristine white. His pen began to trace a doodle on the paper, denting the surface. Ah, she'd annoyed him with her futon comment. She felt rather pleased with herself if only because he'd finally given her some sort of reaction. She wasn't one for splashing her emotions all over the place and neither was Ollie, but she had to know something was going on below the surface. She had to know this was as hard for him as it was for her.

Not long and this would be over, she told herself. A year of battling after dealing with the out-of-the-blue announcement that he no longer wanted to be married to her would finally be finished and they'd never have to sit in the same room again. She exhaled a long, slow breath.

The conversation continued as one solicitor listed things and the other gave a yes or no. It was all very straightforward. After what felt like an eternity had passed, Naomi – feeling aged beyond her years – watched as the two solicitors stood and shook hands. They chatted away as if they hadn't just had their daggers drawn over who got possession of the KitchenAid mixer, the king-size mattress or the SMEG fridge. She rose, and Ollie placed his clean notepad back in his bag. He really hadn't needed to get it out at all but that's what he was like: methodical, organised, prepared for every eventuality.

They stood facing each other across the table, Naomi's eyes darting once more to the Filofax knowing this might be her last chance to fling it at him.

'I hope we can keep things amicable from now on, Naomi,' he said, completely avoiding eye contact.

Her hand reached towards it but the solicitor, without realising what was going through her mind, moved it away. It was true she hadn't taken the news of his intention to divorce her particularly well, especially as he'd done it just before Christmas last year and had then bolted to his parents' house in Hertfordshire. But she hadn't destroyed his clothes, keyed his ridiculously expensive Mercedes or broken any of his favourite arty glass ornaments. Instead, she'd yelled at him while he'd collected his clothes and had argued tooth and nail for the things she'd brought to their relationship. It wasn't much. For all the wealth and financial security she had now, she'd started off with very little and what she had brought to their relationship, she wanted to keep.

Ollie lifted his chin. He'd always been arrogant. She hadn't seen it like that at first. She'd thought it was confidence but over the last year she'd recognised it for what it was: a feeling of superiority. One that she realised now had always, in some ways, been directed at her.

'And I'm sorry things didn't work out,' he added. His tone was robotic too, she reflected now.

He'd said something similar to her before when they'd had meetings like this and she wondered if it was more for the benefit of others, rather than something he actually meant. A stream of expletives entered her head but instead she found herself saying, 'Yeah, me too,' in a way that sounded far more sarcastic than she'd intended. She was genuinely sorry things had turned out the way they had. She still didn't really understand what he'd meant when he'd said he thought it was better they ended things because she hadn't been 'all in' for a long time. What did that even mean? Wasn't 'all in' something football players said to each other at the start of matches? It sounded like meaningless mumbo jumbo to her. Nothing more than an excuse.

She flashed him a small smile and gave a shrug, unsure what else to do. Then he scarpered as quickly as possible, his Italian leather brogues clacking on the floor. He hadn't even put his coat on before he left the room, walking away with the thick, expensive wool and cashmere blend draped over his arm, his briefcase in the other hand. As he reached the door, he gave a final quick glance over his shoulder, but Naomi couldn't tell if he was looking at her or the solicitor following him outside. They'd both been lurking, possibly making sure they didn't come to blows after how heated some of her and Ollie's exchanges had been.

At least it was done now. The worst bit was over and thankfully they'd agreed she could stay in the house. He got the car, which was fine. No one really needed a car in London anyway and she never needed to drive anywhere in the city. It was always easier to get on the tube. She'd never really seen the point in having a two-seater sports car in a built-up city and he'd hardly ever managed to drive it over thirty miles an hour with all the traffic.

Naomi exchanged pleasantries with her solicitor, thanking him for everything he'd done, and after giving Ollie a few minutes to get all the way out of the building so they wouldn't have to share the lift, she too made her way outside.

That was it. They wouldn't have to face each other again and everything now, her solicitor assured her, could be done via paperwork. She wrapped her coat tighter around her as she stepped outside into the cold London streets. It was still raining but she was glad to be out of that office and into the fresh air.

She'd taken the day off work not knowing how long the meeting would take. As it was, it had only been a few hours, but those hours had been arduous, and a headache pounded behind her eyes. She pressed her fingers to her temples, squeezing to try and ease the tension. Perhaps she needed a drink. Water rather than something alcoholic. She was glad she didn't have to return to the office.

The pavements were heavy with crowds: tourists and shoppers darting to and fro, Londoners rushing to wherever they needed to be. Although the street she was on didn't have giant Christmas lights hanging overhead, you could still feel that special atmosphere that London had at this time of year. It seemed to emanate from the people around her and she made sure not to bash into anyone, or else she might catch it.

She took her phone from her pocket. Despite having her 'out of office' on, she could see the notifications lighting up her phone with urgent emails and voicemails that had come in while she'd been sitting across from Ollie. Her hand began vibrating and she could see her secretary was ringing her, but she decided to push the phone back into her pocket. Corporate law demanded long hours, but she couldn't work overtime today. She didn't have the capacity to deal with anyone. Things normally slowed down over Christmas and Naomi wondered what she would do then, when the office was closed. She didn't exactly love her job anymore but what would she do without it when everyone else was posting pictures of stupid Christmas jumpers and enormous Christmas Day dinners? A sense of dread washed over her and she pushed the thought away. She'd think about that later. The last few hours had been draining enough.

She watched the happy shoppers passing in front of her for a few minutes, feeling a frown form on her face. Christmas, in her opinion, was dramatically overrated. The pressure to buy perfect presents, to make sure every type of food was purchased because the shops were closing for one whole day, the excess of it all. It was silly, if you asked her. Ridiculous. And why did it start so early? November was, quite frankly, obscene. How she'd ever bought into it all when she was an intelligent woman baffled her. Christmas was commercialised nonsense designed to give children something to look forward to in winter.

Ignoring the familiar piercing sound of Mariah Carey's whistle notes and other 'classic' Christmas songs clamouring through shop doorways, she made her way around the crowds. She passed a family gazing at the obscenely bright Christmas lights in a particularly gaudy shop window, the child's eyes wide in wonder, and she felt a twinge deep inside. She brushed it off as hunger and pushed on towards home – her home, as it was now – though she wasn't even sure that was where she wanted to be.

Chapter 2

'Full Bridget Jones,' Naomi muttered to herself as she trudged to the living room in her fluffy pyjamas, chocolate ice cream tub grasped tightly. The spoon stuck out of her mouth as she navigated towards the sofa, attempting not to spill the wine in her other hand. She wasn't quite at the singing 'All By Myself' stage just yet, but she was getting close.

She flopped down on the sofa, pulling a blanket over her knees and snuggling into the luxurious seats as she switched on another of her favourite romcoms. Before, she'd always loved *The Holiday* with Cameron Diaz and Kate Winslet, but since last year she couldn't bear to watch it. Being broken up with at Christmas had left a horrible taste in her mouth. One she could feel again now almost ruining her chocolate ice cream. She stuffed another spoonful in instead and allowed her eyes to wander to *The Proposal* with Sandra Bullock. A classic.

She'd turned on the posh-looking electric fire Ollie had had installed not long after they'd moved in. It gave off a pathetic amount of heat, and she couldn't help missing the not so attractive but hotter than the sun one her parents still had at their house. Even with that and the underfloor heating on, she shivered uncontrollably.

The meeting earlier had, in some ways, been like breaking up all over again. In fact, it was worse. When she and Ollie had first split up, after his horrible announcement, she'd assumed he was having some sort of midlife crisis and thought they'd get back together. He couldn't possibly want to throw away the ten years they'd been an item. They'd built a wonderful, comfortable life together full of all the things successful couples had: designer clothes, a nice house in an expensive part of London, luxury holidays. Okay, it hadn't been the most passionate of marriages but not every day was like that when you'd been with someone for such a long time. At least they hadn't got to the 'There's fifteen minutes of half-time; fancy a quick one?' stage.

Naomi circled her feet, feeling the soft fabric brush against a bit of bare skin where her fluffy sock had rolled down. The house she and Ollie had shared was full of possessions. A lifetime of things they'd accumulated, and all this material comfort had made her feel safe. That sort of safety was important to her. Yet, a part of her wasn't going to miss it. A part of her was looking forward to most of it going to Ollie's new flat. She'd loved Ollie and under-stood his love for the trappings of life: a top-of-the-range coffee machine that even ground the beans, a fancy hob and oven that were more like a computer, but deep down she'd never got used to it. To go from having nothing to so much still made her uneasy. With her salary she could afford whatever she wanted, but nothing had made her feel more secure than knowing that money was in the bank. There'd been so many times growing up when it hadn't been, and she'd seen the stress that had caused her parents.

Naomi's eyes fell from the TV screen to the photo of her adoptive parents sitting on the glass coffee table at the end of the sofa. They hadn't had much money, but they'd given her a wonderful upbringing she was more than a little grateful for. Just as her mind was about to wander down a terrifying road of what might have happened had she not been assigned to them to be fostered and then later adopted by them, her phone rang. They'd been due to call her today knowing what was going on. She glanced at the screen but saw her best friend Mia's name flash up along with a photo of her with a cheesy grin and her beautiful, happy face staring out.

'Hey, you,' Naomi answered, wedging the phone between her shoulder and ear so she could shovel some more ice cream into her mouth.

'You had better not be slobbing around in your pyjamas feeling sorry for yourself,' Mia said. Her Swiss-German accent was almost undetectable when she spoke English – though she could speak both German, French and even Italian fluently.

Naomi paused, and her eyes slid down the thick, pink pyjamas decorated with white clouds, landing on matching pink bed socks. She wiggled her toes. 'Of course I'm not. I'm just having dinner.'

'Oh, *excusé*. Shall I call back later?' The concern in her voice sent a pang of guilt through Naomi.

'No, no. It's fine. I can eat and talk.'

The rain was once again battering the windows and Naomi pulled the blanket higher over her. The weather was cold and dreary and didn't show any signs of easing off yet.

'Wait a minute,' Mia said, her voice ringing with suspicion. 'What's for dinner?'

'Umm, ice cream.'

'Naomi!' She'd screeched it so loudly Naomi instinctively pulled the phone away from her ear to protect her eardrum. 'That's not dinner that's pudding.'

'I skipped to dessert. I couldn't bear cooking after today.'

'So you haven't really eaten anything, have you?'

'This is what I fancied. It's soul food.'

'Are you drinking?'

'No.' Silence. 'Yes.'

'So you're basically drinking on an empty stomach.'

'No, I've eaten half a carton of ice cream.' She patted her food baby belly. 'And that's been more than enough.'

'I am not happy about this,' Mia said in her usually bossy tones. 'I'm not happy about this at all.'

'Well join the club but what can we do. Divorce is a bi—'

'Have you cried yet?'

Naomi scowled. 'Not yet and I don't intend to. I told you. I don't cry over men. They're not worth it.'

It had been a running joke between them since they'd met at university that Naomi never cried no matter what was going on in her life. It wasn't that she was an evil emotionless machine, she just couldn't help it. She simply wasn't the crying type. And though sometimes, when she saw friends and family upset, she wondered what was wrong with her, she wasn't able to bring tears to the surface. It was her greatest strength and, a part of her feared, her greatest fault.

'But that doesn't mean I'm not devastated,' she said, swapping chocolate ice cream for wine and taking an enormous gulp. At that precise moment, Sandra Bullock and Betty White were in the middle of a rain dance in *The Proposal* and she thought of her and her parents dancing around the kitchen at Christmas. It sent a shock of something down her spine and she paused the film. 'I'm completely devastated right now. I'm divorced, sitting alone in the house I used to share with my husband, I hate my job—'

'What do you mean you hate your job? You used to love it.'

'I know but—' She scooped out the melting ice cream and dribbled it into her mouth before removing the spoon and waving it around as she spoke. 'Lately . . . oh, I don't know, corporate law, rich people getting richer – not even people . . . companies getting richer, fat-cat bosses – it's

14

just not giving me what I wanted from my career. Not anymore. I loved the money and the sense of job security but—'

'So what do you want from your career? More prestige? A sense of fulfilment perhaps?'

'A sense of fulfilment. Exactly. Like you have.'

While Naomi had left university and entered the world of corporate law, Mia had followed her passion of hospitality, which was lucky as her father ran a very profitable chain of hotels and ski resorts in Switzerland. She'd stepped straight into the family business and had loved every second of it. Naomi had been excited by her job too, at first, but over the last year that had faded just as her marriage had been slowly dissolved.

'Aren't you seeing your parents over Christmas?' Mia asked.

'Mum and Dad are in the Caribbean on a cruise. I made them go. It had been cancelled once and I didn't want them missing out again. I just – I don't know—' She scratched her forehead, still holding the spoon, and chocolate ice cream ended up in her hair. She ran her fingers through it to remove it. 'I thought I'd be fine but I'm not. And as well as having a rubbish love life and hating my job I have no friends—' Mia loudly cleared her throat. 'Apart from you who is the most amazing bestie ever . . . and I have exactly zero hobbies.' Having listed everything she now felt completely depressed and took another swig of wine. 'Oh God, I think I'm having a midlife crisis.'

'You're thirty-four. Much too early for a midlife crisis.'

'Fine,' she agreed begrudgingly, though a hint of a smile played on her lips. 'But what am I going to do all on my own over Christmas? Like I said, no hobbies and no one else to annoy with my presence.'

'Okay, that's it. I've had enough of all this moaning. This isn't the Naomi I know and love.'

It was true she wasn't herself. She was normally positive, upbeat, motivated. In the office she was known as the one who could handle the most difficult or complicated of cases. She was letting circumstances get on top of her and she'd dealt with so much worse before. Living in a foster home had been no easy feat from what she could remember and her early years with her adoptive parents had been full of emotional recalibration. If she could get through that, younger and more vulnerable than she was now, she could get through this.

'Come to Switzerland,' Mia said. Though it was more of an order than a question. 'Stay with me at my father's new place. Le Petit Chateau. We can spend some time together and you'll be far away from all these troubles. All you need is a little perspective. Some time to recharge and relax after the divorce. Le Petit Chateau has just been renovated and redecorated. It is top-end luxury and perfect for a Christmas vacation – not that I'm trying to sell it to you or anything – just trying out some new copy on you. What do you think?'

The idea was very appealing. Perhaps she wouldn't

hate work so much if she took a break from it and she certainly didn't want to be here all on her own. She glanced around the room imagining it bare of all Ollie's things, with a sad Christmas tree in the corner and a pathetic string of lights. She felt sick – and not from eating too much ice cream. Maybe staying somewhere else, somewhere beautiful, would give her something more than her situation to think about. She could take walks, read books, finally learn to ski.

In the last couple of years before their split, she and Ollie hadn't had many holidays. He'd travelled a lot with his work, and she'd thrown herself head first into her career. Her bank balance was nice and healthy. She always made sure of that, unable to bear the thought of missing a mortgage payment. All she'd have to do is get an extended break from work and considering she'd only taken a handful of days off, she was sure they'd say yes. Staring around at the lavishly furnished house, the things Ollie and she had chosen, getting away seemed like a brilliant idea.

'You've gone very quiet,' Mia said, the smile clear in her voice. 'Does that mean you're thinking about it? Le Petit Chateau is exquisite, and Switzerland is beautiful. Snowy mountains, lakes as smooth as panes of glass and the food—'

'You sound like tourist information.'

'But you are thinking about it?'

'I am,' Naomi replied, eyeing the artwork on the walls, pieces she'd never really liked that much, truth be told, but she'd gone with Ollie's decisions because a foster kid adopted by a working-class family didn't know anything about art. Perhaps she should have swallowed her shame and admitted she simply didn't like it whether it was skilful or not. Art is subjective after all. But she'd always carried that stigma with her. She pushed it down again now, burying it deep inside her.

'The hotel is beautiful too. Snowy Christmassy pine trees—'

'I don't care about trees. I'm off Christmas.'

'You're what?' Mia asked, giggling.

'Off Christmas.'

'What do you mean off Christmas? You can't be off Christmas. No one is.'

'Starting this year – well, last year actually – I am.'

'But you've always loved Christmas. You were the one making us decorate our rooms in halls as soon as it was the first of December.'

She thought again of Ollie pushing his wine glass aside after a lovely dinner, clasping his hands together and saying, 'We need to talk,' in a voice that brooked no argument. They hadn't long festooned the living room with Christmas decorations. Expensive glass ornaments hung from the ceiling and an enormous tree sparkled in the corner. They'd even talked about getting some tasteful lights for outside though Ollie had been nervous the neighbours would think it trashy. 'I know but last Christmas kind of changed things.'

'It's newly decorated. Beautiful rich wooden furniture,

luxurious beds, pillows so soft you will sleep like a baby.'

'I don't need all that,' Naomi said, laughing at her friend's really rather good attempt at convincing her.

'I know you don't but there's nothing wrong with being comfortable. Or looked after by someone who cares about you.'

Naomi smiled. 'I'm going down a bit of a self-pitying rabbit hole, aren't I?'

'It's not surprising after today, but you can't go on like that forever.'

'True.' She nodded her head in agreement. It had been a long time since she and Mia had spent any quality time together. They were both so busy their visits to each other had been fleeting and even their weekly video or phone calls had become less frequent.

'So . . . you'll come?'

'I will,' Naomi replied confidently, feeling a tiny bit of herself returning. 'Text me the address and I guess I'll get on the first flight I can.'

'Excellent! Oh, I can't wait to see you, Naomi. You're going to have a wonderful Christmas. I'll make sure of it.'

Naomi smiled, her spirits lifting at the idea. Last Christmas had been one of the worst of her life. It'd be nice to have a good one far away from home to wipe out that memory. Besides, it would give Ollie time to clear all the things they'd agreed would be his from the house, including the futon. She giggled to herself as she remembered the earlier meeting. Still, she didn't want to be around while he was loading everything into a van, or more likely, while people he'd hired loaded everything into a van.

It was time to stop feeling sorry for herself and enjoy her independence. It was time for an adventure.

Chapter 3

As soon as Naomi stepped out of the taxi at the address Mia had given her the cold air hit her cheeks, icy and refreshing. All the anger and hurt she'd felt over the last year leached from her system, cooled by the wind, her mind diverted by the view.

On the plane ride here, she'd seen snow-covered valleys and craggy mountain peaks surfacing through the white landscape. The sky was laced with wispy clouds and looking down she'd seen fog-filled dells. The vast whiteness of the landscape was so different to the muddy fields of England she'd watched disappear from view at take-off. Even on the taxi ride up she'd marvelled at the view out of the window, never realising before the many different shades of white a snow-filled land-scape actually was. The car had followed the tracks already cut into the snow, the brown rocks of the moun-tain lining her path on one side while on the other, a low metal fence warned them away from the sheer drop down the mountainside.

Naomi sucked in another breath and gazed at the sheer beauty of it all. Under a sky of an almost impossible shade of blue and a strong shining sun, mountains surrounded her on all sides. Some were snowy white, covered in thick powder. Others were a little barer, with tall pine trees covering the sloping sides that reached high on the horizon. Behind her, ski slopes wound their way down the inclines, accomplished skiers weaving their way grace-fully to the bottom, exhilarated, and then they trudged to the ski lift to take them back to the top. Further away, heavy clouds threatened another dusting should they move in during the night.

The place was breath-taking. It was even more beautiful than Mia had described, and she'd been sending Naomi ever more tempting snippets since she'd agreed to come. Over the last week as she'd read them and seen photos of the countryside, she'd found excitement building inside. She couldn't wait to leave London with all its over-the-top Christmas decorations to come here, away from the gaudy shop windows. She knew she was being a Scrooge and a total misery guts about Christmas but right now she just couldn't muster the enthusiasm for the festive season. Once upon a time it had been her favourite time of the year, but it had become a sort of to-do list without any of the feeling it had had when she was little. Evidence of the separate lives she and Ollie were leading perhaps.

She had just turned back from the view and grabbed

her bags, which the kind taxi driver had unloaded, when something bashed into her back sending her flying forward. The ground came rushing rapidly towards her face as her body fell headlong over the suitcases, leaving her bum high in the air. She managed to stay in this strange version of downward dog for what could only have been a few seconds but felt far longer before she began to fall sideways, ending up on her back and staring at what had bashed into her.

It was a man in a red ski suit, his visor pulled down and ski poles clasped in his hands.

Was it her imagination or was the taxi driver giggling? Embarrassment made her angry and from her position on the ground outrage grew inside. 'Hey! What the hell are you doing?'

A heavily gloved hand pushed up the visor and she heard what she assumed was a muffled apology, but she couldn't initially make out the language. Finally she heard: 'I'm so sorry. Please let me help you up.'

English – though tinged with a thick German accent. Clumsy ski-man reached out a hand and she took hold, slipping on the flattened snow as she tried to stand up. Perhaps her normal winter ankle boots hadn't been a great idea. Her feet had been freezing since the moment she'd landed and the fact her toes were no longer working wasn't helping her keep her balance.

She began to brush down her coat. 'Why weren't you looking where you were going? I'd have thought that's the first rule of skiing.' Now she really did sound like a

Scrooge, like grumpy old Ebenezer himself – though Charles Dickens never wrote about skiing to the best of her knowledge.

'I was but . . .' Finally upright, she drew level with bright brown-gold irises. Thick dark lashes rimmed kind eyes that were creasing at the corners as he smiled. He let go of her hand and removed his helmet. 'I really am sorry,' he replied calmly, pressing a hand to his chest.

As his helmet and mask had lifted, his red hair had sprung about his face. He had a strong square jaw scattered in stubble, and a rather nice smile. Naomi felt something stir in her belly. For the first time in years, she was feeling an attraction to someone. His smile was slightly lopsided, and she found the warmth of her annoyance cooling. This was unexpected, but it felt good – like she was remembering that she was still a woman who could feel something other than hatred towards a man. Though her marriage had failed a year ago she wasn't dead from the waist down just yet and though her heart wasn't thawing at the idea of Christmas, it was clearly thawing at the idea of meeting someone new.

'You know, I'll be honest,' he said, meeting her gaze. 'I was not looking where I was going. I was distracted by the view.'

There was a mischievous gleam in his eye. Had he meant her? Naomi found her mouth hanging open and cold air seeping in. She might get used to staying here if all the men were as handsome as this one. Deciding that shouting at random skiers wasn't the best way to start her holiday – or to make friends – she said, 'It's very beautiful, isn't it?'

'I never get tired of it. Can I—?' He motioned to her bags as Mia appeared, climbing out of a shining black car.

She was wearing a thick jacket, thermal leggings and heavy boots but somehow managed to look elegant and flawless. Her dark brown eyes weren't visible behind the huge sunglasses she wore to shield against the dazzling glare from the sun, but her long, dark brown hair – the colour of rich gingerbread – stuck out from under a cream bobble hat.

'Naomi!' Mia moved towards her with a smile, and the ski-man stepped backwards.

'I can see you already have a welcoming party. Perhaps next time I can help.'

Naomi tucked her hair behind her ear, though she wished she hadn't as it suddenly seemed very cold. 'Yes, maybe next time. Thanks.'

Mia drew level and replacing his helmet, ski-man headed on past them. 'What was that?'

'What was what? Him? He just offered to help with my bags.' She wasn't going to say he'd knocked her over first. She didn't want anyone else laughing.

'You were flirting!'

'I was not.'

'Yes, you were. Though not very well. You need more practice.'

'Thanks a bunch.' The two friends laughed and

25

embraced each other. Their arms locked, squeezing the other close. It had been far, far too long since they'd seen each other.

'Oh, I've missed you,' Naomi said, muffled into her shoulder.

'I've missed you too. It's been eighteen months since we last saw one another.'

'It can't have been that long.' Naomi let her friend go and Mia stepped back nodding.

'It is, but we can make up for lost time now. Come, come let me show you Le Petit Chateau.'

They both grabbed a suitcase and loaded them into the back of Mia's car before she took the wheel. The journey wasn't far, but the roads were covered in compacted snow. Mia drove expertly up a steep lane, finally pulling into the car park a few minutes later. With her usual energy, within seconds of parking, Mia had unclipped her seatbelt and was out of the car unloading the cases. Naomi stared with her mouth open at Le Petit Chateau: the small castle. She'd assumed that as the place was in Switzerland the word *chateau* was just to make it sound nice. Realising she was alone in the car, she jumped out.

'This is Le Petit Chateau?'

'It is.'

'This?' Naomi pointed at the beautiful, really quite large building in front of her. 'But it's huge! Doesn't *petit* mean small?'

Mia laughed. 'Isn't it funny? We kept the name

because every time someone came to work on the place they all said the same thing. They couldn't believe how big it was.'

Naomi's eyes drank it all in. The building was a mix of a traditional French chateau and a Swiss ski chalet but somehow it worked. The bare bones of the original chateau were still visible in the design of the ground floor which was made of pale French stone. The top two floors were more like the Swiss ski chalets Naomi had been expecting. They were made of wood with a large balcony running all the way around the outside of them. The wooden railing was covered in snow and either side of the windows were lights that accentuated the beauty of the building. A line of pine trees in front of the chateau reached almost to the roof, their branches dusted in white. It certainly wasn't the small ski lodge she'd been expecting. This place screamed five-star luxury.

'I'm speechless,' Naomi muttered.

'You're never speechless.'

'I am today. It's . . . it's . . . exquisite.'

'Christmassy yes?'

Naomi groaned. 'No, it's just gorgeous. I told you I'm not interested in doing Christmas this year.'

'Okay, okay. Well, I'm glad you like it. It's been in our family for years, but we only recently converted it to a chalet. The building was falling apart but we've given it a new lease of life.'

'It really is beautiful.' Taking a suitcase each, they edged closer to the entrance.

'I'm so pleased you're happy. We only finished it earlier this year. That's why I'm here. We've just completed all the internal decorations, so you'll be one of the first people to stay.'

'Really?'

She nodded, her eyes bright with enthusiasm. 'It's not actually open to visitors yet but we have a few house-keeping staff. We have the grand gala party on Christmas Eve when the village will get to come and have a look at what we've done, but that's before we allow any paying guests to stay.'

'But aren't you missing out on revenue? Wouldn't it be better to open before Christmas? I can imagine a lot of people would love to spend the festive season here.'

'We could but we feel it's more important to include the community and they've always been welcoming to my family. They often use our other chalets for community activities and events, and we employ a lot of people in the town. A Christmas Eve party here, them seeing it before more people come to stay, it is a way of saying thank you for putting up with the renovations. Come on, let us go inside.'

Naomi followed Mia around the side of the building to the front entrance. Two tall pillars supported a small gable roof underneath which hung the sign for the hotel. She could see Mia's style and elegance in the branding: the sweeping cursive letters against a pale white back-ground. Smaller pine trees in large ornate pots lined the way to the door.

Naomi had expected something like a hotel reception,

but the entrance lobby was huge, opening up into an equally large open-plan lounge and dining room. In front of her was a sweeping staircase leading up to the first floor, subtle lights shining from the walls to lead the way. On one side of the room, a large stone fireplace drew the eye, the bright orange flames glowing brightly giving the room not only warmth, but the sweet scent of wood. A number of comfortable sofas and armchairs surrounded it, blankets folded neatly over the backs, cushions in neutral colours making them look even more comfortable. On the other side, to her right, was the equivalent of the check-in desk though it wasn't a boring desk with a bell; it was more like a coffee table where you'd sit with a friend, enjoying a hot chocolate after skiing all day. Rich, chunky wood was the theme throughout and the neutral furniture with occasional splashes of colour accented it perfectly.

'Wow,' Naomi said, looking at Mia. 'This is truly amazing. I can't think of anywhere better to spend Christmas.'

Mia squealed and wrapped Naomi in another hug. 'We are going to have the best time.'

'We are.' And for the first time in months, she actually believed it.

'You're going to be on the first floor in one of our most elegant rooms.' She went to the coffee table and picked up a small card that had been sitting on top. 'Once I employ people, they'll do all the room allocations before people arrive so the cards are all waiting for them.

There'll be no hanging about. It'll be straight into the luxury of it all. The top-floor suite is still being finished otherwise I would have put you in there.'

'Everything looks so wonderful, I know I'll be comfortable wherever you put me. I bet even a broom cupboard is kitted out well here.'

'You know me. I like to do things properly. Father and I decided this would be the most high-end of all our properties and I think we've managed that. There's also a gym and swimming pool in the basement and we have a spa already, just down the hill, so everyone will get access to that too. Did you want me to book you in for anything? A massage or facial maybe?'

'No, that's fine,' Naomi replied. 'I can do that myself if I want anything.'

'Well, tell them Mia has said everything is complimentary. In fact, I'll email them now.' She pulled out her phone and began typing furiously.

Naomi smiled. 'You don't need to do that. I'm happy to pay to be here.'

'No, I won't hear of it.' She continued to type and finally looked up once she'd hit send.

Her friend was always working, ticking jobs off her to-do list. It was partly why they'd got on so well at university. They'd both been goody two-shoes, eager to get top marks. Mia, because she wanted to impress the father who had such a successful business and also the highest of standards, Naomi because she knew how much it was costing her parents to support her and she didn't want their hard-earned cash to go to waste. Her father had worked two jobs to help her through university and the first thing she'd done when she'd begun working in London was to pay off her debts and send them money each week. Luckily, things had got easier and though she wasn't sending money every week any more she liked to treat them to things, like the cruise they were now on, as a way of thanking them. She wondered where they were right now. Probably sunning themselves on some tropical island or sitting out on the deck red-nosed. She'd have to call them later to check in.

'Mia?' A deep voice followed by heavy footsteps sounded down the stairs and Naomi's head snapped to follow it. 'Where do you want these red chairs again? Was it guest bedroom four or six?'

The voice sent chills down her spine, almost causing her to shudder as the familiar notes stirred distant and forgotten memories inside her. She felt the urge to turn and run, but her feet were rooted to the spot.

'Gabriel,' she whispered.

Chapter 4

Mia ran forwards towards her brother. 'Gabriel! Look who's here.'

He came to a stop before her, his eyes widening a fraction as confusion turned to recognition. She hadn't remembered him being so tall – perhaps hurt had diminished him in her memory. If it had, it hadn't done anything to lessen how good-looking he was. If anything, he'd aged like a fine wine. Gabriel's pale blue-grey eyes met hers, but she couldn't read anything in them. His skin, flawless, with only faint traces of lines on his forehead showing his age.

'You remember Naomi, right?'

'Yes.' He smiled, pushing a hand through his blond hair. A few strands fell forwards as he brought his hand back and something fluttered inside her again – only this time it was even stronger than with ski-man. 'Hello, Naomi.'

She wanted to speak but her mouth was glued shut. Even if she had been able to talk, all of her words had disappeared and her first attempt at speaking came out as muffled, incomprehensible nonsense. She swallowed and tried again. 'Hi.'

'It's Gabriel,' Mia said, prompting her friend. 'You remember my brother, right?'

'Yes, yes, I do. Hello.' She crossed her arms over her chest feeling suddenly cold and exposed.

The last time she'd seen him, she and Mia had both been eighteen, and freshers at university. A few years older, he'd come to visit Mia, to see how she was settling in and . . . She pushed the rest of the memory away. Anger flared inside, both at the memory and the effect he was having on her now. Even her fingers were tingling. She flexed them to stop, and found the iron will her professional career had given her – not to mention her difficult upbringing – growing stronger.

'It's nice to see you again,' she said, just as she would to any work colleague she hadn't seen in a while.

'It's good to see you too. You look . . .' He paused and her heart rate increased as she wondered what he was going to say. Nice? Terrible? Tired? Like she'd been travelling all day and needed a shower? It was anyone's guess at this stage and the uncertainty only heightened her defences. 'Well,' he said eventually.

Well? That was nice and non-specific. It was also a lie. She didn't look well at all. She knew full well she looked dishevelled from the journey and worn out from the divorce.

Her hair was dry and had probably fluffed in the mountain winds, and her skin had grown duller over the last six months of legal wrangling. She doubted even the crisp, alpine air would be able to give her sallow complexion some colour. She smoothed the hair on the top of her head and brushed it behind her ear. 'Yes, so do you.'

The thick jumper he was wearing accentuated his broad chest and shoulders. His lips were still perfectly formed and eminently kissable. She quickly drew her attention from them. His eyes lingered on hers, not moving from her face until he suddenly turned to his sister as if Naomi was nobody.

'So, Mia, where do you want these red chairs? Bedroom four or six?'

Mia smiled. 'Seven, actually.'

'Okay.' He nodded, running his hand through his hair one more time. 'Nice to see you, Naomi. Enjoy your stay.' He turned and stalked back towards the staircase.

So that was it? Their first meeting after all these years and he acts like she was just some passing acquaintance. Someone he'd known once a long time ago. Actually, he hadn't even treated her with that much warmth. He'd treated her like the hotel guest she was. She was more than a little insulted and anger flared inside. Mia didn't know anything about that night, and Naomi did her best to pretend that Gabriel Mathis was nothing more than a guy *she* had once known. Mia's brother she'd met once a long time ago. She plastered on a smile and turned back to Mia.

'You didn't tell me Gabriel would be here.'

Her friend was back looking at her phone, her thumbs skimming over the screen. 'Didn't I? I've been so busy I must have forgotten to mention it. But you got on well when he came to see me at uni, didn't you?' She finally looked up.

'Yeah, we got on fine. It was so many years ago I can barely remember to be honest.' Naomi shrugged with fake nonchalance.

'Well, he hasn't changed much.' Considering how he'd treated her back then, Naomi was sure that wasn't a good thing.

'Shall we get your bags and I'll show you to your room? You'll want some time to unpack and get settled.'

Seeing Gabriel again had unsettled her more than any amount of unpacking was going to fix but she was happy to do as she was told. 'And I've got a few things to do before we can have dinner together tonight. Is that okay?'

The prospect of relaxing followed by a nice dinner with her best friend brought the smile back to her face. 'Of course. I have a detail-filled plan that includes lots of chilling out.'

'You'll have access to streaming services through the TV in your room so there'll be something you can kick back and relax with, or you can come and take over the lounge if you prefer.'

With Gabriel around, her room sounded like the safest option.

They took the elevator up to the second floor and Mia held the card against the lock. A second later it flashed green, and she pushed open the door, standing aside to let Naomi in first.

While she'd expected the luxury and elegance of downstairs to continue, Naomi still found her hand flying across her mouth as she entered her room. The bed caught her eye first and not just because Gabriel's face still floated in her mind with his chiselled jaw and strong shoulders. Beautifully embroidered sheets enclosed a thick, bouncy duvet and a large stack of pillows. A fluffy silver throw was folded expertly over the end of the bed and innumerable cushions in natural and light cream shades were piled high. She wasn't sure she could bring herself to actually sleep on it; it was like a work of art and it wasn't even the grandest thing about the room. A huge TV hung on the wall opposite the bed, and there was a desk and chaise longue filling the corners as well as a wardrobe made of thick Scandinavian wood.

Naomi darted to the en-suite bathroom to see pale marble combined with thick, deeply grained oak and a bath so deep she could almost float in it. It was luxury, pure luxury unlike anything she'd experienced before. Even with her savings she would never have spent money on something this extravagant. A pang of guilt suddenly came over her.

'Mia, this is all so incredible. Are you sure you don't want me to give you some money towards my stay?'

Mia's eyes widened in outrage. 'Absolutely not. And if you ask me that again I'm going to start making you do

Christmassy things that you'll hate. Though I can't honestly believe that you hate Christmas that much.'

'I really do,' she replied.

'Well, I won't hear anything more about it. You should see the balcony.' Mia led the way from the bathroom and Naomi followed, her body fizzing with excitement.

Her friend had dramatically cast the double doors to the balcony wide open and though cold wind had flooded the room, she couldn't resist joining her friend outside. Mia had taken a seat in one of the wooden chairs, a blanket draped over her shoulders. Along the top of the thick wooden ledge small strings of fairy lights dropped like icicles. Naomi took the seat beside her and together they stared at the vast horizon of snowy mountain peaks and tall, deep-green pine trees. The bright light was fading, the sky a sheet of palest mauve and the clouds she'd noticed earlier were drifting ever closer. She watched skiers in the distance weaving down the slopes, their skis leaving tracks behind them. Amidst the pockets of busyness, there was an overwhelming sense of peace around them.

'Will it snow again tonight?' Naomi asked, pointing at the clouds above.

'Probably. You can feel the temperature has dropped already, can't you?'

Naomi pulled the blanket from the back of her chair and wrapped it around her. Comfortable silence descended as they took in the view, and despite the shadow of Gabriel dancing in her mind, a feeling of comfort descended over her – she'd missed this in her life back home. She felt her muscles relaxing, her mind untying the knots and conundrums that had taken all her energy. Here she was free to unwind, free to be herself. She closed her eyes, breathing in a cool, detoxifying breath. As she filled her lungs, she was sure they had more capacity than they'd had in London.

'So,' Mia said. 'How are you? Really?'

Naomi opened her eyes. 'I'm okay, I think.' Ollie and their divorce felt far away sitting here in the mountains, watching the sun slip below the peaks. She felt better being here than she would have felt at home, alone, surrounded by all their things. Yet, she didn't miss him and the realisation that she was finally putting that part of her life behind her took her slightly by surprise. Was it the year they'd already been apart, or had they been slipping away from each other before then? Gabriel's face appeared in her mind's eye. He'd looked good. Scarily good and her stomach tightened at the thought. 'So what's Gabriel doing here? Is he helping you get this place ready?'

'Sometimes. He's working nearby for a while. It's nice to have him around. We haven't seen each other as much as we both would like but, you know, life gets in the way.' There was a tone of regret in her voice that made Naomi wonder if there was more behind it but Mia moved the conversation on. 'He's been very useful to boss around.'

He'd been studying business when he'd visited her and Mia all those years ago and Naomi suddenly pictured him in a suit but quickly pushed the thought away.

Her frustration at him swelled again but she hid it behind a smile.

'And he always likes to escape here.'

Again, there was an undertone of sadness in Mia's voice and Naomi glanced over to see it mirrored in her face.

'What's he escaping from? An angry ex?' She laughed but the idea made her feel something akin to jealousy, which was utterly ridiculous. Of course he'd have had relationships over the years just as she had. Not that that night constituted anything more than what it was. How could he not? The man she'd known had been kind, funny, intelligent, soulful. At least that's what she'd thought at first. And even if those things didn't sway a woman, his looks would. But looks, she'd found, could be incredibly deceiving and this time she didn't mean her handsome ex-husband.

Mia giggled. 'No. He hasn't dated anyone in a while. He keeps saying he's against the idea of being in love. I think you would call him a lone wolf.'

'A lone wolf? I suppose it sounds better than saying relationships aren't worth the agony.'

'No! You can't mean that. That is a terrible way to look at things.'

Naomi cocked her head. 'You're talking to a woman who's getting divorced, Mia.'

'But surely you don't hate the idea of love?' Mia's dark hair flew around her face as she turned. 'I don't and I've been on hundreds of dates but never found the right person. Love is about fate, and timing. The heavens have to align with the right person at the right moment.'

That wasn't what had happened with Ollie. Naomi felt a flush of shame. Their relationship had never been passionate or fiery. It certainly hadn't been the fates aligning just for them. It had been decidedly comfortable, which sounded shallow, but Naomi had thought herself in love with him. It just wasn't the sort of love you saw in movies. A horrible thought entered her mind that she'd mistaken real love for companionship and security.

'You really believe that?' she asked Mia.

'I do. The last date I went on was nice, but it wasn't right. You know what I mean?' Naomi shook her head in confusion. 'He was nice. I was nice. The food was nice. But it wasn't right. Another time maybe things might have been different. If I was having that date in five years' time, five years older, it might be like fireworks. You never know when the right time is going to be. When heaven and earth line up for everything to be perfect.'

'I suppose you're right.' Would that be the type of love she looked out for now?

'But you can't hate love.'

'Okay, maybe I don't hate love. But I do hate Christmas, so don't ask me to do Christmassy things. I don't care what anyone says I won't be singing Christmas carols, I won't be making gingerbread, and I definitely won't be decorating any Christmas trees. I'm glad to get away from all the commercial rubbish and intend to chill out here without any of the fuss.'

'Wow, that is some kind of attitude. Do your parents know how much you hate Christmas now?'

'No. But I'm hoping by next year I might feel different.'

Her parents had always loved the festive season and made Christmas extra special when she was younger, especially in the years after her official adoption.

Mia reached out and squeezed her friend's hand. 'Does skiing count as Christmassy?'

Naomi thought for a moment. 'No, that's more just a winter sport, isn't it? I've actually never been skiing before.'

'I was hoping you'd say that. I can teach you. It'll be fun.'

'But I don't have any ski stuff.' Her family hadn't been able to afford holidays, and certainly couldn't afford all the equipment needed for skiing. She felt the familiar sting of inferiority plague her deep down inside. No matter how much money she had in the bank she feared she'd always feel this way.

'Don't worry. We have everything anyone could need here. Lots of people who visit haven't skied before and don't want to spend the money on things they may never use again. We'll kit you out in the morning and then we'll have some fun on the hills.'

'Which hill?' she asked, looking around. 'It won't be a massive one, will it?'

Mia laughed gently. 'It's a phrase. Skiers call the slopes hills but I'm sure you'll get the hang of it quickly – and all the lingo too.'

Naomi hoped so. At least it was better than carol singing and going to endless drink-fuelled Christmas parties or something else horribly festive. She stared at the slopes still busy with confident skiers. As the lights flickered on in the neighbouring chalets, a warm, radiant glow of orange enveloped them. She could stay here for the entire evening, but as lovely as that idea was, she had something else in mind for her and her friend. 'I have an important question to ask.'

'Oh?' Mia's eyes glistened, knowing Naomi's teasing tone from their years of friendship.

'Is there a minibar and if not, where can I get a drink around here?'

Mia tossed her head back laughing. 'There is a minibar in that cupboard over there, but I have a better idea. Let's go down to the lounge. It's my favourite place. The chairs are comfortable, and the fire will warm us up. I've designed it to be relaxing, yet chic.'

'I thought you had some work to finish off?'

'Ahh . . . I guess it can wait.'

Naomi gasped and then softened her teasing. 'Are you sure? I know how work always comes first with you.'

'It's fine. I can catch up on it tomorrow and I put a bottle of champagne in the fridge hours ago so it will be perfectly chilled by now and dinner will be ready soon. It's nothing fancy, just a delicious local stew that will warm you up from the inside.' She stood up and rubbed her hands together. 'My fingers are freezing.'

'I'm glad you said that. I thought it was just me being a baby and you were sat there like some superwoman impervious to the cold.'

'Superwoman you say? I like that. Isn't that what I wanted to be when I left university?'

'From the look of this place you've achieved it.'

'I'm not sure my father would agree. He has always had exacting standards and big ideas.'

'He hasn't seen it yet?'

Mia shook her head. 'He's been busy with other things.'

'I can't see how he wouldn't be impressed with this place. It's amazing.'

Mia blushed. 'So, you think you will be happy here for a while?'

'I've been happier this afternoon than I've been in a long time,' she replied sincerely. Even with the reappearance of Gabriel. 'Now come on, enough mushy stuff. Let's get that drink and some food. I can't tell you how much I've needed an evening with my bestie.'

Chapter 5

Naomi woke the next morning from the deepest sleep she'd had in months, possibly even years. After spending the evening in front of the fire with Mia, talking non-stop, giggling and catching up on everything they'd missed, she'd then snuggled down under the plush duvet – head nestled on cloud-soft pillows – and instantly drifted off into a restful slumber. She'd woken eager to see the world outside – this snow-laden paradise – and after getting dressed she descended the stairs raring to go. She hadn't felt this alive in a long time and she certainly couldn't remember the last time she'd jumped out of bed ready to seize the day. After some breakfast, she made her way over to Mia's chalet, buzzing with excitement for a day of skiing.

Snow had fallen again last night, and fresh white drifts dusted cars, branches and roofs. Today, no clouds hung in the sky leaving a wide, unsullied expanse of ultramarine.

As Naomi gazed around her, all the colours seemed sharper and more vivid: the snow on the mountains whiter, the blue sky purer and more striking, the green of the trees darker and deeper.

Following her friend's garbled directions, given tipsily as they said goodnight, Naomi listened to the crunching of snow under the boots Mia had given her as she made the five-minute journey to Mia's chalet. This was more the sort of thing she'd been expecting when she'd first arrived. Not that she wasn't ridiculously happy with Le Petit Chateau. She just hadn't thought chateaus existed outside of France, but Mia had told her that in this area – which was on the French side of the French–German language border within Switzerland – there were a few chateaus still hanging around. Still, Mia's home was much more traditionally Swiss. This chalet was cute and compact with sweet wooden shutters and latticed window boxes. Snow piled high on the gabled roof and she walked up the steps and through a small veranda where chairs and tables were ready for après skiers to sit outside. It must have been one of the older cabins as the wooden balustrades were weathered, the wood lighter. She knocked on the door, taking a deep breath of the cold, crisp air and enjoying the way it woke her mind, chasing away the fuzziness of too much wine from her brain.

'Naomi,' Mia exclaimed as she pulled the door open. 'Come in, come in.' Naomi followed but was surprised to see Mia in a cute jumper, tight jeans and boots. 'Do you want some breakfast? Did you have anything at

Le Petit Chateau? I asked for your meals to be provided.' She could see Gabriel, from the corner of her eye, sitting in the corner of the room reading a newspaper. Suddenly he folded the top down to look at his sister. 'I mean *I* asked for Naomi's meals to be provided.'

There was a sparkle in his eyes as his gaze ran to Naomi. Then he flicked the paper back up and tingles ran up her spine. She ignored him. She'd decided last night, before she fell asleep, that he was choosing to treat her like a complete stranger and pretend the past had never happened. Well, that was fine. If that's what he wanted to do, it was what she would do too. It was no skin off her nose. She wasn't about to let him spoil her stay and she didn't have to think about him at all when she returned to England.

'There was a huge spread laid out for me,' she said to Mia. 'I couldn't have eaten it all if I tried. It was delicious. You must thank the chef for me. There were so many beautiful pastries, meats and cheeses I could have stayed there eating all day.'

'I will,' Mia replied with a strange smile.

'So, are we still . . . you know—' She pointed at the window and Mia gasped, her hand pressing against her forehead.

'Oh no! I'm so sorry! I forgot. How could I be so stupid? I am the worst host.'

'No, no you're not at all. It's fine.' Naomi laughed as Mia cursed under her breath.

'I have a meeting to see the caterers for the gala party.

How can I forget we were skiing?' Naomi held up her hands pleading with her friend to calm down but Mia was in full swing. 'I never double-book myself. I never forget anything either. I'll have to—'

'Mia, it's fine! We can go skiing another time. I don't mind. I'm happy to explore on my own. I might take a walk or—'

'Gabriel can take you,' Mia declared, suddenly brightening.

Naomi spun to look at him. As Mia had said the words, his paper had been pulled down to reveal his entire face. He didn't seem particularly keen on the idea. How could she politely say she didn't want to spend time with him? That she'd rather explore on her own than be alone with the man who could barely remember her.

'No, no it's fine. I'm sure Gabriel's busy and I really don't mind—'

'Please,' Mia said, pressing her hands together, pleading. 'I'll feel so much better and far less guilty if Gabriel takes you. You don't mind, do you?' She turned to Gabriel. 'You're not doing anything today. You said so.'

He stood, folding the newspaper in four and dropping it onto his vacated seat. 'Well I did have grand plans to read a good book, but fine.'

Don't sound too enthusiastic, will you? Naomi chewed the inside of her lip in annoyance. 'You really don't have to, Gabriel. I can just go for a walk or something.'

He turned to his sister as if waiting for an answer, which annoyed Naomi even more. 'No,' Mia said, placing her hands on her hips and glaring at her brother. 'Gabriel doesn't mind, do you?' There was a menace to her voice that brooked no argument.

'No,' he replied, with what Naomi was sure was a slightly huffy edge. 'I don't mind.'

'Great!' Mia clapped. 'We're about the same size,' she said to Naomi. 'So you can borrow my skiing stuff. Let me get it for you.'

Mia bustled off leaving Naomi standing next to Gabriel. Inside she was raging and though she kept an eye on him from the corner of her eyes, his expression was unreadable and she couldn't tell if he was dreading this as much as she was. From the way he tried to wriggle out of it, he probably was.

A painful silence descended, and she looked at the ceiling, then the floor. She tucked her hair behind her ear and then he finally glanced at her, giving the type of awkward half-smile you give the doctor or people on the tube when you accidentally stand on their foot and have to mutter an apology. It was exactly the type of smile you give when you've received a particularly unpleasant Christmas present. Maybe that's how he felt about her showing up at the chateau to see his sister. She turned away. With all these thoughts running through her head she'd managed to put herself in quite a bad mood. The fresh air had been sucked from the room and what was left felt thick and heavy in her lungs. The scent of his cologne drifted towards her: something clean and fresh like bergamot or lemon mixed with something peppery.

She'd spent far too long unpacking the fragrance and glanced at him to see if he'd noticed only to find him watching her, but his gaze darted away once more.

This was excruciatingly awkward.

Should she speak first or leave it to him? She didn't have anything particular to say but politeness dictated one of them should make small talk.

'So,' he said unexpectedly, leaving a long pause. 'You want to ski today?'

'Umm, yeah, sure.' They'd spoken so easily that night, all those years ago, but now talking to him was more painful than a bikini wax.

'Have you . . .' Another long pause like he'd started the sentence then forgotten what he wanted to say. 'Skied before?'

'No. Never. I—'

A loud clatter followed by Mia's cursing drew her attention away from the most boring conversation in history. Honestly, it could have entered the *Guinness Book of Records* for the most mundane small talk ever to have taken place on planet Earth. Where was his soul? The excitement for life he'd had back when she first met him?

Mia's arms were overflowing with skiwear. Poles were sticking out from under one arm while her other hand was just about hanging on to a single ski. Its partner lay a few feet behind her on the wooden floor and had obviously been the cause of the crash.

'Here we are. Everything you could need.' She forced the bundle into Naomi's arms and her legs nearly buckled

49

under the weight. Mia checked her watch. 'I'm so sorry but I really need to go.' After hastily throwing on her coat, she grabbed her enormous handbag full of folders with bits of paper sticking out the top and fled, the door swinging shut behind her as a muffled 'Have fun!' echoed.

Naomi turned to Gabriel and attempted a smile. From his reaction it had looked more like a grimace. 'I'd better—'

'You'd better get changed,' he interrupted coolly.

'That's just what I was about to say.' Naomi knew better than to point out he'd interrupted her and instead answered as if he'd never spoken. Who was this man though? He certainly wasn't the enthusiastic and bois-terous yet tender man she'd met before.

She dropped the bundle and found the clothes from within it. She was just about to open her mouth to ask where Mia's room was when he said, 'Her room is that way,' like some freaky mind reader.

'Thanks.'

'I'll quickly change too and meet you back here.'

She walked on to find Mia's room, wishing it was her friend teaching her how to ski and not Gabriel. Though smaller than the rooms at Le Petit Chateau with darker, less grained wood, it was still tastefully decorated and felt homely. Mia had always had excellent taste and knew how to dress a room. There was a small bookcase and all the other furniture you'd expect to find in a bedroom: a large wooden wardrobe, a chest of drawers, but there were little additions that gave an extra something. A vase of flowers on the windowsill, a beautiful glass bowl on a shelf along with photos in silver frames. Just as Mia's room had been at university, everything was tidy and in its place; no mess or clutter had been left out. Every aspect of Mia's life was organised, and thanks to living with her through university, Naomi had picked up the same habits. In exchange, Naomi had taught her friend how to cook on a budget and together they'd relied on each other throughout those years.

Naomi changed quickly and emerged a few minutes later to see Gabriel staring out of the window. He was head to toe in matching black skiwear, his helmet under one arm, skis and poles expertly stacked under the other. When he noticed her, his eyes scanned her body and she felt suddenly self-conscious even though he was probably just making sure she'd got everything on the right way round.

'Shall we go?' she asked, eager to get them moving.

'Sure.'

Within minutes they were on the beginners' 'blue' slope. A class was under way nearby and she watched as people nervously pushed themselves along, laughing with their family and friends. Gabriel placed their helmets down nearby. She was watching him, wondering why he'd done that and then he did the freaky mind-reading thing again.

'You won't need it for a while. You haven't skied before, have you?' Gabriel asked, helping her into her skis and locking the boots in place before they began. They both had thick hats on to protect them against the cold – but

Naomi was still a bit nervous of cracking her head open without her helmet.

'No. Are you sure we don't need our helmets? They're all wearing them.' She pointed at the beginners' class.

He ignored her and asked again about her skiing experience. 'None at all?'

'Nope. This'll be my first time. The helmets?' He glanced up, his eyes meeting hers and flicking away again.

'I told you, you won't need them yet.'

As he stood and she realised how close he was standing, she lost her balance and nearly fell. Her body reacted, trying to regain its equilibrium, and after jerking backwards and forwards, she settled more or less upright. 'Whoops. Sorry,' she said out of politeness.

'How can you fall over? You haven't moved an inch yet.'

She couldn't tell if his tone was impatient or teasing and she bristled. 'There's no need to be rude. I've never worn skis before. It's a bit . . . weird.'

When he next spoke, his tone was softer. 'Skiing is quite simple, but it does take some practice. Okay, I want you to walk around. Move forward and back, side to side. Just get used to them.'

She began to lift her foot, feeling like she had giant, heavy flippers on.

'No, no, no,' Gabriel said, waving his pole at her. 'Just slide, don't lift your foot off the ground.'

Embarrassment warmed Naomi's cheeks. 'You said walk.'

'I meant glide.'

'If you meant glide, you should have said glide. Walking and gliding are two very different things.'

'Is this the lawyer coming out? I'd hate to be in an argument with you. I think I'd lose.' He was grinning and it warmed his cold blue-grey eyes.

The fact he knew her occupation nearly made her fall again. 'Mia told you what I did?'

'She mentioned it when she said you were coming. I didn't think you were interested in that sort of thing.'

'What sort of thing? Skiing?'

'Corporate law.' He shrugged, the grin vanishing. 'It just seems very boring.'

'It's not boring, and how do you know what I'd find boring or not?' she replied defensively, though lately it most definitely was. 'What had you expected me to be doing? I was studying law when you came to see Mia at university.'

The mention of university and by implication that night sent something electric into the air, like the flicker of a flame would create an explosion.

'I just thought . . . I don't know.' He shrugged, seemingly dropping the subject. Naomi couldn't help but be relieved. She didn't want to talk about that night with anyone, least of all Gabriel. 'Try moving again,' he instructed.

She began to move, her body tilting this way and that. It was like trying to stand on jelly. She hadn't thought it would be this hard. She'd stood on snow before. Not this much of course, but it had snowed in England and she managed to walk on it pretty well, so why was this so difficult? She attempted to walk sideways like a crab and found herself falling into Gabriel as one ski accidentally caught on the other and she toppled to the right. He caught her with an oomph and pushed her upright.

'Okay. This is terrible,' he said airily. 'Maybe try gliding a little.'

'I was just gliding!'

'No, you were shuffling. You might find it easier to be in motion, though I doubt it.'

She met his gaze. 'You're not exactly being encouraging. Have you actually taught anyone to ski before?'

'No, but I've been skiing since I was a toddler. My father used to say I could ski before I could walk.'

'Well, lucky you,' she fired back. 'Not all of us could afford holidays to snowy wonderlands when we were little. Being able to do something doesn't mean you can teach it.'

He tilted his head and though she'd expected to annoy him, there was a hint of amusement in his voice. 'Are you saying I'm a terrible teacher?'

'Maybe,' she replied. 'Actually, yes. Yes, I am. How exactly is getting me to walk sideways in the most unnatural footwear imaginable supposed to help me to ski?'

He looked at her, and the winter sun made his eyes sparkle. 'You are very rude.'

'And you're very impatient.'

'I am not.'

'You are.' She went to cross her arms over her chest

forgetting she was standing in snow and nearly fell again. She managed to stay upright by bending her legs but by the time her body had stopped rocking she was too afraid to straighten them. She stifled a smile. 'Stop laughing,' she commanded as Gabriel spluttered. 'Look why don't I join that class over there and you can go and do whatever it is you do around here?'

'The adult beginners? I think even that might be too much for you.'

Her mouth hung open. 'How— You are unbelievable! How dare you.'

To show him how wrong she was, she tried trudging towards the class but only made it a few feet before her skis had a disagreement. One went left while the other went right and she ended up on her hands and knees perilously close to doing the splits. She heard Gabriel laughing from behind her. If it had been Mia, she would have been laughing her head off too. They'd have tried a bit longer and then headed back to Le Petit Chateau for a drink, probably something alcoholic. But it wasn't Mia, someone she'd done too many embarrassing things with to care about. It was her gorgeous and very annoying older brother, someone she didn't want to make a show of herself in front of – at least not any more than she had already.

'Are you going to help me?' Naomi asked, trying to push herself upright for the third time. She suddenly felt his arms around her, strong and secure as he set her upright facing him. Her hands gripped onto his broad shoulders.

Despite her anger, as she saw him smile, longing tugged inside her. The sexual chemistry had always been a bit lacking between herself and Ollie, but the way Gabriel was looking at her now sent shivers down her spine. Or maybe that was just the weather. For a moment, it felt as though he'd remembered her, like his eyes were searching her face to find traces of the young woman he'd once known. Had he felt it too?

'Are you steady now?' he asked, breathily.

'I – I think so.' She cursed herself for feeling so flustered and pulled herself together. 'You can let go now.' His hands dropped. 'So, what's next then, oh great ski instructor?'

Gabriel thought for a moment then cleared his throat. 'I have an idea. This way. If you can manage it.'

'I'll do my best,' she replied sarcastically.

With his arm hanging behind her like a safety barrier they made their way towards another slope.

'Where are we going?'

'You'll see.'

As they drew nearer, Naomi narrowed her eyes. The slope was tiny. So were the people. 'The kids' class?' she exclaimed feeling heat warm her cheeks once more. 'Are you kidding me?'

'I really think this will be the best place for you.'

'Are you deliberately trying to humiliate me?' She stared at him, her face set.

'What? No.' He was genuinely shocked, as if the idea had never occurred to him. 'This will stop you feeling embarrassed in front of other adults.'

'Other adults yes, but other children? No. I can just see them all giggling at the giant lady who can't manage the simplest of things.'

'Naomi, what are you talking about?' he replied steadily. Then suddenly comprehending he baulked. 'Did you think?' She didn't answer. 'The kids' class is finishing soon. Levi, who teaches people of all ages, is a great teacher. One of the best we have around here.'

'Is he a friend of yours?'

'Not exactly. We know each other a little, that's all.'

Gabriel motioned to the class where a man in a red ski suit was teaching tiny children in skis larger than they were. A young girl slid hesitantly along but she stayed upright and came to a gentle stop just before him. He cheered like she'd won the Winter Olympics, patting her on the shoulder and holding his hand up for a high five. Naomi couldn't help but smile. Whoever he was, he was great with the kids. She hoped he'd be as kind to her though Ivan the Terrible would have been kinder than Gabriel in her opinion.

'Why don't we try some more basics while we wait?'

'Okay,' she agreed hesitantly. 'But if you laugh at me, even once, I'm going to hit you with my ski pole.'

'They're called sticks.'

'Fine. I'll hit you with my stick. Is that better?'

'Much better. At least I know what to look out for.'

Slowly, with Gabriel's help, she started to get the hang of it. She wouldn't be sailing down a mountainside anytime soon, but she was at least managing to stay upright more often than not.

'That's it,' Gabriel declared with a smile a little while later. 'You're doing it. Well done, Naomi.'

It had taken twenty minutes and she'd travelled a total of about three feet, but considering where she'd started, she'd take it as a win. Without thinking, she held her hand up for a high five and was delighted when Gabriel clapped his palm against hers. Even in the thick gloves the contact made her heart flutter.

Suddenly children were filing out behind her to meet waiting parents and the red-suited instructor skied effortlessly over to them.

'Levi,' Gabriel said. 'This is my sister's friend, Naomi. She's staying with us over Christmas.'

His sister's friend? Was that all she was? It was true the day had started out somewhat rockily but they'd definitely been on friendlier terms this last half an hour. She wasn't sure what she expected, but after they'd spent the best part of the day together, she'd assumed he'd present her as something related to him, perhaps his guest or his friend. That he'd felt the need to distance himself from her, as if she was nothing to do with him, was both insulting and hurtful.

The instructor lifted his helmet to reveal familiar flaming red hair and golden eyes. The man who'd knocked her over when she'd first arrived smiled warmly. 'We've met actually, though I'm sure she doesn't want to remember me.'

'Now I've tried skiing I can promise there are no hard feelings,' Naomi replied, smiling. 'But I would have thought a ski instructor would be better at stopping.'

He laughed and Gabriel's brows drew together. 'What happened?' His eyes darted between her and Levi with something akin to suspicion.

'I'm ashamed to say I knocked her over. I wasn't looking where I was going, and I ran straight into her. I was mortified. I'm still very sorry about that,' he added, looking at her.

A smile pulled at her lips. Handsome and sweet? A much more winning combination than aloof and arrogant. 'Don't worry about it. I probably would have fallen over without your help anyway.'

He laughed again and she felt another bolt of attraction towards him, something totally different to the confused feelings she'd had towards Gabriel since her arrival. Perhaps it had all been nothing more than old, unresolved memories stirring inside her. Levi had sent a shot of electricity down her spine in a way that felt more exciting than the heavy past that currently bound her and Gabriel together. Though she wasn't looking for a new romance right at this moment, free and easy was exactly the type of thing she would go for if she were.

'So what can I do for you, Gabriel?' Levi asked.

'We need your help,' Gabriel announced. 'Naomi needs some private skiing lessons, and I thought you might be just the person to help her.'

'I have to warn you though,' Naomi said, less embarrassed about it under Levi's kind smile, 'I really am worse than any of the kids you were teaching.'

'Don't worry about that. Children often pick things up

59

much quicker than adults and if you've never skied before you have nothing to be ashamed of.'

That word stirred something inside her. She'd carried shame all her life because she was adopted, because her adoptive parents couldn't give her the labelled trainers and fancy clothes the other kids at school had. The love and security they'd given had made up for all that, yet – deep down – there were still times when she battled with feeling unworthy. Even now.

'I promise you,' Levi continued, 'I can teach you the basics in under an hour and if you've got a little longer, then by the time I'm done, you'll be ready for some of the smaller slopes tomorrow.'

'I really don't think so,' Naomi replied, shaking off the shadow of the past. 'I'm not saying you're not a good teacher, I'm sure you are, but I think I might be beyond help.'

'You're not that bad,' Gabriel interrupted.

'That's not what you said earlier,' she replied sharply. She hadn't meant to, but his earlier teasing had touched a nerve. Mockery that Levi's kind words had soothed a little.

The challenge sent Gabriel's eyes to the ground. As if sensing their discomfort, Levi spoke.

'How long do you have?'

'As long as you need,' she replied. 'Gabriel, you can go if you like. I can find my way back to Le Petit Chateau.'

'No, no. I can wait.'

She really didn't like the idea of him standing around

watching her, but if he was determined to stay then that was down to him.

Levi gave her a wide grin. 'Shall we get started?'

Naomi nodded and they moved away from Gabriel. He stayed where he was for a few minutes, then moved to lean against the trunk of a giant pine tree. She hoped some of the snow piled up on the branches would fall on his head like something from a movie but unfortunately, it didn't.

For the next hour, Levi gently coaxed her, speaking encouragingly, correcting things when he needed to, but most of all assuring her she was doing fine, that there was nothing wrong with not having done this before. Soon she was actually enjoying it, and as she relaxed she grew more confident. She loved the feel of the snow under her feet, the soft crunch as she moved around. He was a great teacher and laughter filled the air as he cracked jokes.

'You're my star pupil today.'

'Even against all those little ones?'

'Even against my favourite pupil – Tara.'

In their conversation last night over dinner, Mia had told her she needed to practise flirting, and feeling at ease with Levi, she found herself saying: 'I bet you say that to everyone.'

'I promise I don't.'

'So what do I get for being star pupil?'

A sound came from over by the tree, she heard Gabriel muttering something but couldn't make out what it was.

When she looked a bit closer, she could see him scowling like he'd hurt himself. She ignored him. He was clearly fine.

'I normally give the children stickers and a certificate. Would you like a certificate?' The light shone on his tanned skin, dancing off the stubble on his chin.

'You know, I think I would.'

He laughed and promised her one as soon as she'd mastered a snow plough turn. 'We could try tomorrow or—'

'Naomi?' Gabriel called, walking towards them. 'Mia is back. Do you want to stay or shall we go and meet her?'

She'd been having such a nice time it took her a second to decide but Levi and his certificate could wait. She was here to spend as much time as possible with her best friend and after the way she'd had to rush off this morning, Naomi was dying to know more about what Mia was up to. She turned to Levi.

'I've had so much fun, but—'

He held up a hand to stop her. 'You're here to see your friend. I completely understand.'

Handsome, kind, and understanding? Now that was a special combination.

'Perhaps I'll see you again for some more lessons—'

'I'm not sure you'll need any,' Gabriel interrupted. 'You've worked wonders, Levi.'

Levi looked like he wanted to say something else but didn't and Naomi unclipped her skis as he'd shown her. A cold breeze drifted over her as she picked up her skis and she realised the sub-zero temperatures hadn't bothered her as much as she thought. Being so active had kept the chill from her bones but she was looking forward to trying out that luxurious bathtub in her room, soaking down into the bubbles and relaxing her muscles.

'See,' she said to Gabriel as they made their way to Mia's cabin. 'All I needed was a good teacher.'

Again she'd expected a scowl and a grunt but was surprised to see a smile spread over his face. A second later, a deep chuckle filled the air. 'You were right. I was a terrible teacher.'

'You're not going to disagree with me?'

'No, especially not now you can chase me across the snow. Not that you can chase me very fast.'

She laughed too but no matter how hard she tried she couldn't make out the man beside her. He caught her looking and she turned away. 'You wait till I've had some more lessons with Levi. Then you won't be able to insult me.'

His face darkened and he suddenly headed in the opposite direction. 'Le Petit Chateau is that way—' He pointed out the route Naomi should follow. 'I have to go.'

She stood still, like a lemon, holding her skis, sticks and helmet. What had she said? She'd have to ask Mia, as subtly as she could, what had happened to change him so much.

Naomi made her way back to Mia's chalet but all the while her brain was buzzing, replaying the day's events over and over. When he'd held her earlier something had stirred around them. Was it sexual tension that had electrified the air between them? Or was it simply memories of a night long, long ago and the unfulfilled dreams she'd allowed herself to contemplate? Dreams that, as the years had passed, hadn't faded from her mind and still existed as vividly as they had back then.

Chapter 6

The next morning, Naomi was staring at another delicious breakfast spread. In the living room, a young man – one of the housekeeping staff – was dusting.

'Good morning,' Naomi trilled.

The young man smiled. '*Guten morgen.*'

'Can I tempt you to share some of this with me?' she asked, pointing at the buffet table. 'This is far too much for me to eat.'

'Oh, no thank you.'

'What's your name?' Naomi asked.

'Peter.'

'Well, it's lovely to meet you, Peter. And if you decide to grab something, I promise I won't tell.'

He smiled shyly and kept on with his work.

Today, as well as meats and cheeses and small pastries, there was also a bowl of freshly made muesli with different yoghurts on the side. Naomi eyed it warily. She'd never been a big fan of muesli though this looked far more appetising than anything you'd buy from a supermarket. If they were lining up all this for the single guest currently staying at Le Petit Chateau, then what would it be like with a houseful? They'd be impressed – she knew that for sure. She really must find out from Mia who the chef was and say thank you. Naomi took a moment to decide how many pastries were too many when Mia appeared at her side immaculately dressed as usual, with her hair tied back in a high, springy ponytail.

'*Guten morgen*, Peter,' Mia said as she walked through to Naomi. Though she smiled widely when she saw her friend, it didn't reach her tired eyes.

'Are you okay?' Naomi asked.

'I'm fine.' She grabbed a pastry and popped it in her mouth. Her eyes crinkled at the corners, but the dark blue circles were clear underneath them.

'Are you joining me for breakfast?'

'If that's okay?'

'Of course it is. I wasn't sure if I'd get to see you today so this is a wonderful surprise.'

'I'm sorry I've been so busy.'

'Is everything all right? You've seemed a little rushed lately.'

'Everything's great,' she answered a little too quickly. 'You should try the muesli. It's made here on site in the kitchens. They're down in the basement. It's really good.'

It felt a little ungrateful to say she didn't like muesli

and as she'd noted earlier, it was the most appetising she'd ever seen it. The buffet had been laid out on a long dense wooden sideboard that separated the lounge from the dining room. She picked up a bowl and added a couple of spoonfuls. The oats and seeds were dotted with raisins, flaked almonds and shards of grated apple. She added some of the tangy natural yoghurt on top and found herself interested to see what a proper Swiss muesli tasted like.

'Okay but stop trying to distract me.' She gave Mia the side-eye. 'You say everything's fine, but I know there's something.'

'Are you trying to tell me I look terrible?'

'You look gorgeous. As normal. I'm saying you seem a little stressed.'

Mia grabbed a small plate, loading it up with tiny apple strudels. 'I don't normally forget meetings that's for sure.'

Naomi looked sadly at her bowl of muesli. She'd have a few mouthfuls to be polite and then grab some of the golden pastries with squelchy apple and raisin filling oozing from the sides. 'So what's going on?'

They made their way to one of the tables and sat down opposite each other. Naomi ate her first bite of the muesli, giving Mia time to speak. 'Oh my God,' she declared, covering her mouth so bits of food didn't fly out. She knew she shouldn't speak with her mouth full; it was one of the first things her mum had gently taught her when she'd gone to live with them at four years old, but this time she couldn't help it.

Mia smiled. 'Told you it was good.'

'Why does it taste so good? There are a million different brands of muesli in the shops and none of them taste like this. This is so . . .' She couldn't find a word to describe the subtly balanced mix of flavours singing in her mouth. The creaminess of the oats, the sweetness of the apples and raisins, the nuttiness of the almonds playing with the tang of the yoghurt. She'd never eaten anything like it. This was totally unlike the dry bird food she'd stayed away from at home. 'This is perfect. The chef is a genius.'

'I'll pass that on.'

She finished her mouthful and took a sip of coffee. 'Now, can you stop trying to distract me from what's going on with you?'

Mia sighed, picking up a stray flake of pastry and popping it in her mouth. She normally had a voracious appetite and that she was picking at her food heightened Naomi's concern. She glanced over her shoulder and saw that Peter had now disappeared upstairs. 'You remember I told you about the gala party on Christmas Eve?'

Naomi nodded.

'I normally have some help from a friend of mine, an events planner, but due to heavy snowfall she hasn't been able to fly out yet. Now she's told me she's been asked to do a huge charity event and can't make it out. I've been doing everything myself and now that she isn't coming at all, I'm worried I'm going to run out of time. I've been charging around like a crazy woman trying to get everything prepared but there's only twenty-four hours in a day and twenty-two days to go. We're already in December and nothing's decorated yet—' She cast a hand around, motioning to the ground floor of Le Petit Chateau. 'I'm just getting further and further behind and if I don't get something sorted soon it's going to be a disaster.'

'You know,' said Naomi, scraping the last of the muesli onto her spoon and considering a second bowl rather than some of the tiny apple strudels. Those, she thought, she could take up to her room for a snack later. 'For someone as intelligent as you, you can be very dim sometimes.'

Mia's face lightened instantly as she laughed. 'Well that's rude.'

'I can help you, can't I?'

'No.' She shook her head. 'Definitely not. You're my guest. Here for a break of your own.' She sat back, staring sternly at Naomi as if she'd just suggested they'd go skiing naked. 'I won't hear of it.'

'I am here as your guest,' Naomi replied calmly. 'Staying in this amazing place, eating this amazing food for free. It's the very least I can do. I'd like to help. I've discovered I'm not the greatest at skiing—' Gabriel's strong arms around her as she clung to his broad shoulders sprung to her mind. 'And there's only so much exploring I can do. Let me help please. I'm a high-flying lawyer; I'm pretty good at organising things.' She reached out and took Mia's hand. 'You don't have to do this all on your own.'

Mia stared at her friend for a second. 'That's a very convincing argument.'

'They're my speciality.'

'But no.'

'Mia, stop being so stubborn. Why won't you let me help?'

'Because you've been through enough lately. What you need is to relax.'

'I'll have plenty of time for that too. And, if you let me help, it'll mean you'll have more time for us to spend together and it is you I'm here to see. Oh, and if you don't say yes, I'll follow you around all day annoying you.'

Mia laughed, her features softening. Naomi could see some of the stress vanishing from her. 'You're really sure you want to do this?'

'Definitely.'

She sighed, defeated. 'Okay then.'

'So, you'll let me help?'

'I will.'

'Great. What can I do then?'

'How do you feel about decorating this place for me? The decorations are in a storage unit on the edge of town. We had to move everything out for the renovations. I know you didn't want to do Christmassy things but—'

'It sounds fun.' Naomi plastered on a smile even though the idea filled her with dread. She should have known coming to a winter wonderland over Christmas was going to involve some Christmassy things. Perhaps there was a way she could frame it in her mind that wouldn't feel so festive.

'Are you sure?'

'Absolutely. Decorating this place feels more like – I don't know – interior design? I don't fancy being surrounded by lovey-dovey couples giving each other goo-goo eyes under the mistletoe that's all. Decorating here will be different.' She could parcel it up as work if she needed to, but actually the idea of making this place look merry for a community party that just happened to be on Christmas Eve wouldn't be too bad.

'Wonderful. I'll call Gabriel and get him to take you this afternoon unless you had other plans?'

Her stomach tightened. She wasn't ready to spend any more time with Gabriel after yesterday. Especially after the way he'd stalked off at the end of the ski lesson she'd had with Levi. 'Gabriel? No, don't worry. If I can use your car, I'm sure I can find it myself. I'll use Dolly.'

Gentle lines formed on Mia's forehead. 'Dolly? Who's Dolly?'

Naomi held up her phone. 'Dolly's my satnav. I named her.'

'You did what?'

'I named her. I went for a Southern accent, so she sounds like Dolly Parton. It makes journeys much more fun.'

'Please don't tell me you thank her at the end of a journey?'

'Of course I do. It's good manners. And if Dolly Parton turned up I'd thank her for just being alive. She's a legend.'

71

The pair giggled, but despite Naomi's subtle protests, Mia was insistent. She would call Gabriel and despite Naomi's pleas to wait till after breakfast, there was no stopping Mia. She immediately seemed back to her usual self and stuffed a mini apple strudel into her mouth as she pulled out her phone. Within seconds she was dialling his number and before Naomi could stop her, he'd already answered. His voice sounded nearer than she'd expected and Naomi looked up to see him striding through the door, his phone against his ear and by his side, an enormous fluffy dog.

'Yes, my dear sister?' His eyebrows rose as he placed his phone in his pocket.

'Hans!' Mia trilled, ignoring Gabriel as he walked towards her, instead focusing on the dog trotting by his side. 'Come here, you handsome boy.' She lowered her phone, ending the call, and began fussing the dog. He twisted his head from side to side, enjoying the way she tickled behind his ears with both hands. When he noticed Naomi, he decided she too would like to give him some attention.

'Who's this?' she asked as she sat still, allowing him to sniff her and get used to her before she tried to stroke him. She'd learned from a dog-owning colleague that even sticking your hand out to a dog to let them sniff you could be seen as threatening behaviour if the dog was nervous and though she didn't think Hans was, it was better to be safe than sorry. As soon as he was comfortable, looking at her with wide endearing eyes, she began stroking the soft hair on his head.

'You know how to welcome strange dogs,' Gabriel said, his voice lifting. Was he impressed?

'A friend taught me.'

'This is Hans. He's my dog,' he added and Naomi laughed.

'I guessed that.'

His face clouded again.

'What breed is he? A husky?'

'An Alaskan Malamute but they look very similar.' Hans had ice-blue eyes and thick black and white fur that was wonderfully soft to the touch.

'He's lovely.'

As if hearing the compliment, the huge dog rolled over, his legs in the air, wanting her to tickle his tummy. She knelt down on the floor next to him and gently scratched his fur.

Gabriel watched her for a second before turning to Mia. 'What were you calling me about?'

Mia turned to her brother. 'Can you take Naomi to the storage unit? She's going to help organise the gala party.'

'Really?' Why was he so surprised? Did he think she wasn't capable or that she wouldn't want to? Painfully, she realised that with all the years that had passed between them he really didn't know her at all or perhaps he was so arrogant he thought the same of everyone. 'Why?' he asked Naomi directly.

She hadn't realised she'd have to pass a job interview with Gabriel first. 'I'd like to help,' she said, lifting her chin defiantly. 'If Mia needs a hand then it's my duty as her friend to get stuck in.' She sat back on her chair and Hans rolled back on to all fours before pushing his nose under her hand for another fuss. Gabriel was scowling. She liked his dog more than him at the moment. 'I'm happy to do anything she needs me to do.'

'I'm putting her in charge of decorating Le Petit Chateau,' Mia said. 'It'll be a great help and I know she has excellent taste.' Mia grinned at her friend before turning to her brother. 'So I need you to collect all the Christmas decorations and bring them back here so she can get started.'

'Fine,' he huffed and Naomi felt her skin prickle with annoyance. 'When do you want to go? I'll have to bring Hans with me too.'

'That's fine.' She might as well get it over with and then she could spend the rest of the day sorting everything out and deciding where it needed to go. The idea made her feel a little warm and fuzzy inside and she pushed the feeling away. 'I guess there's no time like the present.' She eyed her empty bowl of muesli and glanced at the beautiful ornate clock on the wall. Its traditional face sat in a mount made of pale driftwood showed it was only just nine o'clock. 'But I might have one more bowl of that gorgeous muesli before we leave.'

'See,' Mia said, smirking. 'You can't get enough of it now.'

'All right, smarty-pants.'

'Gabriel, will you join us? I'm going to have one too.'

He hesitated for a moment, taking a small step forward

then back before saying, 'Sure. I haven't eaten yet this morning and I'm starving.'

What was the hesitation about? Was it that awful to be near her? This morning wasn't going to be any fun at all if he couldn't even stand to be in the same room as her. At least she'd have Hans to cuddle when conversation died, which it inevitably would.

'Is Hans allowed anything?' Naomi asked, fussing him again.

'Unfortunately, this greedy guy has to have a specific diet. He might look like he can handle anything, but he has a very delicate stomach.'

'Poor Hans.' The dog eyed the plate of meat on the buffet table sadly and Naomi gave him another ruffle behind his ears before slipping him a piece of ham when Gabriel's back was turned. What harm could it do? She'd fed plenty of dogs ham before. They loved it. Hans must eat bits of food off the ground all the time. That's what dogs did. Gabriel was just being miserable. And what he didn't know wouldn't hurt him. Or her.

Chapter 7

'Are you sure you didn't give that dog some meat from the table?' Gabriel growled, winding down his window. The cold wind blasted in, but the freezing breeze was preferable to the decidedly smelly air currently circulating inside the car.

'No! Absolutely not,' Naomi lied, wishing she'd never slipped Hans the food. She'd thought it would be fine, a treat for Hans. But it certainly wasn't a treat for her right now.

The dog, who was wriggling on the back seat with a seatbelt attached to his harness, scuffled forwards, his stomach rumbling loudly, and he gave off another audible fart that echoed around them.

'Someone must have. I've told Mia not to feed him anything but dog food, but she never listens. Now we have to sit in this stench.'

Realising her friend would take the blame, Naomi

decided to own up. Wafting her hand in front of her face and trying desperately not to breathe in or out, she said, 'All right, it was me. I gave him some ham.'

'What did you do that for? I told you he had a delicate stomach.'

'I thought you were being miserable. I didn't know it was that delicate.'

'Miserable? I am not miserable.'

She decided now wasn't the time to argue. Hans began licking his lips. 'He's not going to be sick, is he?'

Gabriel glanced over his shoulder. 'No. But he probably wants some water. Can you?' He nodded towards the back seat where, next to Hans, lay a water bottle and plastic pop-up bowl. She manoeuvred everything around and placed the bowl in front of him on the seat. He lapped up the water. 'I told you not to feed him,' he grumbled again.

'And I've said I'm sorry.'

'No, you didn't. You just said you assumed I was being miserable.'

She replayed their conversation. He was right; she hadn't actually apologised. 'You should be a lawyer too. All right, I'm sorry. I should have listened to you—'

'As his owner and the one who looks after him.'

'Yes, as his owner and the one who looks after him, I should have believed you.' Naomi turned to Hans, whose eyes met hers looking decidedly sad. 'He'll be all right, won't he?'

'He'll be fine. He hasn't farted in the last five minutes so that's progress.'

Was he making a joke? A hint of a smile played on his lips as he stared out of the window at the road. She remembered the warmth of that smile and how, away from home, settling into university, it had made her feel like a light was shining on her. She turned to look out of the window.

Gabriel drove down the snowy streets of the ski resort and out onto the roads leading to the local town. Naomi had wondered what she'd say to him; what they'd talk about on the journey. Hans, it seemed, had provided a suitable subject. But now, as she concentrated on the scenery lining the busy road into town, it took her breath away – just as it had when she'd arrived.

The winding road, which seemed to have been cut into the face of the mountain, took them down towards flatter ground. The roads were clearer, the tarmac just about visible. To her left, banks of skinny pines and spruces stood tall and dark green, a contrast to the snowy peaks behind them. To the right, where the mountainside fell away, the tops of trees poked up like tortoise heads, level with the road. A part of her wanted to stop the car and go and touch one: to brush her fingers over the needles and branches. The lower they went, where the ground flattened, the green of the fields began to emerge as patches of snow melted.

Hans finally lay down on the back seat, snoozing happily.

'You're very quiet,' Gabriel said, glancing at her quickly.

'I was just enjoying being able to breathe again. And I was admiring the scenery. I stupidly thought it might be boring all covered in snow, just a sheet of white, but it's so much more.'

'You've never been somewhere like this before?'

'No. Whenever we went on holiday, it was to somewhere hot. Resorts and that sort of thing.'

'We?'

'Me and my husband. Well, soon to be ex-husband.'

'Oh.' His gaze shot to her and then back to the curving road. 'I'm sorry, I didn't mean to bring that up if you don't want to talk about it.'

'It's fine,' she replied, surprised at such a sensitive response. 'I'm okay about it.' This time she actually meant it or, at least, meant it more than she had before. 'We split up about a year ago. Our divorce will be finalised soon. It's just been nice to get away from it all.' She turned her gaze back to the window and the awkward silence that seemed to follow them around when they weren't distracted by a dog's dodgy tummy descended again. 'So, how long are you here for?' she asked after a few minutes. 'Mia said you were staying for a bit.'

'I'm not sure.'

She waited for more. Nothing. 'Mia hasn't changed much,' she said to fill the silence.

'No. She's still as driven as always. She loves being busy, but sometimes she can be too busy.'

'Well, I'm glad I can take a load off by helping with this gala thing.' She wondered what Gabriel was doing to help his sister but asking was out of the question. She could only imagine how that would go down, especially after nearly gassing them both by feeding Hans. After seeming to read her mind again, his tone was defensive and hard.

'I'm helping her as best I can.'

'Oh, right. Good.' She didn't know what he meant, or what to say.

'But my hands are tied.'

'What do you mean?'

He took a breath. 'It doesn't matter. Just . . . It's not that I'm not doing everything I can to help. I do know she's stressed.'

'I wasn't implying you weren't.'

'Your face—'

'My face what?' Her tone was sharp, and she was feeling defensive too. She didn't like being attacked for an incorrect assumption.

'Said otherwise.'

'My face never uttered a word.' Suddenly fed up with his mood swings she said, 'Look, don't project your insecurities onto me.'

'Insecurities? I was stating facts.'

'Facts are indisputable truths: things that can't be bent and changed to suit your own needs. Figures are facts; dates are facts. You were stating opinions. Your version of the truth. That's not the same thing as *the* truth.'

'Are you always so lawyerly?'

'Lawyerly?'

'Argumentative.'

'You started it.'

'Fine. Whatever.' He shrugged, keeping both hands on the wheel. 'Just don't judge me.'

'I wasn't.'

Hans gave a bark from the back seat making Naomi jump. Gabriel talked to him soothingly.

'It's all right, boy. Everything's okay. He's a sensitive dog, attuned to changes in atmosphere.' Gabriel gave her the side-eye and she turned to the window, ignoring him.

The atmosphere had definitely changed. It had been tense before but now it was filled with the residue of argument. Even she and Ollie hadn't argued this much. They hadn't really argued at all, which is why his asking her for a divorce had seemed so shocking. Maybe if they'd argued, they'd have worked through whatever problems he'd decided they had. Naomi suddenly pictured their relationship like a heartbeat showing on a monitor, it wouldn't have had the up-and-down moments like this gave; it would have been a level, unemotional line. A flatline, she realised with a start.

Gabriel switched on the radio and the rest of the journey was spent pretending that the songs playing would eventually wipe out the awkwardness. They entered the edge of town and Gabriel said, 'The unit is on the other side of town, but it won't take long to get there.'

Houses began to gradually appear, and suddenly the streets were lined with small, square buildings with red-tiled roofs and wooden shutters at the windows. There was a strange mix of both Gothic and Romanesque architecture that gave the place a distinct character all of its own.

Spruce trees were dotted everywhere, taller than the buildings, making them appear short and squat by comparison. Every roof was dusted with snow. It was larger than she'd thought, sprawling, but as people smiled when they met each other, eager to talk, or threw their heads back in laughter, it was clear this was a community.

They passed a traditional German market as they drove slowly through the busy streets. The stalls were lit up with twinkling fairy lights, steam rising from the ones selling food, queues of people eager to buy or taste whatever was on offer. She wound down her window and the scent of spiced red wine drifted towards her, mixed with savoury sausage. Her mouth watered, even though it hadn't been long since breakfast.

'What was that?' she asked Gabriel, pointing towards it.

'The Christmas market. It's here every year. There's always a small market there, but it doubles in size near Christmas.'

She made a note to visit as soon as she'd decorated Le Petit Chateau. Not that she wanted to feel Christmassy . . . but it looked interesting and she needed to buy a Christmas present for Mia and something for her mum and dad too. She supposed she'd have to get Gabriel a little something if he'd be around on Christmas Day as well. She'd get him something dull and inexpensive given that he kept doing everything he could to keep away from her and hadn't had the guts to mention anything about their past. She wanted Le Petit Chateau decorated as quickly as possible so Mia could stop worrying. As soon as it was done, she'd come down and sample as much food and drink as possible and see what presents she could get for her parents and Mia.

After they had passed through the market, she found the houses were soon dying away again, and they exited the other side of town to a sort of industrial estate with rentable storage units. Gabriel climbed out and opened the door for Hans. After unclipping his seatbelt, the dog jumped down and followed his master, sniffing around as Gabriel found the correct key, unlocking the unit and pushing up the metal shuttered door. Naomi followed, her hands furling into Hans's soft fur. He momentarily paused his sniffing to look up at her then carried on.

'Here we are,' Gabriel said as he stepped inside. 'The Christmas decorations should be in here somewhere.' He began to riffle through cardboard boxes and tentatively Naomi started to help. She didn't want to open one she shouldn't and have Gabriel moan at her for being nosy, but she couldn't just stand around while he did everything either.

'What's that smell?' she asked, scrunching up her nose. Somehow, the air smelled worse than the car; only this was musky and damp.

Gabriel's brow furrowed. 'I think there's been a leak. Some of these boxes are wet.' He looked at the ceiling and then at the floor. It was damp in places, the concrete dark grey. 'That's not good.'

Naomi opened the flaps of a cardboard box to see traditional German Christmas baubles. She picked one up.

It was a star made of thin wood, and a Christmas scene had been carved into the middle of it. But the wood was wet in her hands and it disintegrated into pieces. As she bent down and searched through the box, all she found were more wet and useless wooden decorations.

Gabriel picked up a box and stepped towards her as the bottom fell out and glass ornaments shattered all over the ground. The water had seeped in and soaked the bottom of the box and the cardboard had given way.

'*Verdammt*! They're all ruined.'

'Is this everything?' It didn't seem like enough to decorate the enormous lounge and dining room of Le Petit Chateau.

'No, there are a few more boxes here somewhere.'

'Maybe they're still intact?'

'Maybe.' He ran a hand through his hair, the other resting on his waist. She straightened and he looked at her, his pale blue-grey eyes meeting hers. They were alight with annoyance at the disaster around them but the fire it brought made Naomi's stomach flutter. 'You keep looking,' he instructed. 'I'll clean this up.' He grabbed Hans's lead and secured him to the other side of the room away from the broken glass. Without a broom he began gathering the shards into a pile with the side of his boot.

Naomi opened box after box but everything she found was either wet, broken or smelly. It was all unusable. 'I'm sorry, Gabriel, but there's nothing I can use here – it's all ruined.'

'*Verdammt*,' he said again. 'The removal firm we hired to move everything seem to have carelessly tossed the boxes with no regard for what's inside. We better get back and tell Mia. She is not going to be happy.'

Naomi stared at Gabriel's worried expression, knowing it was mirrored on her own and for a moment they were once again in tune. She turned away. Mia was most definitely not going to be happy and this was the very last thing she needed.

Chapter 8

'Ruined?' Mia asked, eyes wide as they explained what they'd found in the unit. They were standing in the living room of Le Petit Chateau, the fire warming their legs after the cold, damp trip into town. She shook her head, her features tightening in alarm. 'There's only twenty days to go. This should all be done by now.' She gestured to the room and began pacing. 'Okay, I just have to deal with this.' She let out a long breath and Naomi was surprised she'd been able to inhale that much oxygen. Mia pulled her phone from her pocket, her fingers swiping at the screen as she spoke. 'Okay. Think, Mia. Think. First, I'll have to find an online retailer, buy it all, get it delivered tomorrow, then decorate.' She turned to Gabriel and Naomi her eyes wide with stress. 'But with the snowfall who's to say it'll get here?' She began pacing again and Naomi watched with mounting concern. 'Father's been—'

'He's been what?' snapped Gabriel and Naomi was

taken aback at his tone. It hadn't been directed at Mia, but a definite protective edge had come to it. Even Hans had raised his head, awoken from the deep sleep he'd settled into. 'What's he been saying to you? He needs to stop putting so much pressure on you; it isn't fair. He needs to learn—'

'It's nothing.' Mia reached out and took his arm, giving a reassuring squeeze. 'He just likes reminding me of the time frame. You know what he's like. He hates me falling behind schedule.' She sighed deeply. '*I* hate falling behind schedule.'

Mollified somewhat, Gabriel said, 'As long as he isn't putting too much pressure on you. He can always come and do it himself if he's that bothered.'

Naomi felt herself frowning. What was happening in the Mathis family? Gabriel seemed almost angry with his father and Mia . . . well, Mia just seemed overworked and on the verge of exhaustion.

'Let's not get into all of that,' Mia said, removing her hand from Gabriel's arm and swiping manically at her phone. 'I can't take it right now. I need to focus on how to fix this problem.'

'Umm . . . I have a suggestion,' Naomi said, lifting her hand into the air. Mia and Gabriel stared at her. 'I'm still happy to sort out decorating the chateau. Why don't I find some suppliers and order everything we need? Or better still, why don't I just go down to the Christmas market tomorrow and buy a load of stuff? You've mentioned how much you want to support the community and thank them for supporting you, so surely filling this place with locally made decorations is a great opportunity to do that? And you don't have to do anything, Mia. You can still leave it all to me.' She released a big breath,

'Gabriel could drive—'

'I can drive myself if someone lends me a car. I don't need babysitting all the time. I'm not a child. And I know the route now after today. I won't get lost.' She was finding it difficult to be around Gabriel. 'I could even go this afternoon if you—'

'No, no,' Mia said, 'I can't ask you to do that. Oh—' She suddenly flopped onto one of the large comfy-looking chairs by the fire. 'I'd blocked off some time for us this afternoon so we could see each other, as tomorrow is full of meetings. There just isn't enough time in the day. I need to choose the wine for the party and—'

'Mia, if you need to work, I understand,' Naomi replied gently.

'She needs to stop working for a while and relax,' Gabriel added, and Mia nodded her agreement.

'I know. I'd thought I could help decorate if everything was brought back here and combine spending time with you, but now, I need to think about a new budget for the decorations and decide where the money's going to come from and—'

'Listen,' Naomi said. 'You need to calm down and take a breath. This isn't like you, Mia. You're normally so unflappable.'

'It's just my workload is . . . what can I say? A bit crazy right now.'

'It's been crazy for months,' Gabriel interjected. 'Too crazy.'

Naomi smiled soothingly at her friend. 'I have an idea. Why don't we grab a drink and go through each room making a list of what we need. That way you'll get an idea of budget, and we can still spend some time together.' Though she was still against all things Christmas, at least this way she got to spend time with Mia and they could feel like they were making some headway with the party planning.

Mia suddenly brightened. 'We could even taste the wine samples for the gala party. They're at my office. I could go and grab them before we start. I need to tell them by the end of the week what we want.'

'It sounds perfect.' Naomi grinned. She was happy to see Mia relax a little.

'Tomorrow, I'll give you my company credit card and—'

'Mia,' Gabriel began, his voice carrying a warning note. 'Father won't like it. He doesn't like rules being broken – you know that.'

'Father won't have to know. And I trust Naomi implicitly. Don't you?'

Gabriel batted the comment away. 'Of course, but—'

But? That but was another reminder of how little he knew or remembered her. 'I'm not going to run off with the company credit card and book a flight to the Bahamas.' She kept her tone light but tension grew between them again. 'I know it's not an ideal solution but—'

'It'll be fine,' Mia said, regaining some of her composure. 'And if he ever finds out, I'll take the blame. It's my decision.'

'He will find a way to blame me anyway,' Gabriel said. The siblings looked at each other as if having an unspoken conversation, then Gabriel shrugged. 'Okay. Naomi, you can use my car. I have to work tomorrow so I won't need it. Here.' He handed her the keys and as he dropped them into her hand, his fingers brushed her palm sending a tingling sensation up into her arm and across her chest. She looked up and found his eyes wide as though he'd felt it too, then he scowled again. He turned back to Mia. 'I'd better go. I'll put in a complaint to the storage unit.'

'It's fine – I can do it.' She began typing on her phone again.

'No,' he said with a smile, resting a hand on her shoulder. 'I will. Stop trying to do everything.'

With a sigh, she relented, her shoulders sagging in relief. 'Thank you.' Gabriel left, calling Hans to follow him, and Mia turned to her friend, her energy renewing. 'Hot chocolate or something stronger?'

'Something stronger, I think. Shall I help you fetch the wine we're going to taste? I've never done anything like that before.'

Ollie had suggested it once but she'd baulked at the idea. The type of people who went to wine tastings knew things about wine and generally came from a class very different to her own. Luckily, she'd been able to talk him out of it without admitting the truth.

'I literally just drink a bit of each one and decide which I like best,' Mia said. 'I don't know anything about the flavours or smells. Sometimes, I even decide based on which label will go best with the colour scheme.' She grinned. 'Shall we get started?'

'Let's have five minutes by the fire first.' Naomi looked at her friend. She seemed exhausted. 'It'll do you good to sit down for a while.'

'Wait, I must just make a quick call first.' She picked up her phone again.

'Mia,' Naomi said, gently pressing the phone down towards her lap. 'Five minutes. The world won't end if you take a five-minute break. I promise.' Mia smiled and her eyes became glassy with unshed tears. 'Do you need to let them out?'

Just as Mia always teased Naomi about her inability to cry, Naomi would joke when Mia decided she needed a therapeutic sob.

She shook her head. 'No. I'm fine. I'm so glad you're here. It's been . . . things have been tough recently. I won't go into it all now but thank you for helping with the decorations.'

They sat quietly for a few minutes, Naomi making conversation about this and that. Before the full five minutes were up, Mia was itching to move and shifting in her chair.

'Which room shall we start in? Here? We always have

a massive tree out front of Le Petit Chateau bought from a seller in town. We've placed the order already so that is one thing ticked off. Though we'll probably need some hardy outside decorations for that. The ones from storage are beyond saving.'

Naomi marvelled at her friend's drive and her usual ability to deal with whatever was thrown at her but there was definitely something wrong, and Naomi was determined to find out what it was. Mia had always put pressure on herself to be the best but after the exchange between her and Gabriel, a niggling thought grew in her mind that at least some of the pressure Mia was under was coming from her father.

Mr Mathis had always been focused on his business – Mia was following in his footsteps and taking the lead. Gabriel too, must be working for him, though in what capacity she wasn't sure. She clutched the keys still in her hands, remembering the feel of his skin brushing against hers. She shook the thought away. He'd proven again today he was difficult and defensive, not the man she'd known before. And yet, the softness with his sister, the wish to protect her, had shown a big heart underneath his arrogant exterior. Naomi had never met a man so confusing and attempted to banish him from her thoughts – though she knew full well he'd linger there for the rest of the day.

Chapter 9

The fairy lights of the Christmas market twinkled against the pale white sky as Naomi pulled into the nearest car park and exited the car. The sky was veiled in a tapestry of clouds – all grey-white and fluffy – their formations carrying an ominous arrival of snowfall. Without the sun shining the temperature had dropped again. According to the people she passed – older couples talking about the weather and younger children excitedly hoping to play out in the snow later – there was no possibility of the forecast being wrong. Naomi didn't mind either way; she loved watching the snow fall from the fireside of Le Petit Chateau, staring out of the window as it tumbled from the sky. It was a world away from the busy, LED-lit London streets.

As she strolled between the small wooden chalets, the whole place was an assault on her senses in the most heavenly way possible. As well as the warm glow of sparkling lights, the myriad smells from the different foods that were cooking made her hungry. Her appetite sprang to life and she wanted to eat everything. From the sweet apple strudels, crepes and roasted chestnuts to the savoury *bratwurst*, newly discovered *reibekuchen* and potato fritters. She wanted to eat it all, and though she'd had another wonderful breakfast at Le Petit Chateau – this time with muesli made with dried cranberries and hazelnuts – she couldn't resist a bag of roasted chestnuts as she perused the stalls.

The night's fresh snowfall crunched underfoot just as the sweet chestnuts crunched in her mouth. She heard a child squeal and tilt her head to the sky as snowflakes started to fall down gently, landing on her nose and eyelashes. The Scrooge inside her that had existed in London began to melt even though she'd intended to treat today like nothing more than another job to be completed. She had the list she and Mia had prepared yesterday, a pen to tick things off and Mia's company credit card. She felt both happy to be trusted with it but nervous at the same time and kept checking her wallet was safely in the bag slung across her body. Yet, she couldn't deny that being surrounded by the sights and smells of Christmas – choral festive music playing all around her, the snow under her feet and mountains encasing her – caused an excitement inside her that she hadn't experienced since she was a child. A smile began to tug at her mouth, and she dropped her head worried that people would think she was crazy smiling at nothing. It wasn't nothing though, a small voice in her head said. It was a change. A release. A childlike enjoyment that, for once, she didn't feel ashamed of.

Growing up, when she'd first come to live with her adoptive parents, Christmas had been exciting but scary. She'd never known how long it would last. Would she end up back in foster homes again? Would they change their minds and send her back? Over the years she'd hoped that feeling would disappear but even as she'd grown up, and each Christmas had brought a new tradition, a little part of her remained worried that this one would be the last. That at some point, the love would run out. It had for her biological parents, so what would be the difference here? She'd wondered if there was something deep inside her that was simply unlovable. She shook the thoughts away, happy to be walking around this winter wonderland on her own, with thoughts of a family Christmas distant in her mind.

Next to the chestnut seller was a stall selling hand-carved wooden ornaments. A large four-tiered Christmas scene complete with wings at the top hung down behind the vendor's head. The top tier had angels with trumpets, the second the three wise men, the third Mary and Joseph on the donkey and the fourth baby Jesus in his manger. It was beautifully crafted, and she could just picture it hanging in the entrance hall to Le Petit Chateau. She made a note to come back for it later.

Feeling the cool wind on her face, she tugged her hat down tighter and walked on, stopping a couple of stalls down at one selling shining Christmas baubles. They hung from ribbons at the front of the stall and were laid out neatly in rows. She joined the queue to have a look, holding them gently and admiring the hand-painted swirls on the glass.

With Mia yesterday, as they walked around Le Petit Chateau drinking wine and making notes on what decorations they should have, it was decided that bright colours would contrast beautifully with the natural décor. Mia loved splashes of colour and where she'd used them it really made the wood stand out. Red, green and gold were going to be the main colours and the decorations in front of her were perfect. She'd also add a few white ones here and there, like the beautiful diamond-shaped bauble she was holding now, to add a little something special. When the busyness had died down, she spoke to the vendor.

'*Morgen!*' the man said heartily. He was in his early fifties, his nose red from always being in the cold and his kind brown eyes creased at the corners as he smiled.

'*Morgen,*' she repeated cheerily.

'You like this one?' He pointed to the row of ornaments similar to the one she was holding.

'Was my accent that bad?' she joked.

'Not at all. I already knew you were Mia's English friend staying at Le Petit Chateau.' He gave a friendly grin that put her instantly at ease.

'Oh, I see. News travels fast around here, doesn't it?'

'My son Peter works there. He said you were very kind to him, trying to share your breakfast.'

Naomi smiled. 'I remember him. They keep giving me way too much food! Honestly, he'd be doing me a favour if he took some.'

'I will tell him.'

'Thank you.' She shifted on the spot to keep warm. 'Everyone here is very friendly.'

'It's why I've never left and why so many people who visit come back year after year. There is a sense of being home here.'

There *was* a sense of home here, particularly in the market area where everyone gathered together. She watched the stallholders chatting as soon as they were able, huddled together in little groups and then darting back to their stalls to serve. He smiled warmly and she turned her attention back to the ornament.

'These are absolutely beautiful. I was wondering if I could order some for Le Petit Chateau.'

'Le Petit Chateau?' he asked confused.

She didn't think it prudent to explain why they were changing the Christmas decorations and instead said, 'As the place has had a revamp, Mia wanted to do the same with the Christmas decorations and she wanted to use as many locally produced things as she could.'

'Wonderful.' He beamed. 'How many does she need?'

'Well—' She and Mia had sat and argued good-naturedly over this for more than an hour after touring the hotel. They were going to have one Christmas tree in the lounge and another in the dining room as everyone would be mingling in those areas, with smaller ones in the hotel bedrooms that would be filled after Christmas with paying guests. Mia had asked if Naomi wanted one for her bedroom, but she'd declined. She didn't need a whole tree but had agreed to a few decorations. A memory of decorating the tree with her family popped into her head.

They hadn't had a lot of money growing up. Her parents still didn't now, which was why she'd bought them the cruise for their anniversary. Holidays were a rare treat for them, and she wasn't going to drag them home to spend Christmas with her when they deserved to go off and enjoy themselves. As a child, she hadn't had as many presents as other children whose front rooms had been full of prettily wrapped boxes, but they'd always given her what she could – the main toys she'd wanted – and as she'd got older, the designer perfumes and trainers that had felt so important.

They'd felt important with Ollie too and with the people at work. She had to look the part of the high-flying corporate lawyer with designer handbags and shoes, yet when she thought back on her family Christmases, she only remembered the things that hadn't cost much money: making gingerbread men with her mum, decorating them with her dad and all hanging them on the tree together. She remembered making reindeer food on Christmas Eve, never realising that it was all the old stale cereal from the cupboard, and some crushed-up blusher from her mum's make-up box because they hadn't any glitter. She remembered snuggling on the sofa between them on Christmas Day once all the presents were opened, watching a festive movie. She smiled at the memory, feeling it warm her from inside.

Abruptly snapping back to reality she said, 'I think we're going to need about a hundred.'

'A hundred?' he asked incredulously.

Naomi went on to briefly outline their plans for Le Petit Chateau for the festive gala party on Christmas Eve. 'Is that possible?' she asked, concern growing inside her at the frown pulling his brows together.

'I don't have that many as these are all handmade. And I don't think I could make enough in time. But I know someone who might be able to help.' He called across the crowd of people filling the walkway to the next aisle. 'Elias, come here.' He beckoned him over and though he spoke in German she could see he was outlining everything Naomi was asking for. If she'd been expecting rivalry between the two businesses she was wrong, because after a moment he and Elias turned to her, smiling.

'We can do it. Elias will help too.'

Elias, who was about the same age, nodded. 'It's wonderful they want to use our handmade decorations. I know they have used mass-produced ones before. Some of my fellow neighbours have commented on it, though we didn't like to say anything to the Mathis family as they are always very good to us hosting community events and giving us space for the youth groups. Everyone will be very pleased the hotel is using local craftsmen and women.'

'That's wonderful,' Naomi replied. 'When do you think you can have them ready by?'

'Between us? A week? Or maybe ten days. We know how important the gala opening is to Mia.'

That would take them to the fifteenth of December. She still needed to pick the Christmas trees and have them delivered to the hotel so that would have to do. She had a feeling they would let her know if they were able to deliver them early and she wouldn't be surprised if they did. 'That's fine. Thank you so much. I'm Naomi by the way. Naomi Winters.'

'Winters?' he repeated with a smile. 'That's a good name for out here.' His smile was warm as he signalled to the snow still gently drifting down. 'This is Elias and I am Noah.'

She went to get out her wallet, but Noah shook his head. 'We will send the bill to Mia.'

'Wonderful. Thank you.' That should keep Gabriel and the senior Mr Mathis happy as she wouldn't need to use the company credit card. Now she needed to find some smaller decorations to fill the spaces in between, and there were certainly enough to choose from.

'You should visit Caspian's too. He has a shop two streets away and he sells the most beautiful hanging decorations and Christmas scenes. They will be perfect for the gala. He doesn't come to the market, but he is one of the best artists in Switzerland.'

'Ah, I will, thank you. Why doesn't he come to the market?'

'He prefers the quiet of his shop, though he does like to visit the schools and teach. He likes to show the younger generation how to make traditional decorations, so the art is not lost.'

'How wonderful. Well, thank you. I'll see you soon, I hope.' She continued through the market passing endless stalls selling Christmas cards, homeware, cushions and blankets. She scraped at the bottom of the bag holding her chestnuts and frowned as she looked down to find the small paper packet empty. They'd been so delicious she hadn't realised she'd eaten them all. Suddenly craving the comfort of a warm drink, she treated herself to a hot chocolate complete with a perfect swirl of cream, marshmallows and shavings of rich, dark chocolate. She took a sip. It was divine and would definitely give her the energy to make it through till lunch. Her feet were beginning to ache, so she sat on a bench, the warm hot chocolate keeping the cold wind from her fingers. Her phone rang, breaking her concentration as she studied the perfect-looking drink and she looked at the screen, frowning. It was Ollie.

Why would he be calling her now? They'd almost finalised everything now and he'd been the one to suggest all communications went through their respective solicitors. Fear settled hard and stonelike in her stomach. Maybe something terrible had happened?

'Oliver?'

'Naomi. Hi.' His voice was calm, like they chatted this way every day. Like they were friends.

'Is everything all right?'

'What? Oh, yes. Everything's fine. I just wanted to ask you something.'

In the millisecond before he spoke again, her brain conjured different scenarios of what that might be. She only knew for certain he wouldn't be asking her to come back. That simply wasn't Ollie's style. Once he'd decided on something that was it; he'd never accept another option. He was inflexible, secure in the knowledge he was right. That he'd weighed up all other options and made an informed decision that this was the right course. There were never any 'maybes' or 'what ifs' with Oliver. And, even if he had said he'd changed his mind, she was sure she would say no. Though it would have been nice to hear.

'What do you want?' she asked briskly. She'd been enjoying her day in town and didn't want her divorce creeping in and ruining it.

'It's about the picture in the lounge. The one on the alcove wall opposite the windows.'

'Yes? I thought we'd decided I was keeping that one as you were having the other pieces.'

'Right . . . So you definitely want it?'

Even though it was freezing, her skin flushed with anger. It washed down her spine, pricking like needles. 'Yes, I do want it. That's why I said so in the meeting the other day.' After all that, he was trying to change the terms they'd spent a year thrashing out. It made her blood boil. It wasn't an extravagantly expensive piece. It wasn't a well-known or even an up-and-coming artist. She'd seen it in a gallery window when they'd holidayed in the South of France and had fallen in love with it.

'Yes, but, you don't even really care about art, and it got me thinking whether—'

'Whether you'd appreciate it more?'

He was silent for a second and she knew she'd hit the nail on the head. 'Well, I wasn't going to say that exactly but—'

She began walking in a small circle at the end of the bench, trying her best to keep her voice down. After everything they'd been through to get to this point it felt underhand and devious to call her and try and get more of their stuff. 'I don't get why you want it, Ollie. You've got literally everything else.'

'Except the house.'

'Which you're welcome to buy me out of. This was one of the only things I really wanted. I'm not giving it up.'

The holiday had been a few years after they'd married. They were both so busy with their careers it had taken a long time to arrange time off together and they were determined to make the most of it. It had been a perfect holiday. They'd never stopped talking and spent their days strolling arm in arm around tiny French villages. Then one evening she'd seen the picture hanging in a gallery window and knew she'd treasure it forever. The beautiful mix of colours, the way it seemed to capture everything special they'd seen so far had stayed with her through the night.

The next morning, she'd been waiting outside the gallery for it to open. She couldn't risk anyone else getting there and buying it before her and though it had cost a fortune to ship home, as soon as she'd hung it in the living room, she'd known it was perfect. Even now, though things had ended between them, she didn't want to part with the reminder of all the good times they'd had. She wasn't prepared to wipe out the years of their marriage as though they'd never happened. They were a part of her and helped her become who she was today. She also just really liked the painting!

'I'm happy to buy it off you,' he continued, as if she hadn't even spoken. 'Just name a reasonable price.'

The proviso 'reasonable' irritated her more than the offer to buy it and though she worried he might try to change their agreement, leading to weeks or months of more legal wrangling, she wouldn't give in. 'It's not for sale, Oliver,' she said firmly. 'Let it go. I'm keeping the things I brought to the marriage – which I know isn't much. Mainly my photos and odd little bits – but I brought that picture. You have every other painting, every other arty object you've collected over the years, the car and most of the possessions in the house itself.' As it was, she was going to have buy a new fridge and washing machine when she got back.

He sighed as if she were an exasperating child. 'Fine then. Goodbye, Naomi.'

She stared at her phone, the call now ended. Her hand tensed around it. Adrenalin was buzzing around her system just as it did after a day at work, battling for her clients. She took a sip of the hot chocolate, remembering how she'd felt before hearing his voice. She wouldn't let him ruin her day. Not when it had been going so well. She slid her phone back into her coat pocket and made her way towards the shop Noah had told her about.

With only the general directions given, Naomi wandered around the small streets, lined with the typically Swiss houses she'd grown used to on the way in. She turned down an alleyway to see a quaint little shop with orange light emanating from the windows. The walk had done her good and her anger had faded just in time for her to meet Caspian. The commercial Christmas music she was so used to hearing in London was absent and in its place was the gentle tinkling of miniature bells and the chimes of tiny musical instruments. The door stood open, and she climbed the three stone steps inside. An old man sat behind the counter, working, and all around her were beautiful Christmas scenes.

She'd often seen knock-offs of these sorts of things in shops but they were nothing compared to the expert craftsmanship and painstaking attention to detail of the real thing. Every item was hand-carved and hand-painted, the tiny brushstrokes visible on the rosy-cheeked faces of the angels and the brown beards of the wise men. As well as the Christmas scenes, festive decorations hung from the ceiling.

'*Morgen*,' the man replied, his mouth barely visible under a white Santa Claus-type beard.

Naomi smiled. 'Hello. These are all very beautiful.'

'Thank you. My father used to make them and his

father before him. This shop has been in my family for generations.'

'You must be very proud of it.'

'I am.'

As she turned on the spot, examining the room, a large star hanging on a green velvet ribbon caught her eye. Made from wood, it would fit perfectly with the décor of Le Petit Chateau and being so big it would make the perfect focal point for the dining room.

'If I'm not mistaken, you're Caspian, aren't you? Noah recommended I come and see you.'

'I am. And I'm always open to visitors.'

'I'm Naomi, staying at Le Petit Chateau.' She held her hand out for him to shake.

'It's good to meet you.' His grip was firm, his hands calloused from the manual work he did.

She went back to studying the decorations. 'These really are very beautiful. Can I ask how much is this?'

'That is one hundred euros.'

It was expensive but she could understand why and handed over the credit card with ease. He seemed surprised she wasn't making an excuse not to buy it.

'Would you like me to wrap it for you?'

'Yes, please. I don't want it to get damaged before I get it back to Le Petit Chateau.' His eyebrows raised at the mention of the hotel, and she felt the need to explain she was on a shopping trip for decorations. 'I was thinking it would look beautiful in the centre of the dining room for the gala party. Are you coming?'

'Oh yes, everyone goes to that. We are all eager to see what it looks like now. Before it was rather sad and needed a lot of work, but I hear Mia has done a wonderful job. That's what Peter, the son of one of the stallholders, says.'

'Noah, yes? I met him earlier this morning.' Suddenly, as she watched him wrap the star in tissue paper and place it carefully in a thick paper bag, an idea occurred to her. 'Do you have any more of these stars?'

'Not of this size. Smaller, yes.'

'That's even better. How many do you have?'

He sat a little straighter and stroked his beard. 'About twenty of different sizes.'

'Can I take them all?'

'All of them? Now?'

'Whenever I can come and get them.'

'I can send them up to the chateau tomorrow. I will need to get them from upstairs and package them up. My son can bring them.'

'Does he work at the chateau too?' she joked.

'No.' Caspian laughed. 'But he will be around tomorrow to be my delivery boy.'

'That would be brilliant. Thank you.' She could already picture exactly where these were going to go and a little burst of excitement filled her. 'Does your son work with you?'

He nodded. 'He will take over from me one day.'

Naomi thought how beautiful that was and hoped this store would be here for more generations to come.

Morning was falling into afternoon as she left the shop,

and her stomach began to rumble as she made her way back to the market. Perhaps she could get just a little something to quell her hunger. Without realising it, she had begun to walk towards a stall with a chalked sign stating *Flammkuchen*. She'd never heard of it before but seeing the other customers walk away with the thin flatbreads covered in delicious toppings like crème fraiche, bacon and onions, she knew she had to try one. The smells made her mouth water and as soon as the tiny food parcel was in her hands, the first bite forced her eyes closed and she could focus on nothing else. It was delicious and exactly what she needed after Ollie's phone call.

Walking while she ate, Naomi had just finished and was wiping her hands with the napkin, scooping up the crème fraiche that had dripped down her fingers, when her phone rang again. She prepared herself for it to be Ollie trying a second time, readying herself for another exchange. He was nothing if not persistent.

Chapter 10

When Naomi looked at the screen, her anger ebbed away to be replaced by concern. It was her secretary from back in London. She thought about ignoring the call. She was, after all, on holiday, but her assistant knew that and wouldn't be ringing unless it was something urgent. With a sigh, she answered.

'Hi, Danielle, everything okay?'

'Umm, no, not really. I'm really sorry but there's a bit of an emergency.'

'What's happened?'

'Damien needs some papers.' Damien was her colleague and they often worked on cases together. 'He said I should try and get you to do them because you're much better at them than him.'

Naomi hated these sorts of compliments. Compliments that were used as an excuse to fob your own work onto someone else. Damien was an expert at it. 'Did you tell him I'm on leave?'

'I did, but he wanted me to try anyway. He said it's business-critical.'

'What's it for?'

'The Johnson-Bradmore case.'

'Damn.' That was their biggest client and their biggest earner. She'd be expected to get it done and she knew full well that if anything went wrong, Damien would be the first to say she'd been too busy on holiday to help out the team, or that he'd asked her, knowing how critical it was and she wouldn't play ball. It was one of the things she found most challenging about her career lately. All the hours she put in would be fine if it was for a good cause, something she felt passionate about. Or if she was helping someone who desperately needed it, but the only people she was helping at the moment were rich bosses. How had she fallen into this trap? Still, she needed her job. It was important to her for a number of reasons. The thought of being out of work terrified her almost as much as the loss of financial security she'd worked so hard to gain. Gritting her teeth, she said, 'Send me the emails and I'll see what's needed. When's the deadline?'

'Tomorrow,' she replied, quietly. 'First thing.'

'Great.' Naomi scratched her forehead. 'Looks like I'm working through the night then.'

'I'm really sorry, Naomi.'

'It's not your fault, Danielle. I should have suspected something like this would happen.' She'd been so caught up in this place she'd let everything else slip from her mind. Every holiday she'd been on in the last few years had ended up with either her or Ollie taking some time out to do something work-related. She should have known this would happen. 'Send everything over and I'll deal with it, okay? Luckily I brought my laptop.'

'Are you having a nice time?' Danielle asked cautiously.

'I am and the food is divine. I'll bring you back some gorgeous Swiss chocolate.'

'You're the best. Much nicer than Damien. Don't tell him I said that though.' She laughed.

'I won't but it's not hard to be nicer than Damien,' Naomi joked. 'Don't work over Christmas, okay? You deserve some time off putting up with us all.'

'I promise I'll be turning my phone off on Christmas Eve.'

'See you soon. Tell Damien I'm on it.'

'Thanks, Naomi. You're a lifesaver. I hate to think how he'd have kicked off if I hadn't got hold of you.'

No doubt he'd have been using Danielle as his own personal assistant. Corporate law was full of men like him and, in her mind, it added another tick to the list of things she hated about her job.

Naomi rang off and felt the irritation coursing through her muscles. She walked directionless for a while, listening to the crunch of the snow beneath her boots and feeling the cold air on her hot cheeks. If she'd been at home, she would have dived straight in but being here she felt the snowy peaks tugging at her, demanding her attention. As she rounded a corner, an older lady struggled towards her, her small fingers straining under the weight of full carrier bags. Suddenly one of the handles snapped and the contents of the bag filled the road. Naomi threw her rubbish into the bin and jogged across the snow-covered street to help. Others had stopped to help too and soon the lady had everything back into a bag.

'Can I take that for you?' Naomi asked. 'Or perhaps give you a lift somewhere?'

'No, no,' the old woman replied, shaking her head vehemently so her fluffy grey-white hair bounced around her head. 'I don't live far. I can manage.'

'In that case let me help you carry this home. Here—' She gently took the carrier bag from the old lady and presented her arm for the woman to lean on. After a hesitant second, she took it gratefully.

'You're English, aren't you?'

'I am.'

'Holiday?' Her questions were blunt and to the point and Naomi wondered how much of that was simply her way of speaking and how much was her trying to catch her breath.

'Something like that. I have a friend out here who asked me to come and stay and as I'm getting divorced, I decided I'd rather be here with her than at home on my own.'

Why had she just blurted that out? Ollie's phone call must be lingering in her mind. She'd never have said something like that back home to a complete stranger.

'Very sensible. Who is your friend?'

'Mia Mathis.'

'Ah, Mia and the handsome Gabriel.'

'Yes.' Naomi chuckled nervously as thoughts of Gabriel floated into her brain. Handsome and arrogant too. 'I'm staying at Le Petit Chateau.'

'Lucky you. I've heard it is very beautiful now.'

'It is. Will you be coming to the gala party? Everyone in the area is invited.'

'If my son arrives I will. He is a human rights lawyer and cannot always get away but he said he would come with me.'

'You must be very proud. I'm a lawyer myself but in corporate law. He must get a great deal of satisfaction from his work.'

'He does. Do you not?' The woman's small, dark eyes watched her. Her face was graced with deep-set wrinkles, each line telling a story of a life well lived.

A sly smile pulled at Naomi's mouth. 'You're very astute.'

'I have lived a long time.'

'I don't like it as much as I did before.' Whether it was the fresh air, the old woman's easy manner or simply being away from home, she found herself opening up again and this time the little voice in her head that had always stopped her before stayed silent. 'I used to love it and I love the financial security it gives me, but it isn't as fulfilling as it once was.'

'Well, it is never too late to change.'

'Isn't it? Sometimes it feels like it is.'

The old woman laughed. 'How old are you?'

'Thirty-four.'

'Your whole life is ahead of you. Do you want to be miserable for the rest of your life? Doesn't it seem a long time to be miserable?'

'It does,' she conceded. The idea of being unhappy from now to retirement seemed too much to even contemplate.

'If it's too long to be miserable, then there is enough time for change. And there are many people in this world who could do with the help of a good lawyer. That's what my son says anyway. Ah, here I am.' She pointed at a house and after slipping her arm from Naomi's she rummaged in her pocket for her keys.

'I didn't get your name,' Naomi said, placing her bags on the doorstep. 'I'm Naomi.'

'Alina. It was nice to meet you, Naomi.'

'You too.'

She waved from the bottom of the steps and made her way back to the car as strange sensations roiled inside her. Alina's words echoed through her mind: *if it's too long to be miserable, then there is enough time for change*. Change was scary. Change didn't always work out. The prospect of working through the night didn't appeal to her at all and pressed on her chest: a physical reminder of how much she was falling out of love with her job. Was there a middle ground? A way to feel satisfied professionally while still retaining the financial stability that growing up with nothing had made important to her?

She climbed into the seat of the car, grateful for the shelter it offered, and sat for a moment, the keys in her lap, thinking. An answer didn't readily present itself, but Alina's words wouldn't shift from her mind. As she drove back from the market, the wide expanse of mountains and trees opened out before her. She could feel herself unfurling too, opening up to new ideas in a way her brain would never have let her at home. She had space to think here and, as it turned out, she had a lot more to think about than she'd originally believed. Naomi smiled. Suddenly, Ollie and the divorce seemed like a long way away, the world a lot fuller than it had been before. Though she'd be working through the night, she was beginning to feel that change – if planned and prepared for – could perhaps be a good thing.

Before she got out of the car, she took out her phone and out of curiosity googled community care law. A special branch of law that focuses on helping children who need to be fostered or adopted. As she did so, a warm feeling grew inside her. It was a subject very close to her heart and she wondered why she had never thought of it before. She suddenly felt like her life had been stuck in neutral, coasting along, but now it was time to ram the car into gear and move forwards. As long as she didn't get cold feet first.

Chapter 11

The next day, Naomi began hanging the beautiful star decorations delivered by Caspian's son. He'd been there bright and early and the boxes had been waiting for her when she'd come down in the morning.

After working until the early hours, she'd finally hit send on the case notes Damien needed and collapsed into a fitful sleep. She always found it difficult to switch off after a heavy work session. She'd slept in this morning and appeared groggily in the dining room at around ten o'clock, rubbing her tired and gritty eyes. Thankfully, the breakfast buffet was still laid out for her. Everything was freshly baked and warm and she wondered where the chef hid. She hadn't seen them yet and really wanted to thank them for the gorgeous meals they were preparing for her. She'd have to lie in wait for them one day. Now full from breakfast, she felt re-energised to dive into the box of decorations. She studied each beautiful object, deciding where it should go.

Just as she was hanging the largest star on one of the beams in the dining room, Mia walked in, casting aside the jacket she'd worn outside with the snow pattering onto the ground. The log fire was burning brightly, and Mia stood in front of it warming her hands as she spoke to Naomi.

'Where did you find those? They're gorgeous.'

'Caspian's.'

'The shop in town?'

Naomi climbed down after securing the ribbon. 'Aren't they gorgeous? I've got loads more to hang, all different sizes, and I've got a tonne of handmade baubles being delivered soon too. Don't you think these will look lovely in here with the Christmas tree over in the corner there?'

'They'll look wonderful,' Mia said, finally leaving the fire and making her way across the lounge to the open-plan dining area. 'You know, for someone who hates Christmas, you seem to be enjoying yourself.'

Naomi scowled. 'Do you want my help or not?' she teased. 'Because I could easily leave this to someone else. How about Gabriel?'

'No!' Shook her head emphatically. 'No way. He never got the hang of interior design, I can assure you. No, it's much better it's you. But aren't you enjoying it just a little bit?'

'Maybe a little bit,' she conceded, retying one of the decorations so both sides of the bow were even. 'The people in town were happy we – or should I say you – were getting local handmade decorations. I think it's done wonders for your reputation.' She suddenly panicked, seeing Mia's eyes widen. 'Not that it needed any help – everyone was saying how respected the Mathis family were – but—'

Mia laughed, holding out a hand to stop Naomi from worrying. 'It's fine. I knew what you meant. Before we redeveloped this place, we just ordered bulk retail ones. They were cheaper and I have to confess, easier. But I'm realising now that the extra expense is more than worth it. It's only right this place should be decorated with things from the town. I'm even thinking we could have some decorations for visitors to buy. Maybe here?' She went to a small alcove in the corner of the living room. 'I'm thinking shelves with baskets on, each displaying the decorations. I don't think we'd even charge commission. We'll just pass the profits straight on.'

'That's a great idea. I think the locals would really love that.'

She continued to examine it with her hands on her hips. Naomi could see her calculating the dimensions and how they'd display things in her mind. She was probably even deciding how the money would be processed. She was nothing if not thorough. Mia turned, smiling. 'It just goes to show, sometimes good things can come out of bad situations, don't you think?'

'I do,' Naomi replied, taking another decoration from the box and running her fingers over the ribbon. Her thoughts ran to the lady she'd met in town, Alina, and her son the human rights lawyer. If she hadn't been desperate to get away from home for Christmas she'd never have come here. And if she hadn't come here, she wouldn't have met Alina and now been thinking about community care law. An idea that over the last twenty-four hours had firmly taken root in her brain. But she wasn't quite ready to talk to anyone about it yet. There were still things she needed to get her head around. Things to understand, decisions to make and little things she needed to address herself before she could think about talking to anyone else.

'You've got a talent for this,' Mia said.

'I don't know about that. I think the decorations kind of speak for themselves. They're so well made they can't not look good. I could sling them anywhere and visitors will think they're fabulous.'

'Not quite true,' Mia replied, studying her friend. 'Are you okay? You look tired.'

'I'm fine. I just need more caffeine. I was up most of last night working.'

'But you're on holiday. I mean—' She signalled to the box of decorations. 'A working holiday, which I'm very grateful for, but you know what I mean.'

'It's fine. Something came up and I had to deal with it. It goes with the territory, I'm afraid.'

'I hope you don't have to do it again.'

'Me too.' It surprised her just how much she meant it. There was a time when she'd loved pulling all-nighters. Working into the small hours ensuring everything was perfect, that the client would be happy. But things were different now. Over the last year, as her marriage had faded, so had her love for her work.

As if sensing her tiredness, Mia changed the subject. 'Gabriel will like these, I think. He hates over-the-top Christmas decorations and has always liked the local crafts.'

Naomi worked hard to ensure the mention of Gabriel didn't bring any emotions to her face. The memories of long ago had been surfacing again, being around him and the fact she didn't like the man he'd become would be a definite barrier between her and Mia if she ever said anything. 'What's it like working together? Do you enjoy it? You've always been close. It must be nice to—'

'We don't work together.' Naomi paused as Mia giggled at the idea. 'I think we'd kill each other if we spent all day every day together.'

'But I thought he worked for your father, like you do.'

Mia shook her head, her face darkening. 'He's never worked in the family business. Gabriel and our father haven't spoken for years. Not long after he came to visit me at university – you remember that visit, don't you?' Naomi nodded. She remembered it all too well. How special it had been, and how heart-breaking. 'After that visit he told our father that he didn't want to enter the family business, that he was going to study to be a chef.'

'A chef?' Naomi couldn't hide the shock in her voice. Not at the prospect of him being a chef – they'd talked about it when he came to visit Mia – but that he'd actually done it.

120

'It was his passion, and he's very good, don't you think?'

'I don't know.'

A slight smile pulled at Mia's lips, though her eyes were still tinged with sadness. 'Yes, you do. Who do you think has been making all your meals?'

'Gabriel's the chef *here*?'

Mia nodded. 'Here and at another place nearby. He's very good, isn't he?'

'Very good.' It was all she could manage to say. She felt numb. His food was amazing. But how had she not known all this? She and Gabriel had lost touch after that night. The hurt she'd felt then burned in her chest again now. She'd wiped him from her mind. It had been the safest thing to do. After that, whenever she and Mia were together, she never asked about him. The hurt had been too strong. Over the years, their conversation naturally turned to other things: their plans for their own lives, work, boyfriends, lovers.

Seeing sadness fill Mia's face, she felt guilty for not asking after him. At least then she'd have known what had happened and could have supported Mia, who clearly needed it. 'What happened?' She edged into a chair, abandoning the decorations, and Mia did the same.

'They had a terrible, terrible row. You remember what my father was like? How I described him? Especially back then. He had set ideas for what he wanted us to do – what he wanted the business to do – but Gabriel never wanted to be a part of that. He became more determined than ever to follow his passion. Luckily, I'd always loved hospitality.

121

I loved growing up in hotels and being behind the scenes of it all, and I loved meeting customers or planning the business side of things. We thought Father would be okay if one of us entered the business, but he wasn't. He was so angry with Gabriel. Father didn't want him to follow his own dreams and after the row, they just . . .' Mia shrugged unable to finish the sentence, sweeping her ginger-bread-coloured hair behind her shoulder.

'Never spoke again?' Naomi finished the sentence and Mia nodded. 'How awful. And how awful for you being caught in the middle of it all.' She reached out and took her friend's hand.

'I love my father and I love Gabriel too.'

'But it must have been hard for you. Do they know what it's doing to you?'

'It was years ago now. Gabriel does his best and it's been easier for me than it has been for him. It was harder at first, but now, when my father and I are together, we just never mention Gabriel, and when I'm with Gabriel, we never mention my father – if it can be helped. I hate it, but what can I do? Father cut him off without a penny and he's been struggling to make ends meet ever since. He loves what he does, and he is making a name for himself, but it doesn't always pay very well. I try to be a good sister and help him as much as I can, which is why he's here, helping you and working at the restaurant nearby. When I heard they were looking for someone, I recommended Gabriel and he agreed to come back as long my father wasn't here.'

'Does your father know he's back?'

'No.' She shook her head vehemently. 'He lives a little further away now he's older. He's almost semi-retired. But it's like it's easier for him if he pretends Gabriel never existed. Though he has been asking about him more recently. I don't know why.'

'Maybe he regrets how things have turned out.'

'My father makes a point of never regretting anything.'

Emerging from somewhere within her brain, Naomi remembered a discussion she and Gabriel had had all those years ago almost as if she'd supressed the memory. She'd suppressed most of her memories from that night, but now, this one was breaking free. After Mia had gone to bed, she and Gabriel had talked honestly about their hopes and dreams. He'd mentioned wanting to be a chef but that expectations were holding him back and he wasn't sure what to do. She'd encouraged him to take the leap and they'd talked long into the night discussing different options.

Had he made up his mind that night as they'd talked so intimately? They'd been so full of dreams then. He'd spoken passionately about recipes and food he was going to make one day, dreams of his own restaurant. She was sure she was going to help people – do pro-bono work along with making money to support herself and her family. Yet reality had taken them far away from the idealistic daydreams they'd had then. She'd never imagined being divorced at thirty-four and he couldn't have imagined losing his relationship with his father. A horrible sadness swept over her.

It must hurt Gabriel deeply – not having a relationship with his father. She knew how difficult it was to navigate those feelings of abandonment. Feelings that had never really gone away. Naomi swallowed as her thoughts veered towards her birth parents. She didn't remember them and had never found out who they were. She'd been lucky to find adoptive parents who loved her and gave her everything she needed, but there was still a void within her, a hole that nothing seemed to fill. Growing up with little money, she'd thought building a life that offered financial security would do it but it hadn't.

Emotion rose within her, pushing the air from her lungs and she took a breath. Gabriel suddenly had a vulnerability to him she hadn't credited him with when she'd first arrived, but he clearly had his own problems to deal with. Was she a reminder of all that he'd lost?

'I wish I'd known,' she said to Mia, taking her hand. 'I could have been there for you. I should have been there for you.' She tightened her grip so Mia knew how much she meant it.

'You couldn't know,' Mia replied, meeting Naomi's gaze. 'I didn't say anything at the time, and I should have but it was all so difficult, and we were both so busy. Father had expanded the ski resort, and I had my hands full with work. You were busy moving to London and starting your career. I'm glad I've told you now though.'

'Me too. And you can always call me anytime, about anything. You know that, don't you?'

They shared a moment, both glad to be together again.

'So,' Naomi said, feeling it was time to lift the mood. 'Where do I get Christmas trees around here?'

Mia laughed, the residual sadness leaving her face. 'There's a Christmas tree farm on the outskirts of town. It's where we order our enormous tree for outside from. Gabriel can take you.'

'That's okay,' she replied a little too quickly. The memory of her and Gabriel's discussion that night – one of the most intimate moments of her life – was still reeling inside her. She'd needed space from him, and her feelings for him, yesterday and still wasn't quite ready to see him again. Not until she'd had time to process everything Mia had just told her. 'Just give me the directions and I'll go on my own.'

'Can you haul a giant tree onto the top of a car?'

'No,' she replied reluctantly. 'But someone there can probably help me.'

'Actually,' Mia said, fondling one of the ribbons on the decorations still to be hung, 'Gabriel will need to use one of the business vans. With all this snow you'll need a good four-wheel drive.'

'Can I just go and look and get them to deliver?'

'Sorry. You'll have to go with Gabriel.' Mia suddenly scowled. 'Why don't you want to go with him? Has he been rude to you or something?'

Yes, repeatedly, she thought, but admitting that might lead on to a conversation about the past. She'd kept the truth from Mia all these years and guilt swept over her. With everything she'd just said, Naomi didn't think now was the time, especially with Christmas coming up and her stress levels already being through the roof. 'I'm just sure he's busy, especially if he's working as a chef nearby. He doesn't want to spend his days off ferrying me around everywhere.'

'He doesn't mind. I know he's a bit . . . difficult at the moment, but I promise he isn't always this bad. He's being particularly weird right now and I don't really know why. I know he's looking for a permanent job but he's been worse recently, like something's bothering him, but he won't tell me what.'

'Maybe with Christmas approaching he's thinking about your father?' Naomi always felt the fact she'd been given up for adoption most keenly at Christmas. Not that she wasn't forever grateful for the life her adoptive parents had given her. It was just that there was nothing better to mess with your emotions than knowing someone hadn't wanted you.

'Maybe. Anyway I'll get him to pick you up tomorrow at ten. If that's okay?'

'Ten will be perfect.' She tried to inject as much enthusiasm as possible into her voice, but her stomach squeezed at the idea of spending the day with Gabriel now knowing his situation. She couldn't help but wonder how much their conversation that night had led to his decision to go against his father's wishes. How much of that decision and his subsequent hardship was her fault? Was that why he was being so weird with her? Did he blame her for the way things had turned out? Her stomach vaulted.

'Everything all right?' Mia asked.

'Yes, all fine, just tired,' she replied, standing and taking up the decoration again.

If only Mia knew the truth about that night. If only she could come clean to her best friend about everything that had happened with Gabriel all those years ago . . . but she couldn't. It had been too long and the time to tell her had long passed. She'd have to bury it all deep down inside and forget about it. She turned and began tying the ribbon, locking the memories away.

Chapter 12

Later that day, after Mia's revelation and a long morning inside decorating, Naomi decided some fresh air was in order. She was ready to get back out into the snow and feel the cold freshness of the air hit her cheeks. She loved the way it refreshed her soul and, even more than that, she loved the feeling when she was back inside, resting next to the fire in the lounge on one of the comfy chairs and her bones were thawing out.

After watching the slopes – streams of powder flying out behind skiers in bright, thick skiwear – she decided she was too tired for skiing. Not so much physically, but she still had to concentrate so much on what to do, and she didn't have the capacity for it after working through the night. Not only that, but it would take far too long to get into all the gear and, despite practising, she still wasn't that great, but she could easily throw on the good boots Mia had given her along with the thick ski jacket to keep her warm. With her fluffy hat, scarf and gloves, she'd be fine to explore on foot once it had stopped snowing.

Following the signs for one of the walking routes, she made her way along the snow-ridden track, enjoying the feel of the cold wind on her face revitalising her skin and the crush of snow under her feet. The normal routines of her life felt a long way away and she couldn't help but smile at how this holiday was doing her good. Having the space to think and look at her life from a distance was helping her leave behind her divorce and reconsider her future in a way she hadn't anticipated. When she crested the hill, the most beautiful view came into sight, and she paused.

Below her, the multicoloured lights of the ski resort shone brightly in the hazy glow cast by a setting sun. The sky was paling as the sun dropped behind the dark, rocky mountains, turning dusky with pastel hues of pink and mauve. Clouds were gathering once more, a mixture of white and grey, and she knew she shouldn't be out too long. She didn't want to get lost, though if she stuck to the track and followed the signposts there was no reason why she should. Still, she'd try and get back before it got too dark.

Other walkers nodded greetings as they passed and she smiled happily at them, enjoying the space that surrounded her. London was so closed in, so tightly packed. There were parks and trees for a little bit of respite – not that she saw much of them during her lunchbreaks.

Those were normally spent working or eating a sandwich at her desk with the only scenery available being the skyscraper office blocks and glass windows of the city. Nothing that compared to the clean air, snow-capped mountains and the pine trees that seemed as tall as the Shard. Still, a part of her missed the buzz of the city and she realised again that it wasn't the city that was the problem. It was what she was doing there.

The idea of switching career came once more into her head and she decided that this evening she'd spend some more time online looking at community care law. It would mean a drop in pay and instantly the thought brought a feeling of worry and insecurity. She'd worked so hard to feel equal to others. But had it worked? She had to concede it hadn't. No matter how many paintings she and Ollie had owned, how many expensive gadgets they had, it hadn't stopped her feelings of shame about her background. She'd worked hard to build a new life for herself but had she lost herself along the away? She was beginning to realise that no matter what you surrounded yourself with, it was still you in the middle of it all.

'*Guten tag,*' a man said, walking towards her. She replied automatically and carried on, but noticed he'd stopped. 'Naomi?'

She paused and turned around. 'Yes?'

'It's me, Levi.'

'Oh, Levi! I'm sorry! I wasn't really paying attention.'

'I can see I made a big impression on you then.'

Naomi laughed as he lowered his eyes shyly. He really was very cute. He was dressed in his skiing gear but without his skis and sticks. His helmet was tucked under his arm and his red hair shone in the light, the setting sun catching flecks of gold.

'You honestly did. I've just been so busy. My mind has been racing at a hundred miles an hour.'

'Oh? Is everything okay?' His concern sent a thrill through her. Who didn't love a man who actually cared and asked questions. Her and Ollie's communication had been one of the most difficult parts of their relationship and they'd never quite seemed to figure it out.

'Everything's fine. Really. You know what it's like when you go on holiday. Being away from home makes you think about things.'

'It does and especially here. The mountains make you feel so small. Life's problems become so insignificant.'

'That's true.' She smiled and he mirrored her, their eyes meeting. She thought he was going to say something more when he took a small step towards her. His mouth opened slightly, but then he closed it again and adjusted his grip on his helmet. 'Well—'

'I was just on my way back down if you wanted some company,' he said quickly.

'Actually, I was heading that way.' She pointed in the opposite direction.

'Ah, I see. Maybe next time?'

'Yes, maybe.'

Again, an expectant silence fell and after a second, she

said, 'I better get going. I'd quite like to be back before it's dark.'

For a moment, Naomi got the impression he was preparing to ask something but then he glanced at the track leading down. 'Goodnight, Naomi. Be safe.'

'I will,' she replied, admiring the swing of his shoulders as he confidently walked away. She liked a man with confidence. It's what had attracted her to Ollie, but at some point, his confidence had morphed into arrogance, or perhaps it had always been that and she'd only noticed during the divorce proceedings.

She carried on, feeling the pressure in her legs as the snow and the steep incline slowed her pace until the ground suddenly levelled out. She could see the patch of flat land through a small group of trees and decided to take the arm of the track that led towards it. Perhaps there'd be a bench or somewhere she could sit for a few minutes. The revelation from Mia about Gabriel and all the realisations about her own life were a lot to handle in one day.

As she walked into the open, she saw that the flat land sloped away back towards the resort, creating a long, shallow hill. On top of the hill stood Gabriel kicking a football for Hans. He looked handsome against the picturesque backdrop, his blond hair lifting in the breeze, the profile of his strong jaw. She felt her stomach tighten again and she turned, eager to walk away before he could spot her. It was too late.

'Naomi?' he called out.

She closed her eyes, wishing she'd been just a tiny bit

quicker, and reopened them, spinning around to face him. She walked towards him, just as Hans came running towards her, his tongue lolling out as he panted. 'Hello, Hans, and you,' she said to Gabriel before crouching down to give the soppy dog a fuss. He sat at her feet, the football between his paws.

'He loves it up here,' Gabriel said, manoeuvring the football with easy movements before kicking it for him one more time. The ball was far too big for a dog to grip in his mouth, but he was chasing it around with his nose, pushing it in front of him like a footballer dribbles with his feet. As he sped over the hillside deep tracks appeared in the snow. It was utterly joyful to watch, and Naomi found herself smiling.

'He seems to be enjoying himself,' she replied, feeling the atmosphere tense between them as Gabriel's eyes focused on her.

'You haven't brought any food with you, have you?' His tone was light and teasing and she realised he was referring to being trapped in the car after she'd fed Hans ham. A smile lit his face. He was the young man she'd known before. Before life and difficult decisions had weighed him down.

'No,' she conceded with a grin. 'Believe me, I learned my lesson the last time.'

'Good, because I think my lungs are still recovering.'

'Even with all this fresh air?'

'Even with all this good alpine air. I've been having nightmares.'

They laughed, both staring at the scenery, not meeting each other's gaze. It was if they'd gone back in time, returned to how well they'd got on when they were younger. But that night had been dangerous, leading Naomi to places she hadn't expected to go.

The view from the plateau was similar to the one she'd seen only moments ago on the path but now the resort was down to her right. Away to her left were rows upon rows of mountains and at the base were small wooden chalets, orange lights from inside blinking in the gloom. In places, the grey-brown of the stony mountainside poked through the blanket of white. It looked treacherous, wild and dangerous yet beautiful. The earth untouched and free from human development. She didn't know how long she'd been staring at it, but when she turned, Gabriel was watching her and her chest constricted under the brightness of his grey eyes.

'Sorry, did you say something?' For him to be watching her like that she must have not heard something he'd said.

He dropped his eyes back to Hans. 'No, I was just . . . You seemed entranced by the scenery.'

'I was,' she admitted. 'It's so beautiful here. Like I said before, I assumed it would be a bit boring. Everything covered in white and unreachable, but I've never seen mountains and a view like this. It's breath-taking.'

'It is.' They fell into silence, both watching the world before them, sharing a moment of peace. 'So I'm taking you to buy a Christmas tree tomorrow?' he said a moment later, looking back to Hans and kicking a clod of snow at his feet. He didn't sound very happy about it and the harmony of the last few moments vanished.

'If that's okay? Mia thought it would be a good idea. We can do it another time if you're too busy. I said I was happy to drive but she said we'd need a van.' She hated the way he made her feel like she was putting him out. She also hated the fact she was going Christmas tree shopping when she'd decided Christmas was going to be quiet and understated, if indeed it happened at all. The idea that she'd package the things she was doing for Mia up as work wasn't working as well as she'd hoped. Being here, in a winter wonderland, it was proving difficult. 'I just think she'd like to get everything sorted as soon as possible.'

'I don't mind.'

'Oh.' She was surprised at his sudden change of tone. 'Good.'

'Why do you say it like that?' he asked, kicking the ball again after Hans had nosed it back to his feet.

'I didn't say it like anything.' She went to cross her arms over her chest, but the thick jacket was too bulky and instead she pressed her foot into the snow, seeing how far it would sink down.

'Yes, you did. You said it like you thought I was being unhelpful.'

She hated being caught out and tried to hide it. 'You're imagining things, I'm afraid, Gabriel.'

He was calm, not rising to her responses. 'I'm not.

135

You thought I was being unhelpful and you still hate Christmas, don't you? That's it, isn't it?'

She looked at him, wishing she'd kept her eyes down. Damn him and his mind reading. 'My feelings about Christmas are neither here nor there. Mia needs me to do this for her and I will. She's letting me stay at Le Petit Chateau; I'm happy to help her in any way I can. It's the least I can do.'

'I don't mind helping either, but that doesn't answer my question. You're being a lawyer again.'

'No, I'm not.'

'Yes, you are.' Hans flopped down at Gabriel's feet, keeping the ball close so it couldn't be hit away. Gabriel thrust his hands into his pockets. 'Why do you hate Christmas so much?'

'I don't hate all Christmases—'

'Then it's just this one? Why?' There was a hint of vulnerability in his voice. Did he wonder if it was him?

'It's not that I hate this one either. See you're not as clever as you think you are.' A smile pulled at his lips, and she hated how it made her feel light and heady. 'I'm just off them for a little while. I don't really know how long. I didn't really enjoy the last one and this one is proving a bit more full-on than I expected.'

'Isn't being here making you feel festive?'

'Yes, and that's the problem. I'm not sure I'm ready to feel festive again.' Why was she being so honest with him? It wasn't that he was a great conversationalist; he just seemed to ask the right questions at the right time. Or perhaps it was their history reminding her of the secrets they'd once shared. 'Being here's making me feel better about some things,' she conceded. 'But that doesn't mean I fancy going full-on Mrs Claus and if Mia asks me to dress up as an elf at any point I'll be flying back to England before she can say tinsel.'

'You are very angry,' he said matter-of-factly, and the bluntness of his words shocked her. She'd obviously meant it as a joke, but she realised now how harsh her voice had sounded.

She stared at the ground, watching the snow pile up around her boots. She did feel angry sometimes. Ridiculously angry. Anger had been her shield through the divorce, through the horrid feelings about being adopted that had plagued her all her life. Anger had been a weapon and defence. 'I'm not always angry.' She kept her voice deliberately soft. 'But it was at Christmas last year when my ex-husband decided to tell me he wanted a divorce so you'll have to excuse me if I'm not bringing out the Christmas jumpers and singing "Away in a Manger" every two minutes.'

'I see.' He nodded and her anger disappeared into the vacuum of snow and space in front of them. 'Maybe tomorrow will make you feel different.'

'When we buy the Christmas trees?' She shook her head. 'I don't think it will.'

'Have you ever been to a Christmas tree farm?'

'No.'

He smiled knowingly. 'Then you will change your mind.'

'I can promise you I won't. I can't imagine rows and rows of undecorated Christmas trees are going to suddenly make me full of cheer.'

'How much do you want to bet?'

'What?'

'We can make a bet. If I win, you let Christmas back into that cold, cold heart of yours.'

'And if I win?'

'Then I will . . . cook you any meal you like.'

'Oh, really? Even if I want a dirty burger? You chefs don't like food like that do you?'

'Dirty burgers are the best kind of burgers.'

Their eyes met for a moment as he smiled. She turned away, back to the view. 'You're a good cook,' she conceded with a smile.

Gabriel gasped and placed a hand on his chest. 'A compliment? Surely not?'

'Don't get too carried away – I'm sure anyone can make muesli.' She knew that wasn't true but didn't want him growing arrogant. 'Okay,' she agreed, feeling her spirits lift. She'd always loved a challenge. 'You're on.'

'It's a deal?' He took off his glove and held out his hand for her to shake.

'It's a deal.' She did the same and slid her palm into his. When his skin touched hers, memories flashed into her head and he looked at her, his eyes wide as if the same had happened to him. As soon as she could she withdrew her hand, feeling it tingle as she pulled her glove back on.

'All you need is some Christmas magic.'

'All I need right now is a large wine.'

He threw his head back and laughed. 'We can do that too, if you like.' Was that an offer? Was he asking to buy her a drink? Before she could respond, he said, 'Shall I walk you back to Le Petit Chateau? It's getting dark and it's easy to get lost out here – even with the lights and the trail signs.'

'Sure.' She couldn't think what else to say, confused by his last remark and the feelings stirring inside her again. They began walking.

'Hans, come.' The dog did as he was told, still panting from the fun he'd had.

She glanced at Gabriel as they walked along, the conversation stilted once more. A part of her hoped he was right. Somewhere inside her, she wanted the magic of Christmas to come back. She wanted to put last year and Ollie's declaration firmly behind her and look to her future. She didn't want to spend every Christmas feeling like this. Ever since she'd been adopted into a loving family she'd always loved this time of year and didn't like that he'd robbed it from her, or that she was letting him. But she still wasn't convinced a bunch of undecorated Christmas trees was going to be the answer. The only thing she was sure of was that she desperately wanted to win that bet.

Chapter 13

'How are you supposed to choose?' Naomi asked the next morning as she and Gabriel exited the van at the Christmas tree farm. Rows of beautiful spruces grew higher and higher the further back they went. Though she hated to admit it, it was an exceptionally wonderful Christmassy sight and her soul was sprinkled with just a little bit of Christmas magic. Even though they weren't decorated with lights and baubles, there was still something special about them. Each tree would go home to someone, making their Christmas special. Just shopping for them was magical. She watched as children ran around, gazing at each one as if they'd never seen a tree before and then being called back by parents who were struggling to keep up.

Hans hopped out of the van and stood beside her. She stroked his fluffy fur and he leaned against her legs in appreciation. Remembering she was off Christmas, she pulled the smile from her face and reined in her enthusiasm. This was all work. Jobs to help Mia. Things that needed doing. And she had a bet to win.

'Why have you stopped smiling?' Gabriel asked. She hadn't realised he'd noticed.

'I haven't,' she replied defensively, tucking her caramel-blonde hair behind her ear and wedging her hat down further onto her head.

'Yes, you have. You were smiling like a kid in a candy store when you got out and then all of a sudden, it's gone. Why? Are you starting to feel Christmassy? Already worrying I'm going to win our bet?'

This freaky mind-reading thing of his really needed to stop. She didn't like it one little bit. 'No, not at all. I was smiling because I was enjoying a cuddle with Hans, that's all. It had nothing to do with this place.'

'Oh really?'

'Absolutely.'

'So it was nothing to do with you enjoying seeing all the Christmas trees, the kids running about and the sheer happiness of the place?'

'Nope. Absolutely not. Where – how – do you start looking somewhere like this?'

'First things first – we start with a hot chocolate. That will always get you in the mood for Christmas tree shopping. Come on.' She followed him to a small cart selling hot chocolates. 'These are the best hot chocolates in the whole of Switzerland.'

'Really?' She raised her eyebrows and pushed her hands

into her pockets. 'Because I had one in town the other day and it was pretty special so that's a big claim, Gabriel.'

As she said his name a flash of something powerful passed between them and she tried to ignore it, reminding herself of the hurt she'd felt before.

'I guarantee this will blow you away. They have a secret ingredient that no one else has.'

'It's not that secret if you know it, is it?'

'Always with the lawyering. I know because I suggested it. That's how I know it's the best hot chocolate in town.'

'Because you helped make it?'

'Exactly.'

She laughed. Again, he was the young man he'd once been. Lighter, happier and full of hope. 'Come on then, astound me.'

He ordered two hot chocolates, and she sat on a bench admiring the scenery, watching as the man grated dark then milk chocolate into a cup. He poured in hot milk and stirred gently. A second later he added some spices, more grated chocolate, and then topped it off with freshly whipped cream and homemade marshmallows. She could tell they were homemade since they were small and oddly shaped, but the texture looked delicious, like tiny white clouds but with sticky, ragged edges.

Gabriel came back, carrying them carefully. Seeing his owner return, Hans curled up at her feet. 'Here.' Gabriel handed one to her and sat down.

The first hot chocolate she'd had was amazing, but this was something else entirely. She'd never known food could affect her body like this and felt suddenly at ease, as if the world had blurred and wrapped her in a warm hug.

'Do you like it?' Gabriel's voice penetrated the velvety bubble.

'Oh my God, it's amazing.' She took another sip, feeling the delicious chocolate cover her taste buds. It tasted so different from the other hot chocolate or any she'd had in her life before. 'What are the spices?'

'I'm not sure I should tell you. You might sell my secrets.'

'I promise I won't. I'm a lawyer after all. We can call it client confidentiality.'

'Really?'

'I swear.'

'Hmm.' He thought for a moment. 'Okay. I think I trust you. It's cinnamon, cardamom, and a tiny dash of nutmeg.'

'It really is amazing.' Hans was watching her every move and she ruffled behind his ears. 'Poor Hans. He doesn't get to have any treats.'

'I'll give him something later. But he loves running around here. This is treat enough.'

'Don't the owners mind?'

'They're used to him by now. He's been coming here almost as long as I have.'

'Shall we start looking for a tree then?'

'Definitely.'

She followed him into the maze of trees and though one looked much like another, she knew exactly the size

143

and shape she wanted for each room. The enormous one that would stand outside Le Petit Chateau had already been ordered and would be delivered by a special truck. She wanted a fat bushy one for the lounge and one that was a little bit skinnier for the dining room.

In the middle of the farm, surrounded by greenery, it felt like it was just the two of them and, of course, Hans who was sniffing every tree trunk he came across. After examining a tree, and Gabriel from the corner of her eye, she said, 'So, why didn't you tell me you were a chef?'

'I don't know. I just decided to follow my own path and do something I loved.'

'I've been meaning to thank you for all the food you've prepared for me. The breakfasts have been delicious. I would have said something before but I didn't know it was you until yesterday.'

'I'm glad you like it. It is more homely cuisine – not all fancy restaurant food.' He sounded almost apologetic.

'No, but that's my favourite. Breakfast should always be something hearty and filling. What do you prefer cooking?'

'Honestly . . .' He pushed a hand through his hair. 'Both. Family cooking is different to a restaurant meal. Food should evoke different things, different emotions.' She listened to him speak, seeing his enthusiasm grow. An admiration for his passion rose inside her. He clearly loved what he did; she just wished his father could see it too. Perhaps it would change his mind about pushing his very talented son away. To Gabriel, food was more than just sustenance. It was about emotion. 'Family meals should be comforting, hardy. The connection is between the people there together, not with the food. The food should be delicious but in the background: something people enjoy but that doesn't steal the topic of conversation. At a restaurant, the food should have a seat at the table. It should be a talking point, a guest in its own right.'

'I've never thought of it like that,' she admitted. 'But I think I understand.'

'Not everyone does.'

The sadness in his voice resonated around them. 'Mia mentioned about your father,' she said tentatively. 'I'm sorry. That must be tough.'

His posture stiffened and he let his attention fall to Hans, stroking his back with the flat of his hand. 'It is, but I'm proud I'll have achieved it without his money. He built the business up from nothing, so I thought he'd understand I wanted to do the same, but he didn't.' She waited, holding her breath, wondering if he'd mention their conversations from all those years ago. 'Now, what about this one?'

It was clear he didn't want to talk about it anymore, and she wasn't going to push. She'd never liked people prying into her life either. There were things about herself no one knew and the fact she was adopted wasn't something she told everyone. Or anyone, really. She'd learned long ago that admitting such vulnerable things didn't always work out how she'd hoped.

145

She shook her head at the tree. 'Too squat.'

'What do you mean too squat? It's as tall as me.' He stood next to the tree, running his hand from the top of his head across to the top of the tree. The tip of its trunk ended just under his palm. 'Are you saying I'm short?'

'No! But that tree is too short and fat for the lounge. We need something taller and slimmer, or everyone will be bashing into it and it won't fit where I want it to go.'

'Are you always this fussy when it comes to trees?'

She playfully ignored him, flashing her eyes at the comment and continued to search. 'What about this one?' She pointed at one slightly thinner than the last.

'Too skinny. It will look sad in the corner.'

The laugh that escaped shocked her and she pressed her hand to her mouth to stifle it. 'Sad? It won't look sad.'

'It will. It'll look like it doesn't want to be there. We need something halfway between this one and that one.'

'Okay. What about him?'

'Him?' He stared. 'You think the tree is a he?'

'Of course. Don't you?'

'I've never thought of it as anything other than a tree. But we can call him Tree-mothy if you like.'

She laughed again and the release of tension it gave made her feel like herself. The version of herself who laughed and loved Christmas. The version of herself who felt safe and happy in the bosom of her family. She hadn't laughed a lot lately and she'd forgotten how it made her body and mind feel. Combined with the warmth of the hot chocolate, she could feel her walls melting away. Gabriel too seemed more relaxed. Happier too. She tried to stop the laughter but the more she tried, the worse it got and before long she was doubled over, holding her stomach.

'Tree-mothy!'

'Yes, and the other one can be Tree-vor.'

'Oh God.' To her horror she began to snort as the urge to suppress her laughter battled with the urge to let it out.

Gabriel threw his head back, laughing with her. 'Are you okay?'

'No! I don't think I am.' They laughed together, one starting the other as soon as they gained control of themselves. Finally, after a few more minutes and many, many deep breaths, she regained control of herself and straightened up wiping her eyes. 'Okay. I'm okay. I'm calm. I'm fine now.'

'Sure?'

'Yes.' She met his eye and the laughter almost started again. 'Okay, let's find Tree-vor. Tree-mothy needs a friend.'

They carried on looking, strolling in and out of the rows of trees. The heavy scent of pine filled the cold, fresh air and her taste buds tingled from the last of her hot chocolate.

'I'm sorry to hear about your divorce,' Gabriel said, blindsiding her. She'd felt so relaxed that her defences didn't automatically go up.

'Thanks. I appreciate it.'

'For him to do it at Christmas? That's horrible.'

'It was a difficult time. You must find Christmas hard too. With your father, I mean.'

'Relationships can be difficult.' He glanced at her after speaking, seeing how the words resonated. Was he referring to what had happened between them? Not that it was any sort of relationship.

'Is that why you're off love like I am Christmas?' He frowned in confusion. 'Mia said you were a lone wolf. Not interested in relationships.'

'I'm not off love. I just . . .'

'Yes?'

'Nothing. It doesn't matter. But no, I'm not off love.'

'So you've never been married?'

'No.'

She could feel him closing down again and did her best to lighten the mood once more. She'd actually been enjoying herself, getting to know the man he was now. The arrogance she'd seen when he'd first arrived had vanished. 'Should it be Tree-vor or should it be a woman? We could have Tree-sa or . . .'

'Yes?' He lengthened the word, filling it with expectation.

'I can't think of any more.'

He chuckled. 'Let's decide when we find it. Come on, Hans.'

They continued searching through the different trees and finally came across the one they wanted.

'It's definitely a Tree-vor,' Naomi said. 'Definitely a boy tree.'

'I agree. What else do we need?'

'Lights. Lots and lots of lights.'

'You sound almost excited.'

'I'm not. I just . . . need the toilet.'

She wasn't sure she'd got away with it until he said, 'It's that way. You can go while I get some help with the trees.'

Naomi exited the stall and looked in the bathroom mirror. She was older and yet, the way she and Gabriel had spoken was so reminiscent of all those years ago she could have been eighteen again. The same feelings that had stirred inside her then tried again now and she pushed them down, staring at her reflection until they'd disappeared. She looked better than she had in a long time. Her hair was fuller, her skin brighter but though she was enjoying her holiday, Gabriel was definitely complicating matters. Knowing she couldn't linger any longer, she exited the toilets and met Gabriel and Hans back in the car park.

'Shall we get some of these?' she asked, pointing to a row of vibrant red flowering poinsettia as the trees were loaded into the tree baler and wrapped in netting. 'I love these plants.' She knelt down and caressed the flowers. 'My mum and dad have always loved these. Our house would be full of them at Christmas.'

'They'll look beautiful in Le Petit Chateau. How about some holly too?'

'Sure. And I guess we should get some mistletoe. I'm sure some people will want to snog at the gala party.' She felt Gabriel's eyes on her but couldn't turn around in case she was right.

'When was the last time you were kissed under the mistletoe?'

'Me?' This time she did turn around. 'Do you know, I'm thirty-four and I've never been kissed under the mistletoe. Isn't that sad?' A tension filled the air and suddenly she felt self-conscious, darting her eyes back to the plants. She'd let her walls down too far and was determined to bring them up again. Quickly.

'Your ex-husband never kissed you under the mistletoe?'

'He wasn't the mistletoe type,' she replied, feeling a tightness in her chest, but this time it wasn't sadness at talking about Ollie, or even Gabriel mentioning him. It was more that her boundaries were tightening. She could feel them physically building back up, closing her off from others. For the first time she wanted to fight it, just a little. 'We never really went in for public displays of affection. That wasn't really Ollie's deal.'

'What happened between you? If you don't mind my asking.'

'I don't know really. A year ago he decided he didn't want to be married to me anymore. Right before Christmas, like I said. I guess—' She toyed with the end of her scarf. 'I guess, perhaps things had got a little' – she shrugged – 'quiet. Our lives were a bit separate, I suppose. He did his thing and I did mine.'

'Was that what you wanted?'

'I don't know. He was busy and so was I. We worked long hours. It was hard to make time for each other and—' She cut herself off, turning away from Gabriel.

'And?' he asked gently.

'It doesn't matter.' She was going to say that in the end she didn't always want to. There were things even Ollie didn't know about her and, she was ashamed to say, she'd never quite felt his equal or that of other people. 'Come on, let's get back to the chateau.'

Yet the question resounded in her head. *And?* And, the answer was, she'd never fully confided in her husband. He knew she was adopted, but she had never told him of the fears that had plagued her mind. The fear that there was something simply unlovable about her and that's why she'd been given away. That one day, the love would run out and they'd decide they didn't want her anymore. Just like he had in the end. Ollie had never really understood her, but how could he when she hadn't ever been open with him? Her mood had darkened this time, but she refused to let it stay that way.

'Let's grab an amaryllis too,' she said, picking up a pot and thrusting it at Gabriel. She gave her brightest smile, but he looked at her sceptically, as though he could tell she was simply pretending.

A few minutes later, with the trees being loaded into the van, Naomi carried the poinsettias, one under each arm like twins. Only, the blooms and leaves were so big she could barely see where she was going. She felt her arm hit someone, knocking her sideways.

'Oh, I'm so sorry.' She lowered the plants to see Levi smiling at her. 'Oh hello. What are you doing here?'

'I've come to get a Christmas tree. Just a small one for

my chalet. Everyone comes here for their trees. Wow, you really like plants, don't you?'

'I'm decorating Le Petit Chateau for Christmas.'

'Sounds fun. Can I help with anything?'

'No, it's fine. Gabriel's helping me.' She nodded to where he was helping load the Christmas trees into the back of the van, Hans running and sniffing around them. Feeling one of the plants slip from under her arm, she squeaked.

'Can I take those from you?'

'That'd be great, thanks.'

He grabbed hold of the pot, their eyes meeting above the beautiful red blooms. Out of his bulky ski suit he was even more attractive. Black jeans snuggled around his strong thighs and a thick jumper spread over his chest. His jaw was covered once more in stubble and flecks of gold were sparkling in his eyes. 'Listen,' he began nervously. 'I was wondering if you'd like to have dinner? Maybe Friday?'

Surprised by his offer she stared at him, unspeaking. His cheeks began to colour attractively. There was a shyness to him she rather liked. It would be her first date since Ollie left and she wasn't quite sure how to feel about that. A part of her felt sadness should have been her first response, but then she felt proud. She wasn't entirely unattractive after all. Her eyes darted towards Gabriel of their own accord.

'I was just checking on Hans,' she said, in case Levi had noticed and thought something was going on between them. 'Friday?' she repeated, while her brain caught up with the situation.

'Is that okay? Or we can make it another night. I just – I had a great time skiing with you the other day.' He placed the plant on the ground.

'Me too.'

'So . . . Friday?'

'Yes. Friday's fine. That'd be great.' Why was she still holding a plant? She looked like an idiot, clinging on to the pot like it was a child. Or a puppy. She put it on the ground.

'Shall I pick you up at seven? From Le Petit Chateau? I know a great local restaurant.'

'Yeah.' She nodded. 'That'd be great.'

'Until Friday, then.'

She smiled. 'Until Friday.'

Tentatively, he leaned forwards and gave her a peck on each cheek. The feel of his skin touching hers sent a shiver through her. Levi stepped away and waved goodbye to Gabriel as he rounded the van and took the plants from the ground.

'What was all that about? Does Levi think you need more skiing lessons or has he given up trying to teach you too?'

'Ha ha.' Gabriel closed the van doors and climbed into the driver's seat. Naomi made her way to the passenger side and squeezed in next to Hans. 'Actually, he asked me on a date.'

'A date?'

'Yes.' She watched him, hoping for some kind of reaction. Just a hint of emotion. Something that spoke to their shared history, to that night perhaps, but his face was unreadable.

'Well, I hope you have a nice time. Levi's a nice guy.'

Disappointment tinged her mind. She stared ahead wishing she hadn't let him weaken her defences as he swung the car around towards the exit. Hans barked and Naomi stroked his head.

'I think it's fair to say I won our bet,' he said when they were back on the road towards Le Petit Chateau.

'What? No way have you. I'm still one hundred per cent off Christmas.'

'A hundred per cent? You mean to say you didn't enjoy today at all?'

'I enjoyed it,' she admitted, watching his face to see if he'd enjoyed it too. 'But I'm still not feeling particularly happy about singing Christmas carols and watching *It's a Wonderful Life*.'

'So you're not a hundred per cent off Christmas then?'

'Maybe not a hundred per cent, more like eighty per cent, I suppose. If I had to put a figure on it.'

'So I did win.'

'You did not. You said you'd make me feel festive and I don't; I just feel a little less grumpy about it.'

'Always with the lawyer talk.'

'Maybe we need an adjudicator.'

'Mia.'

Naomi shook her head. 'She's not impartial; she's your sister.'

'And your best friend. She's still more likely to side with you than me.'

'You think so?'

'What about Levi?' Gabriel's jaw tightened and he kept his eyes on the road. For a second the thought crossed her mind that, after today, she wished it was Gabriel she was going on a date with, then she pushed the thought aside as stupid. She looked out of the window, the scenery passing her by, but she couldn't focus on any of it. Inside, she was picturing her walls growing higher and higher again. She'd already let them down too far today and she could never forgive Gabriel for what he'd done all those years ago. No matter how much he seemed to have changed.

Never.

Chapter 14

'I can't believe you're going on a date! Talk about holiday romance!' Mia squealed as Naomi searched through her friend's wardrobe for something to wear. She'd only brought jeans and massive jumpers and she couldn't turn up in either of those, though she would at least be warm. Naomi couldn't believe she was going on a date either. She'd only been there a week. She hadn't anticipated anything like this happening.

'What do I wear to a date in the middle of a mountain range?' Naomi's gaze fell to the glorious sunset outside her window. The sun cast a bright orange glow as it fell behind the mountains, spikes of light shooting out from it, painting the sky in stripes of dazzling colour from white to deep gold. As the light flickered, the mountains looked black where the snow had melted. It wouldn't be long until more fell and Naomi was looking forward to it. Every time it started it gave her a childlike pleasure, and she hadn't yet got bored of the way the flakes drifted to the ground.

'Simple,' Mia replied, taking over the search. 'A beautiful dress under a big coat. He's picking you up, isn't he? So you don't need to walk anywhere and the restaurant will be warm inside.'

'That's true. I hadn't thought of that.' Naomi pulled out a beautiful black dress from the wardrobe. 'What about this?' She held it up to her body. It had small sleeves for some extra coverage and a V neck that wasn't too over the top. She didn't want everything on display on a first date. She'd never really been one to show her cleavage; it always made her feel uncomfortable to have men leering at her. The length was good as well, stopping just on her knee. She'd look elegant and hopefully not freeze.

'Perfect!' Mia jumped off the bed and grabbed a thick, cream woollen coat with a tie waist. 'And this coat.'

Naomi whistled. 'Talk about classy. Wow.'

'You'll look amazing. This is one of my favourite date dresses.'

Naomi turned back from the mirror and looked at her friend. 'All these dates but none of them up to scratch?'

'I guess none of them have been able to compete with my first love – my career. I'm sure one day I'll meet someone who makes me want to switch off from work but right now I'm happy to date casually when I want company and enjoy the rest of my life alone.'

'I love that.' Naomi grinned at her friend. She loved

her confidence and the way she knew exactly what she wanted out of life.

'Enough about me though. Come on then, let's get you ready.'

They transferred to Naomi's room at Le Petit Chateau and Mia sat and talked with Naomi while she applied her make-up and curled her straight hair. After slipping on the dress, Naomi ran her hands down the sides of her body. The fabric outlined her hourglass shape, emphasising her curves and hiding the bits she didn't altogether love. She stepped out of the bathroom and her friend wolf-whistled.

'You look amazing. Levi's jaw is going to drop.'

'It's not too much, is it?' This would be her first date in over ten years and nerves were beginning to bite.

'Definitely not.'

'But what if he turns up in jeans and a shirt and I'm done up to the nines like this?'

'Then he should have made more effort,' she said forcefully. 'And you look effortlessly beautiful – you're only wearing a nice dress and coat.'

'You're right.' Naomi again smoothed the lines of the dress. 'It's not like I've turned up in a ball gown or anything, is it?'

'Even if you had, you should wear what you want, when you want.'

Naomi giggled. 'Except when I go skiing. Skiing in a ball gown wouldn't be a good idea. Not as bad as I am anyway.'

Mia joined her laughter. 'No, for that you should wear appropriate clothing. No matter how good at skiing you are. The wind can really whip around you. No one wants a frozen—'

'Mia!' Naomi scolded, overcome with laughter again. She'd forgotten how cheeky her friend's sense of humour could be when she was relaxed and happy. With the decorating of Le Petit Chateau off her hands, Mia had relaxed a lot more and Naomi was glad to see the dark shadows fading under her eyes.

Naomi gave herself another look in the mirror. Her skin had gained a luminescence since being here and she glowed with good health. Her hair was softer, thicker, less weighed down by life – just as she had been – and her eyes sparkled. The brush of glittery shadow over the smoky eye make-up she'd applied was, admittedly, helping in the sparkle department, but she didn't look bad, even if she did say so herself.

A car beeped out front and Naomi grabbed the small clutch bag her friend had loaned her. 'Right, show time.'

'Have fun!'

'I will,' she called, slipping on the coat but leaving it open until she got outside. She could hear her mum's voice in her head telling her she wouldn't feel the benefit if she did it up now. She left her room and made her way downstairs with Mia following behind. She was just bustling through the lounge towards the door when Gabriel appeared in her peripheral vision. He was adjusting one of the Christmas trees they'd placed in the corner of the room.

'Hey,' Naomi called to him. 'Leave Tree-mothy alone. His branches are settling before the decorations arrive tomorrow.'

He spun and his eyes widened as he took her in. Naomi watched as his eyes floated up and down her body in a way that made her tingle. 'Wow, you're—' He tilted his head. 'Ready for your date I see.'

'Yep. It's Mia's dress. She let me borrow it. What do you think?' She knew it was a leading question by the way he'd looked at her. It had stirred something inside her and she wanted to know what he thought.

'You look . . .' She waited for him to finish the sentence, just as she had when they'd met again for the first time in years. But if he said *well* again this time she might hit him with her bag. 'You look beautiful.' Her heart thudded inside her chest as a slight pinkness tinged his cheeks. He turned away. 'Are you watering Tree-mothy? He needs topping up every day.'

Pushing her disappointment aside that that was it, she replied, 'Every morning when I come down to breakfast.'

'Good.' Gabriel was in his chef whites and the brightness of his outfit made his grey eyes even more vivid as he looked at her again.

Silence descended until the car horn beeped for a second time. She'd almost forgotten Levi was waiting for her outside. Though why he hadn't knocked she couldn't understand.

'I better go,' Naomi said, motioning towards the door and Gabriel echoed her own thoughts with his strange mind-reading talents.

'He's not coming in to meet you?'

'I guess not.' She would have preferred if he had instead of beeping a car horn like a teenager avoiding her parents. She forced the judgement away. It was cold, literally freezing outside. She couldn't blame him for wanting to stay warm.

'Have a good night,' he said, turning back and running his hands over the pine needles.

In the hour it had taken her to get ready, night had descended. She stepped outside into a mass of velvety blackness. One or two of the brightest stars were glittering and more popped into view the longer she looked at it, though touches of hazy navy cloud were visible.

Levi stood by the driver's door of a rather sporty-looking car. The red paint shone in the lights of Le Petit Chateau and though the car looked sleek and expensive, Naomi couldn't help but think it a little impractical for snowy mountain roads. Surely something sturdier like a good four-wheel drive would be better suited to their location.

'You look beautiful,' Levi said, stepping around the car to greet her. Had he been waiting out of the car for her to come outside? Why not just come in if he was getting out into the cold anyway?

He opened the door for her and she realised he must have only got out to be a gentleman. She shivered as she climbed in, tightening her coat against the cold air that felt icy on her skin.

'Don't worry, she has heated seats,' Levi said as she climbed in. He rounded to the driver's side.

'I'm sorry?' she asked.

'The car – my car – she has heated seats. You'll warm up in no time.'

'Great.' He was looking at her like he expected more of a response. 'That's brilliant,' she added unsure what else there was to say about heated leather car seats. He smiled and she had to admit he looked handsome. His coat was buttoned up, but she could see he'd worn trousers not jeans, so that was a relief. Stubble still coated his jaw and she matched his smile with one of her own. For some reason Gabriel's smile popped into her head but she quickly shook thoughts of him away. There was no place for him tonight. 'Where are we going?'

'There's a great restaurant nearby. I booked us a table. The food is the best in the region and the views are to die for. Not literally of course.' He laughed loudly, and it took her aback. Like a donkey crossed with a goose. She wondered if he was nervous.

She'd thought she would be, but a calmness had washed over her. A little of her old self was returning: the confidence that got her through her job, that enabled her to argue and win cases. The confidence that shielded her from the inadequacies she felt deep inside. She chuckled along with him out of politeness. 'It sounds wonderful.'

'Are you hungry?'

'Starving.'

'Let's go then.'

He put his foot down before she'd even secured her seatbelt, launching them forwards with a velocity she

162

thought only existed in space travel. When they arrived at the restaurant, Naomi felt like she'd been in a Formula One race. She hadn't realised they were being chased by gangsters or outrunning an avalanche. There hadn't been any need to drive quite so fast on snowy, icy roads. During the journey, Levi had glanced at her often and every time she'd silently pleaded that he'd turn his eyes back to the road. She didn't fancy dying this way. She wanted to die in bed, in her sleep, not ploughing off the side of a mountain into the tops of pine trees.

When they pulled up at the restaurant, her fingers were sore from gripping the side of her seat and she couldn't help but worry that she'd left little nail marks in the precious leather. She was also worried about how much she was cold-sweating from the terrifying journey. She didn't want to spend the rest of the night unable to lift her arms up for fear of sweat patches. She took a deep breath to calm her elevated heart rate. She'd had less scary rides at amusement parks.

'Isn't she gorgeous?' Levi asked as they climbed out of the car once he'd finished edging it backwards and forwards into exactly the right spot. His hand was resting on the roof of the car as he gazed at it adoringly.

A sudden swell of nerves shot up her spine as she realised she didn't really know Levi at all. Getting to know someone was the purpose of a date, but she hadn't had him down as a car-loving speed freak. After seeing him teach children how to ski, she'd had him pegged as more of a sensitive, nature-loving outdoorsy type. His love of the car was so reminiscent of Ollie and his love for all things materialistic, so this wasn't the most auspicious start. But given how well they'd got on when he'd given her such a good skiing lesson, she'd have to reserve judgement.

'Shall we go inside?' Naomi asked, feeling the cold bite under her coat.

'Sure.' He held his arm out, leading the way.

The restaurant was beautiful, lit up like a beacon of warm light against the dark backdrop behind it. A mountain range framed it, the peaks looming up higher than its roof, but the mix of wood and glass was welcoming and friendly. The building reminded her more of Le Petit Chateau than it did a ski chalet, being a mixture of stone and wood. The windows were wide and glowing, and a small set of steps led to a glass front door. She opened it just as Levi darted towards it.

'I was going to get that for you.'

'That's okay,' she replied with a smile. 'I can get it.'

The warm air hit her immediately and relief flooded her system. Perhaps she'd been too harsh about the car thing, grumpy with cold. She could feel her body relaxing now the cold air was shut firmly outside. Within minutes, their coats had been taken and they were seated near floor-to-ceiling windows, revealing the beautiful scenery around them. She could see the whole of the ski resort from here and on the horizon, snow-topped mountains reached high into the dark night sky.

'Snow and stars,' she said to herself without thinking.

'Pardon?'

'Nothing, sorry. I was just thinking how the nights here can be summed up in two words. Snow and stars.'

'Right.' He did the laugh again and Naomi really hoped it was down to nerves and he didn't always laugh like that. It wasn't exactly a deal-breaker, but she couldn't imagine putting up with that for longer than a few hours.

A few minutes after she'd settled into her seat, under a modern glass chandelier, a smiling waitress stopped at their table. 'Can I get you anything to drink?' She had a strong American accent.

'Oh, umm—' Naomi picked up the menu. 'Sorry I haven't even looked yet.'

'Would you like me to come back?' she asked with a warm smile.

'No,' Levi replied. 'Just wait.'

The hairs on the back of Naomi's neck bristled. She couldn't stand people being rude to waiting staff. It was just so unnecessary, but perhaps he hadn't realised that's how it came across. She quickly scanned the menu and ordered a glass of wine. 'Thank you.'

'I'm driving,' Levi said to Naomi, ignoring the waitress again. 'So a Coke for me.'

He didn't look at the young woman when he ordered, keeping his eyes on Naomi's and she felt the need to relay the order politely, even though the woman was already writing it down. 'And a Coke, please.'

Had he meant to be rude? She really hoped not. He hadn't seemed the type when they'd met before. He'd been so kind and attentive. Perhaps he'd just been distracted or again it was nervousness? Perhaps he was like her and hadn't been on a date in a while.

The waitress disappeared and Naomi searched for something to say. 'How long have you been out here, Levi?'

'A few years now. I came out with some friends on holiday in my early thirties and never left.'

'Wow, what did you do before?'

'I worked in finance.' She shuddered involuntarily. Ollie had worked in finance, but she wouldn't hold that against him. Just because he'd once had the same profession as her ex-husband didn't mean he was like him. 'It was pretty boring,' he continued. 'But when I came here and got the skiing bug I couldn't face going back.'

'Not at all?' she asked, admiring his sense of adventure. She'd never have the guts to do that.

'Not at all. I called the office on the Monday and handed in my notice over the phone. Luckily, I had a trust fund to fall back on so it wasn't a big deal. I had all the money I needed.' He smirked as if he was proud.

It was a big deal to Naomi whose parents had had to scrimp and save for everything. 'You're very lucky.'

'Am I? I'm not sure I believe in luck. Fate maybe.'

'I mean to have had money to fall back on. Most people don't.'

'No, but then, I'm not most people.' He flashed her a grin she assumed was supposed to be flirty but his response had sent a warning shot into her brain.

She took a moment to admire the view and tried not to let his cavalier attitude to his privilege prejudice her.

'I took skiing lessons and then trained as an instructor, and I've honestly never looked back.'

The young waitress came back over, delivering their drinks. She could only have been in her late teens or early twenties and was probably working here on a gap year. 'A white wine for you,' she said cheerily, placing it on the table. 'And a Coke for you, sir. Are you ready to order?'

'Five more minutes,' Levi said with a dismissive wave of his hand.

Naomi bristled as the waitress coloured, turning to her. 'I'm so sorry. Can we just get five more minutes. We've been too busy talking.'

'No problem.' She smiled politely at Naomi but Naomi wasn't blind to the wary glance she'd given Levi. She didn't blame her.

Naomi wondered if she should say something. If she phrased it subtly, she might be able to get away with it without causing any offence. She'd done it enough times in her job. 'We probably should hurry up and order,' Naomi said to him.

Levi took a long sip of his drink and chuckled. 'Why? I'm not rushing just because they want me to. I'm a paying customer.'

She didn't comment, knowing that if she opened her mouth, she'd say something rude, but this wasn't an attitude she admired. She took a large mouthful of wine. Surely any nerves he'd had would have dissipated by now.

A worry began to form that this was the real Levi and the man she'd met on the slopes and at the Christmas tree farm was nothing more than a public image. She hoped she was wrong.

Unfortunately, her hopes were dashed as the date only went downhill from there. When the waitress came back to take their order, Levi barked it out from the menu without so much as a please or thank you and Naomi felt the need to overcompensate for his poor manners by thanking her profusely and smiling like a maniac. Even the nearby diners had noticed his arrogant tone and had glanced over after the waitress had left. She seriously considered leaving, but kept wanting to give him the benefit of the doubt.

As she was now obliged to stay until at least the main course, Naomi did her best to restart their conversation, unable to shake his rudeness from her mind. 'So you don't regret giving everything up for skiing?'

'Not at all. Why would I? I've got a great house. I'm my own boss. I work the hours I want. I can do whatever I like when I like. There's no downside as far as I can see.'

'Do you miss the money you were earning?'

He laughed as she took the napkin from the table and spread it over her lap. 'Trust fund, remember!' He laughed again, even louder this time, and Naomi couldn't help but stare, wondering where the sound actually came from. She didn't think human people could make that sort of noise. 'I've got more than enough. I can buy anything I want. I got a whole new kit the other day. I'm the best dressed man on the slopes. And my beautiful car's new too. Speaking of beautiful, you look gorgeous tonight.'

'Oh, thank you.' She wasn't sure the switch from car to her quite worked as a compliment, but she was trying her best to be open-minded.

This whole thing was turning into a disaster and she wondered when would be the most polite time to make her excuses and leave. She wished the restaurant had been within walking distance because even in heels she would have taken her chances and left by now if she could. At least the food would be amazing, she thought. She'd struggled to pick just one thing off the menu; every dish had sounded tantalisingly delicious.

The waitress brought over their food and Naomi smiled warmly, thanking her as the delicious smells lingered in the air. 'This looks wonderful. Thank you.' She'd ordered lamb cutlets served with asparagus and courgette. The lamb was beautifully seared on the outside nestled next to three fat stems of bright, perfectly cooked asparagus, and slices of green and yellow courgette decorated the plate. A red wine jus had been artistically drizzled over the top and the smells wafting up made her mouth water. This was the restaurant food Gabriel had talked about and she understood exactly what he'd meant when he'd said it should have a seat at the table. She wanted to taste it and talk about it. She wanted the experience of eating it to override conversation until she'd finished, then she could wax lyrical about it.

Levi's plate was put down in front of him, but he

didn't even look at the young woman and Naomi took a breath in. 'Thank you,' she said in place of Levi, nodding towards him.

'Would you like any more drinks?'

Levi shook his head. 'We're good.'

'Actually, I'll have another wine, please.' Naomi slugged back the last of her glass and grinned cheekily at the waitress. She wasn't going to have a man answering for her. He might still have half his drink left but she'd been sipping hers in place of correcting his manners and was almost out. A moment of understanding passed between the two women.

'Large?'

'Oh, I think so.'

'Are you sure?' Levi asked, his brow furrowing.

She sat back, her frustration suddenly mounting. So, he was the type to disapprove of how much she drank as well as being rude and superficial. She stared down at her plate. The food was too good to miss and she was starving. She'd have this and leave before dessert. 'Absolutely sure,' she said to him before turning back to the waitress. 'A very large glass, thank you.'

Although the date with Levi was proving to be horrific, he had at least been right about the food. It was amazing. The flavours delicately balanced the textures. As soon as she'd finished, she could have eaten it all again and not because the portion was small and she was hungry, but because everything about it had been perfect. Levi had ordered a steak and devoured it without speaking, giving her strange grins as he tried to smile with his mouth full. Naomi consumed her second glass of wine as swiftly as she could.

As he pushed his plate away he said, 'I nearly had to send that back.'

'Why?' she asked, chuckling. 'You barely stopped for breath.'

Levi shuffled in his seat, but Naomi was past caring if she'd offended him. He shouldn't have been so rude to the waitress. 'It was a little tough. I asked for it rare and it was definitely more medium.' He scrunched up his napkin and tossed it onto his plate.

'You probably should have said something before you finished it.'

'I might ask to speak to the chef.' To her abject horror, he clicked his fingers to summon the waitress. Wide-eyed customers stared at them both and humiliation burned her neck.

'What the hell are you doing?' Naomi asked, unable to hold her tongue any longer.

'Getting her attention. I think she's deliberately ignoring me.' He clicked again and as she looked up, he began waving her over.

'I don't blame her,' Naomi muttered into her wine glass.

'Pardon?'

'Nothing.' She tried to calm down. 'Look, Levi, she hasn't stopped all night. You can't just go clicking to get her attention. That's really rude.'

'Then she should pay more attention to her customers.'

'What? She's been more than attentive. She's been great. What more do you want her to do?'

'She works in the service industry, doesn't she? It's her job.'

Something finally snapped within Naomi. She remembered sitting quietly while her and Ollie's solicitors battled it out. She'd felt powerless then and it had been alien to her, damaging in a way she hadn't realised at the time. Before that, she'd never been one to sit with her mouth closed when something needed saying and part of her reason for being here was to reclaim the woman she'd once been. She placed her wine glass down and spoke calmly. 'Levi, do you realise how rude you're being to the staff here?'

'Me?' he asked, looking shocked. 'It's their job to look after us. We're the customers.'

'Yes, but you don't have to be rude. You wouldn't like it if your students were rude to you, would you?'

'No, but . . . this is different.'

'How?'

'They're providing a service.'

'So are you.' Aware that some of the other diners were looking over, Naomi lowered her voice. For all Levi's good looks and apparent kindness, he wasn't the type of man she'd hoped he'd be. It just went to show it could sometimes take a while to really know who someone was. 'It's just basic manners.'

Her calling him out had clearly shocked him and she prepared herself for more bluff and bluster but instead he said, 'Right. Well. I guess you won't want dessert then. Waitress?' He shouted this time, his voice drawing the attention of not just nearby diners, but everyone in the restaurant including other staff. 'The bill please. Now.' He turned back to Naomi. 'We can each pay for what we've had as I've only had Coke and you've had half a bottle of wine.' He picked up a menu from the empty table behind. 'And I'm sure – yes – your main was more expensive than mine by fifty cents.'

Naomi sat back unruffled by his arrogance and rudeness. She'd dealt with far worse in her job. Not to mention the institutionalised sexism that formed part of her everyday existence. But she couldn't believe how different he'd turned out to be. Where was the flirty banter she'd enjoyed during her skiing lesson? The waitress approached and before he had chance to speak, she said, 'Could you split out his meal and I'll pay for mine after dessert, please? Oh, and another glass of wine when you have a second.'

Levi sat open-mouthed, too shocked to argue. Then in one athletic movement, he stood, forcing his chair back. Everyone began to clap her as he followed the waitress to her workstation, eager to pay and leave. Naomi shrugged, feeling proud for standing up for herself but a little disappointed her first foray into dating again had been such a disaster. He glanced over his shoulder while paying, clearly hoping for a response from Naomi, but she kept her eyes on the view in front of her, aware of him toying with his car keys from his reflection. After he'd gone – no doubt without tipping – the waitress came over with a refilled glass and the dessert menu.

'Dessert is on the house.'

'No!' Naomi shook her head in horror. 'Honestly, I'm happy to pay. You don't need to do that. I'm just sorry he was so rude to you.'

'Chef's orders I'm afraid, and once he's made his mind up there's no arguing with him.'

She laughed. 'In that case it would be rude not to. What would you recommend?'

'The torta di pane is delicious. It's one of my favourites.'

'I'll have that then please.'

Described as a rich chocolate bread pudding cake it would round off her meal perfectly and, it had to be said, would be much better enjoyed on her own. The other diners gave her warm smiles. They'd clearly had enough of Levi's attitude too.

Naomi sat back, staring at the snow-covered world outside. She'd have to get the number for a taxi or call Mia to come and pick her up. Disappointment fought with pride as she stared at the lights punctuating the dark, turning the snow an orange hue.

'Your torta di pane, madam.'

Gabriel's voice penetrated the mishmash of emotions inside her and she spun to look at him, a smile ripping at her face.

'Don't tell me you're the chef here.'

'I am.' He placed the plate in front of her and motioned to Levi's seat. 'May I sit?'

'Of course. My date had to leave unexpectedly.'

'Yes, I saw.'

174

'You saw?'

'And heard. Kaylee, the waitress, was telling us about him. I'm glad you told him his behaviour was unacceptable.'

'He was going to complain about his steak.'

'He was what?' Gabriel was so shocked at the idea she laughed, her spoon halfway to her mouth.

'He said it was more medium than rare.'

'He was wrong.'

'Yes, I thought he might be.' She placed a spoonful of the pudding in her mouth and savoured the rich choc-olatey flavour. 'Wow.' She placed her hand over her mouth. 'This is gorgeous.' The texture was smooth and creamy, the chocolate rich and luxurious. It was the height of decadence. 'This is really, really good.'

'Thank you.'

'You'll have to thank Kaylee for recommending it.' He watched her eating and she felt strangely uncomfortable, like they were sharing an intimate moment. Eating with Levi hadn't seemed remotely intimate especially with the way he tackled a steak. 'Do you know where I can get a taxi? Levi drove us.'

'He's a real catch, isn't he? Abandoning you here.'

'Yes, but I'm a big girl. I can make my way back to the chateau. Did you know he was like that?'

'I had no idea. I only started working here a little while ago. But tonight, Kaylee said he has brought a few women here and treated the staff the same way.'

'That's horrible. Does he think it's appealing or some-thing? I hope the other women weren't impressed.'

'Many were here on holiday and left soon after, so who knows. When I saw it was you, I was about to come to your rescue, but I should know you don't need rescuing.'

'I try not to.'

'No, you've always been so determined. Ready to take on the world.' His words hit home and she looked into his pale eyes. He'd said something similar that night . . . A sensation of longing mixed with frustration at the way things had turned out gripped her. But he hadn't turned away as she'd expected him to. He held her gaze before saying, 'If you'd like to stay for a coffee and petit fours, I can drive you back when I've finished, but it will be a while yet.'

'Don't you need the table?'

'We can manage.'

It didn't take her long to agree. 'A coffee would be great then. I'm afraid Levi kind of drove me to drink.'

Gabriel smiled and stood up. 'One coffee coming up.'

She spent the next hour relaxing in the charming atmosphere of the restaurant, watching the stars shine in the sky and chatting with Kaylee whenever she came past. Naomi had been right: she was on a gap year and enjoyed skiing when she wasn't working. She planned to head back home soon and settle into a career in sports massage. Her excitement for the life ahead of her was infectious and Naomi's mind wandered to the jobs she'd seen advertised in community care law when she googled them the other day.

Though it would mean a drop in salary, she had everything she needed. She didn't need, or want, half the trappings she'd had in her life with Ollie. Le Petit Chateau was beautiful, but she was beginning to realise that all the luxury in the world couldn't make a person happy. Happiness came from inside.

Before long, the evening was over, and the restaurant sat empty with only Naomi at a table. The staff were joking and chatting, laying up the tables for the next day. Every time the kitchen door opened, she could hear snippets of conversation, some of it English, some of it German but always punctuated by laughter. Gabriel appeared, his chef's jacket hanging open and a crisp white T-shirt straining over his chest. Her heart fluttered, and she turned, pretending to gaze once more at the view. As she had with Levi, she watched his reflection in the glass. He had a strong, powerful walk, his shoulder swaying as he came towards her.

'Shall we go?' he asked.

After her disastrous date she was eager to get this night over with and replied without hesitation. 'Sure, let's get out of here.'

Chapter 15

Kaylee retrieved Naomi's coat. She'd already paid for her meal, adding a generous tip. It was the least she could do given the aggravation and embarrassment Levi had caused the poor woman.

Gabriel drove them back in his car – thankfully much more suitable for snowy mountain roads – and Naomi sank into the unheated seats in relief. 'What a night,' she muttered.

'Not the date you had in mind, huh?'

'No, not really. I was hoping that my first date after however many years of being part of a couple would be much more . . .' she searched for the right words '. . . sweepingly romantic. I didn't think I'd be dealing with a rude man-child.'

He laughed at her description of Levi and she joined him. 'Perhaps Levi will change his ways now.'

She gave him the side-eye. 'I'd love to believe you, but

I think we both know men like that are set in their ways. Thank you for the lift and for the food. It was the only thing that made tonight bearable.'

'My pleasure,' he replied.

The cold fresh air stroked her skin as they stepped out of the car and walked towards the entrance. 'I'm sorry your date didn't go well.'

'It's fine. I don't think I hoped it would lead to anything really.' He looked confused and though she wasn't exactly sure what she meant herself, she tried her best to articulate it. 'It was nice he asked me but I'm not sure I thought anything would come of it. I mean, it definitely won't now because I don't want to be with someone who treats other people like that, but even before that—'

'You want someone who makes time for you and treats you and others well.' He'd remembered their conversation from earlier when they were at the Christmas tree farm. 'Maybe someone who knows you inside and out.'

Her skin flooded with goose bumps, raising the hairs on her arms. She was speechless, words caught in her throat. 'Yes,' she answered quietly, realising how much she meant it. 'I do.' They both went quiet, their steps slowed. 'I'm glad you followed your passion for cooking,' she said, feeling the painful silence. 'You have a real gift.'

'I don't know about that.'

'I do,' she replied. 'Ollie used to love going to fancy restaurants in London and the food you served here was equal to if not better than any of those.'

'That's high praise.'

She glanced at him to make sure he wasn't teasing her. 'I mean it. I wouldn't say it if I didn't.'

'I know. You've always said what you think. It's admirable.'

'It can land me in trouble sometimes too. As evidenced tonight. I'm sorry if I made a scene in your restaurant.'

'It isn't my restaurant. I just cook there. But I bet it makes you a good lawyer.'

Again, their eyes locked. Naomi was the first to look away, turning to the sky. A shooting star raced passed, illuminating the dark night and outshining everything else.

'Look,' she said, pointing and bouncing on her tiptoes. 'I've never actually seen one before.'

'A shooting star?'

She nodded. 'I was starting to think they were made up. I've wanted to see one my whole life.'

'You should make a wish.'

What should she wish for? She looked at Gabriel from the corner of her eye. The wind ruffled his hair, and his smile was warm and enticing. She wouldn't wish for him though. So much had passed between them, and they still hadn't discussed that night or what had happened after. She felt the weight of unfinished business press on her shoulders and closed her eyes, wishing instead for the courage to change her path. To be brave enough to step out of the comfort zone money provided and follow her heart.

'Snow and stars,' she said quietly as she opened her eyes.

'What did you say?'

'Snow and stars. This place. It's like another world all made up of snow and stars.'

'That's beautiful.'

He edged forwards and she turned towards him, finding herself only inches from him. Their hands were touching, his fingers brushing her skin. She scanned his face, so close to hers she could feel the warmth of his breath on her cheek. In that instant she forgot about the past and saw the man he was now. The man who'd been with her tonight, who'd taken her to the Christmas tree farm, who despite everything seem to understand her better than anyone else. She wanted to kiss him and could imagine his lips pressed against hers, his arms wrapping around her. She had a sense he wanted to kiss her too but when he didn't move closer, fear gripped her chest like an ice-cold gust of wind.

She'd opened up to him once before and it hadn't ended well. She couldn't risk it again. She stepped away.

'We should get inside. It's late.'

His eyes flashed with something she hoped was disappointment, but it could easily have been tiredness or annoyance. He stepped back motioning for her to lead the way. 'Yes, of course.'

As she walked ahead, she was more than ever aware of his strong body following closely behind her. They stepped through to the lounge, and she laid the coat Mia had loaned her over the back of a chair. The fire was still burning, and she warmed herself by it wondering who

181

would be brave enough to speak first. It turned out to be Gabriel.

'You know, you're a very difficult person to get close to.'

'Am I?' She kept her tone light, trying to edge the conversation off.

'You've changed.'

'We all change as we get older. I – I think I'm going to head off to bed.'

But Gabriel was insistent. 'You've changed more than I thought you would.'

Was it any wonder? 'Like I said, everyone changes as they get older. Are you working tomorrow? You don't need to make me breakfast when you've only just finished work now. You'd have to be up at the crack of dawn.'

'Why do you always change the subject when people get too close? Push them away?'

'I don't,' she replied, crossing her arms over her chest knowing full well she did. After his behaviour years ago she wasn't about to admit it. 'I just don't talk about my feelings with every single person I meet.'

'You don't open up to anyone.'

'And how do you know that? You don't even know me, Gabriel.'

'I think I do.'

His arrogance astounded her and she spun to stare at him. His expression wasn't angry or annoyed. It wasn't haughty or arrogant either. He was concerned, caring, and that affected her even more. 'You remember the person I was years ago, after meeting me once. You don't know who I am now.'

'I'd like to.' She felt like she'd been shot. Like a bullet had hit directly at her heart. 'But you have to let people in for that to happen and I don't think you know how. Not really.'

'If I don't then whose fault is that?' He looked confused but wounded too. 'You know why I'm like this. Don't pretend you don't.' She felt her breath hitch. 'But I've learned from my mistakes.'

'I know you find it hard. I remember what you told me before but—'

'But what?'

He shrugged, his tone calmer than hers. 'I don't know. I thought life might have changed you. I thought being married might have led you to trust someone. That maybe you found someone you could—'

'You have no right to talk about my marriage,' she said firmly and his eyes widened in shock. 'And trust? How can you talk to me about trust? I trusted you and look what happened.' She fell silent not wanting to speak about it anymore, but her anger bubbled below the surface. How could he sit there as if nothing had ever happened between them? As if he hadn't hurt her so fiercely all those years ago. How could they have nearly kissed just now? She turned her back as if it would block out some of the emotion swirling in the room and bouncing around between them, but she could feel his eyes on her, burning into her skin. 'You were the first person I told everything to. Everything.'

'Naomi, that night—'

She began to shake. This was it. This was the conversation they'd been skirting around and ignoring since she'd arrived. Since they'd met many years ago. Her breathing grew ragged, and she tried to calm it, keeping control of the difficult feelings beginning to rush and collide inside her.

'It . . .' He struggled to speak, and she turned to look at him. 'I tried to—'

'You tried to what?' He didn't reply, wouldn't look at her either, and she hated how her voice rang with pain. 'Why did you leave without saying anything?'

'I don't know,' he whispered.

'That's not good enough.' This time, her voice was as hard and cold as ice. Harder and colder than her angry lawyer voice. She hated how severe she sounded, how unkind, but it was all she could do to control her emotions. 'I told you everything. Everything! You were the first person to know that I was adopted. Even Mia didn't know that. She still doesn't unless you've told her.'

He dropped his eyes in shame. 'I haven't. Naomi, I'm . . .'

The day he'd come to visit Mia at university, Mia had insisted Naomi come along to meet him too. She and Gabriel had hit it off instantly and though other girls had tried it on with him that night in the student bar, he'd stayed with them, talking about everything and anything. They'd gone back to the house they shared and once Mia had gone to bed, they'd sat in Naomi's room talking for hours, baring their souls to one another. There'd been an instant connection. Not just attraction but a meeting of minds and souls, as if fate had decided they were both meant to be there at that exact moment together. The alignment of time and place Mia had talked about before. Their worlds had collided, and Naomi had felt certain they were bound together somehow, in a way she couldn't explain. And for some reason, in the euphoria of that special connection she'd trusted him with the biggest secret of her life.

'I told you things I'd never admitted out loud to anyone. I'd never told anyone I was adopted. No one. I never told anyone that I was terrified my adoptive parents would change their minds and send me back to foster care. That one day they'd wake up and not want me anymore. That all my life I'd felt like I wasn't good enough because we grew up without much money. I was so scared I'd never be good enough for anyone. That I wasn't good enough to be loved and you—'

'You are good enough to be loved,' he said, stepping towards her, his hand outstretched, reaching for her. 'Naomi—'

She backed away, reliving the pain she'd felt then. 'And you told me everything about yourself too. That you wanted to be a chef but didn't know if you could go against your father. That you were scared of letting him down but you wanted to be your own man. You wanted to be brave enough to follow your own path. I admired that about you. I thought you were different. That we understood each other. Were you just saying those things to get me to sleep with you?'

After they'd confessed their deepest darkest secrets, he'd kissed her. Gently at first, then building in intensity until they were naked in her bed, as close as two people could ever be. As she stood in the luxury of Le Petit Chateau, in front of the roaring open fire and opulent furnishings, she realised that all the luxury, all the material comfort in the world could never protect her from her feelings. Even the ones she buried deep down inside. The hurt, the pain, the insecurity and inadequacy.

'I meant everything I said that night,' he replied and she wanted desperately to believe him but experience held her back. 'I never lied to you about anything. I promise you.'

'You were the first person I slept with,' she confided and finally his eyes shot up to meet hers. She didn't expect it was the same for him and when he didn't answer she knew she hadn't been his first but that wasn't the point. She didn't care about how many people he'd slept with, but that he'd been her first had made him even more special. What she cared about most was what had happened after. 'Then you left. Just slipped out when I was asleep. I woke up alone wondering where you were or what had happened to you. And when I saw Mia she said you'd gone. Completely. You left us both to come back here. She didn't know why either.' She let the words sink in. She'd learned the importance of timing in court and she gave him time to understand everything she'd just said. 'She doesn't know what happened between us by the way and I've never told her but . . .' Her voice broke and he lifted his head again, his eyes flicking to hers but unable to fully meet them. 'I felt so used and embarrassed.'

As the words had flowed, a truth had emerged in her mind. A truth she had never admitted even to herself. With Gabriel, she'd allowed herself to be open, revealing her truest self to him, her flaws, her fears, the insecurities that drove her to be the best version of herself. But despite that, despite knowing how much she feared it, he'd abandoned her, and she'd never recovered from those wounds and the scars they'd caused. Even with her husband. She knew it was silly and tried to blame youth and naivety but, really, it was all due to the connection they'd had and the secret he'd forced her to hide from Mia.

Gabriel's eyes met hers. She could read shame and guilt in his pale grey irises, but he didn't speak.

The next morning, after hearing he'd gone, she went back to her room on the pretext of studying and wept. That was the last time she'd cried. The last time she'd opened up fully to anyone. The last time she would allow herself to be vulnerable and unguarded. It only led to hurt. From then on, the walls had come up, building on the foundation her fears about being adopted had already laid. No one would ever break them down again. He'd confirmed the fact that she was broken, unlovable.

'Aren't you going to say anything?' He didn't speak, but she could see his jaw clenching. The muscle in his cheek

187

squeezing as something happened inside him. If only she knew what it was. She waited but he didn't move. Pain shot through her and she clenched her hands against it. 'You should go.'

He looked at her without saying a word, then stood slowly as if in a daze, holding on to the edges of the furniture as he made his way to the door. He didn't look back.

Naomi collapsed into a chair, her legs shaking. Her whole body trembled, and she wrapped her arms around herself. A slight stinging in her nose proved she was the closest to tears she'd been in years, and she stared at the fire until the feeling subsided. Fifteen years of emotion, buried and forgotten, had come to the surface and it was exhausting. She slipped off her shoes and curled her legs underneath her, allowing her heart rate to calm down.

Gabriel had left without a word. Without giving any kind of defence of his actions. She'd expected something. Had hoped for more. Shouting, arguing, justifying . . . anything to mitigate his decisions but he clearly had no excuse. He'd used her that night. She'd called him out on it and he couldn't even bring himself to apologise. She was suddenly transported back to her university bedroom. She felt as disappointed in him now as she had then. Perhaps even more so because he was a grown man now. Older and supposedly wiser.

She pulled one of the soft cream throws from the back of the chair and covered herself with it. He had broken something within her that night. Something that had never been fixed. Because of him, because of her fears, she'd never fully opened up to Ollie. She'd told him about her adoption eventually and he'd been kind and supportive, even suggesting that should she wish to find her birth parents he'd do everything he could to support her. But she'd never taken that route. She'd always been focused on moving forwards, creating a financially stable home so she could repay her parents for everything they'd done for her. Yet, she'd never told Ollie of the underlying fears she'd admitted to Gabriel. Not being open with Ollie had contributed to the breakdown of their marriage. She'd always closed a part of herself off from him. Perhaps he'd known there was a part of her he'd never reach and eventually it had proved too painful. Like banging his fists against a closed door.

With a shudder, she realised that he hadn't simply decided he didn't want to be married to her anymore. He'd had enough of battering against her defences, never making his way inside and she realised that that was her fault not his. There'd always been a wedge between them, a divide he couldn't cross, and if she didn't change, the rest of her relationships would be just as doomed.

Chapter 16

Naomi didn't sleep at all that night. She'd been there just over a week, her sleep, up until now, mostly restful. Though the sumptuous bed and soft pillows engulfed her, her mind and body were tense, unable to let go of the realisations plaguing her brain. She knew she had to stop hiding. Her fears had kept her from opening up to Ollie, and she had never told Mia the truth about her history and what had happened between her and Gabriel. She somehow felt that if she was ever to move on with her life when she returned to London, she had to start making changes now and this was a discussion she wanted to have with Mia face to face.

The next morning, she couldn't face breakfast and she didn't want to risk seeing Gabriel, so instead made her way straight to Mia's chalet.

'*Morgen*, Naomi,' she said as she opened the door. 'I wasn't expecting to see you till later.' Mia was up and dressed and ready to tackle the day. She was just about to take a sip of coffee from her enormous mug when she noticed Naomi's dark expression. 'What's wrong? You look tired and upset. You didn't have to work through the night again, did you?'

'No, but . . .' She hesitated as her courage wavered, but an iron-like resolve surged through her spine, empowering her to remain strong. 'Have you got time to talk?'

'Absolutely.' Mia moved aside, ushering Naomi in. 'What's happened?'

Naomi slipped off her thick coat and walked in, grateful to be out of the cold. Though she'd grown to love it and the way it blew the cobwebs from her mind, today her tired body shivered in the wind. She took a seat at the breakfast bar separating the living room and kitchen, where a box of cereal and a carton of milk were laid out for breakfast. Mia followed, sitting back down and spooning yoghurt and berries from her bowl into her mouth.

'Sorry to bother you.'

'It's fine. You're not bothering me. What's wrong? Is this about your date? Did you get drunk and do something you regret?'

'Not quite. But there's something I need to tell you. I should have told you ages ago but . . .' She toyed with her nails, running her finger over the small, manicured edges. She'd have to get a top-up manicure soon. 'I don't know why I didn't really.'

Mia left the spoon in the bowl, her face clouding with concern. Her dark hair hung around her shoulders and she began to tie it back, securing it with a band on her wrist. 'What is it? Has something happened with Ollie?'

Naomi watched the flakes of cereal swim in the milk as she gathered her thoughts. She tried to structure her ideas as she would for work, introducing the problem and then demonstrating how they could fix it, but she couldn't do that here. Her brain wouldn't let her. All she kept thinking was that she should have said something to her best friend before now. She should have told her everything during one of their many heart-to-hearts at university or in the years since. Her mind was overwhelmed with worry that her friend wouldn't forgive her for keeping such a huge secret for such a long time, and with all these thoughts lapping in her head she opened her mouth and the words just fell out.

'I'm adopted.'

She frowned. 'You're what?'

'Adopted.'

'That's what I thought you said. So your parents—'

'Aren't my birth parents. They're still my parents, obviously. They always will be. They raised me. But my mum isn't the one who gave birth to me and my dad isn't my birth father.'

'Naomi, wow. How long have you known? Have you only just found out?'

Guilt stabbed at Naomi. Why had she left it so long to admit it? It had been so easy to say the words to Mia now. She felt so stupid. 'Since I was young.'

'Oh right. I see.' She dropped her eyes to her bowl and pushed it aside.

'I know I should have told you before now,' Naomi said quickly. 'And I'm sorry.'

'Why didn't you tell me before?' Her tone was quizzical but not accusatory and Naomi felt her tension lessen.

'I don't know.' She shook her head feeling a familiar block of shame, but this time was determined to push through it. 'I just . . . when I was younger, I was embarrassed about it and when we met at uni it never really came up. After a while, I kind of forgot you didn't know and—' She knew she was making excuses. Pathetic ones that weren't even true. 'No, that's not true. Not really. The only truth is that I've always been ashamed of the fact and—'

'Why?' Mia interrupted as Naomi looked up at her. 'Why would you be ashamed of that?'

'I was ashamed my birth parents didn't want me. That there was something wrong with me, something unlovable.' Sharp, painful memories of her saying those words to Gabriel sprung into her head, piercing her heart. 'It's not that I'm ashamed of my adoptive parents,' she added quickly. She'd never be ashamed of them. She loved them and was grateful for everything they'd done for her. Despite their limited finances, they'd always given her a loving, stable home – which was everything she could have asked for. She'd felt listened to, protected by them and was always told she could achieve anything she put her mind to. 'I know it's not healthy but I just . . .

I've always thought about the fact that my birth parents either didn't want me or couldn't cope and gave me away.'

'Did Ollie know?' Mia asked gently, reaching over the counter and holding her friend's arm.

'Eventually yes. But I didn't tell him for a long time. You remember what he was like, always bothered about reputation and what we looked like to other people. He came from money, and I didn't, so it took me a long time to trust him with my secret. We used to shop at charity shops when I was younger and that would have appalled him. Meeting and being with Ollie, paired with the shame I had about being adopted, is probably why I became so obsessed with earning money. I thought having the designer labels would make me feel good enough, but it never really did deep down. After we were married and my career was on the up, I felt safe enough to tell him because I'd created a Naomi he could be proud of. One that wasn't going to be too much trouble.'

Mia got up and hugged her friend. 'No one who knows you could ever think that. I mean I knew you probably didn't have a lot of money spare during university, but that's only because you worked every hour under the sun. I had no idea you felt like this though.'

The allowance Mia received from her father had meant she didn't have to work throughout university, though she'd chosen to work anyway to gain experience for her future. For Naomi it had been a necessity. She was already going to be burdened with student debt. She didn't want to make it worse by adding credit cards and loans to it.

Her parents had sent her as much as they could, but it didn't cover everything.

'I'm sorry I didn't tell you before,' she said again, feeling the warmth of their friendship in the embrace. 'Please understand it wasn't that I didn't trust you with the information. It was just that . . . I wasn't ready to share it.'

Mia released her friend and smiled. 'I understand. Thank you for telling me now.' She studied Naomi's face. 'No tears?'

She shook her head. 'Sorry.'

'I've told you before it's not healthy to keep things bottled up like you do. Maybe you telling me this is the start of something good for you. But what's brought all this on?'

'That's the other thing I need to talk to you about.' The familiar pull of silence threatened to close her mouth, but she refused to let her old ways continue. She brushed her blonde hair behind her ear. 'You know the atmosphere has been a bit frosty between me and Gabriel?'

Mia nodded.

'It's because . . .' She hesitated, feeling her walls close around her, but she'd come so far with Mia she wouldn't stop now. She valued their friendship too much to keep this a secret any longer. 'That night he came to uni to visit, after you went to bed we stayed up all night talking and I told him everything. I told him I was adopted, how it had always made me feel less than.'

'He wasn't horrible to you about it was he?' Mia's eyes were wide with surprise.

Naomi shook her head. 'No, but . . . God I don't even know how to say this, Mia. That night, something happened between us.'

'Oh my God! What! Did you sleep with him?' Mia's face had scrunched up like she was smelling something unpleasant. Naomi nodded, panic flooding her mind. What would Mia think of her now? Mia pretended to throw up and Naomi couldn't help but laugh. 'Urgh, I think I'm going to be sick.'

'Don't!' Naomi replied, giggling at her friend's expression.

'I'm only joking. I mean, it is icky that you slept with my brother but I'm not stupid. I see women throw themselves at him all the time. If only they knew what he was like to grow up with . . . but still, I get it.'

'You're very relaxed about it.'

Mia shrugged.

'There is a reason why I'm telling you all this. It's not just to put you off your breakfast. It's because last night I realised something.'

She outlined the argument she'd had with Gabriel and how she had finally understood that even though all of this had happened a number of years ago, she'd never really got over it. It had affected her as an adult, destroying her ability to open up to people and rather than face up to it, she'd hid from the fact, building walls and barriers to keep people away and buried her emotions deep inside her.

'I can't believe he did that to you,' Mia snapped, her cheeks reddening and eyes narrowing. 'I'm so angry with him. The next time I see him I'm going to—'

'No, don't,' Naomi pleaded, her hands shooting out across the countertop and reaching for Mia. 'Please. After last night, I think it's best we put the past behind us. At least I've got it all off my chest now. Him saying "I don't know" as an answer for why he left though isn't really good enough.'

'It definitely isn't. Stupid man.'

Naomi smiled. 'I just . . . I don't want to lie to the people I love most anymore. That's why I'm here. I want you to know everything about me. I don't want our friendship to disappear like my marriage has.'

'That won't happen to us. We've been friends for too long. I won't let it. And I haven't always told you everything either. Remember I didn't tell you about Gabriel becoming a chef or the argument with our father? Sometimes life gets in the way but I promise to be open and honest too.' Mia paused, smiling at Naomi. 'But seriously, back to Gabriel, I can't believe he just left. I remember when it happened, I thought it was strange. He was all set to stay for a few more days but he gave no indication it was anything to do with you. Perhaps he'd realised something.' Mia paused and as she thought, she gently ran a fingertip over her lips. 'Come to think of it, it wasn't long after that that he and my father argued.'

'So you're saying I scared him off and caused the argument with your father?' Her tone was teasing and she pursed her mouth in mock annoyance.

'Of course not. How could it be? Gabriel's made his own choices. That's nothing to do with you. I'm so angry with him for making you feel that way. He shouldn't have been such a coward. What were you supposed to think when he did that to you? Of course you'd feel used and abandoned.' She reached out and took her hand. 'Men are so stupid sometimes. I'm sorry.'

Naomi tried to laugh it off. 'It was a long time ago and I'm not exactly angry about what he did.' She was, she just didn't want to make Mia feel any worse than she clearly already did. 'I think it's more that I'm angry that I allowed it to shape me the way it has. And it's time that stopped. Being here, away from home, it's given me the space to realise a few things. Get some perspective.'

'I'm glad something good has come out of the trip. Seeing Gabriel again must have been difficult for you.'

'It was.'

'You hid it very well. I always knew you'd fancy him, and I remember you guys were still talking and laughing when I went to bed but—'

'Let's not talk about it anymore.'

'So how did you and Gabriel leave things last night?'

'Uneasily,' was all Naomi could think to say.

Mia began ducking and turning her head, studying Naomi.

'What?'

'Any tears yet?'

'No. Not yet.'

'Not even last night?'

'No, not even last night.'

'It's really not good for you, Naomi. I've said this before. You have to let your emotions out.'

'I am,' she replied. 'I've talked more about my emotions in the last ten minutes than I have in ten years.'

'But that's not the same as the physical release of tears.'

'I can't force them to come,' Naomi said sadly.

'I could peel an onion?'

Naomi giggled and kept her tone light as she said, 'Let's not talk about it anymore. I want to enjoy this feeling now I've told you everything. I feel lighter, better than I have in a long time.'

'That's good. I suppose it'll have to do for now.' As she finished speaking, Mia stood on tiptoes as a van she didn't recognise drove past the window. She went over and looked out.

'What is it?' asked Naomi, following.

'It's the guys from the market delivering your Christmas decorations.'

'That's earlier than expected. They must have worked hard to get them ready.'

This morning she'd woken up anxious, ready to put Christmas back into the bin, but now that relief washed over her, her treacherous tummy bubbled with excitement. The trees looked bare with only the lights wrapped around them and she couldn't wait to see them decorated with the beautiful handmade baubles she'd seen in town. With the hanging stars in the dining room, it was the final festive touch inside and that only left the outside tree, which would be delivered soon.

'What are you doing today?' Naomi asked her friend.

'I've got a meeting later but nothing for a while. I was going to prep for a new venture my father's thinking of.'

Naomi smiled widely. 'Fancy joining me for breakfast and some tree decorating? That's if Gabriel will have bothered preparing the buffet.'

'He will have. You're our guest.'

'Then let's go and get some food and a huge cup of coffee. I have to tell you about my disastrous date with Levi and the Tree-mothy and Tree-vor saga.'

Mia threw her head back and laughed. 'Gabriel told me you'd named the trees, ha ha. I can't believe it about Levi though; I thought he was nice, handsome too. I'm just sorry it didn't work out.'

'Oh, it's fine. He might have been good-looking on the outside but inside he was an absolute idiot.'

After grabbing their coats, they made their way over to Le Petit Chateau. The snow felt dense and solid under Naomi's feet, grounding her to the earth. She took a moment to take in her surroundings. Feeling lighter after opening up to Mia, she wanted to take in the world around her again: the sprawling craggy mountains, their sides and peaks covered in snow, the pine trees, the expanse of white that surrounded her. She breathed in the cold air, feeling it cool her lungs. She stared at her footprints in the snow, a metaphor for how she was changing her own path.

Elias and Noah, from the market, were chit-chatting as they unpacked the boxes from the back of the van.

'Thank you so much for delivering them early,' Naomi said. 'You must have worked day and night. Here, let me help.' She took a box from him and they all went inside. She put it gently on the sofa and opened the lid. The handmade glass baubles sparkled in the light. They were strikingly beautiful, and Naomi just knew that the assortment of colours and shapes were going to make the trees look perfect: traditional with a modern edge, just like Le Petit Chateau.

'They really are incredible,' Mia said, holding one up by the ribbon so it spun in the sunlight pouring through the window. 'I should have been using these before. I'm sorry I didn't.'

Noah waved a hand dismissively. 'It doesn't matter. You do enough for us all. You employ my son, and for that, I'm very grateful. I'm not sure anyone else would.' Mia and Naomi laughed, knowing he was only teasing.

'Peter's wonderful,' she replied with a genuine smile. 'He's a great asset to the team.'

'I'll tell him you said so.' Noah's chest puffed with pride. 'But we are very happy you're using our decorations now. The town is so excited to see Le Petit Chateau reopen.' He peered around. 'And I'm lucky to get a peek inside.'

'You are. What do you think?'

He took in the open ground floor. A few of the rugs had been changed from pale, neutral colours to dark, earthy greens and with the red and gold colour theme the place already screamed Christmas. 'You have done a wonderful job. Your father must be very proud.'

'I hope so,' Mia said with a smile that didn't quite reach her eyes. 'Actually, I'm glad you're here. I've had an idea for the big outside tree I'd like to ask you about.' She took him to one side and Naomi surreptitiously watched as a smile spread across his face. Whatever it was, it was going down well. She made conversation with Elias, complimenting him on his work too. He explained how they were all made by hand, starting off with a glass cylinder that is heated over a flame and then blown.

'It sounds dangerous,' Naomi said.

'Once you know what you're doing it is fine.'

Mia and Noah came back to join them.

'Have you two had breakfast yet?' Mia asked.

'Not yet,' Elias replied. 'We'll get something at the market.'

'Are you sure you won't join us?' Naomi motioned to the buffet. As usual Gabriel had laid out more food than she could ever eat on her own. Even with Mia there'd be far too much left.

'No, no,' Noah replied, waving his hands. 'We couldn't possibly.'

Elias was more easily swayed, his eyes roving over the plates of meat and cheese, the pastries and the muesli. 'We could take a few things with us.'

'Yes, please do.'

Noah looked to Mia. 'Are you sure?'

'Absolutely. Please, come and sit down. You have time for a quick coffee, don't you?'

Without waiting she began taking cups and saucers and pouring coffee. Naomi helped and they shared a congenial breakfast, talking about the town, the people and how they were all looking forward to Christmas.

'I just hope Alina gets better soon.'

'Alina?' Naomi asked, her ears pricking up.

'She's been unwell and her son hasn't arrived yet. He couldn't get away from work.' Knowing he was a human rights lawyer, she knew that must be difficult. 'I will see her tomorrow – see if there's anything she needs.'

'Let me,' Naomi said quickly. Mia, Elias and Noah all gave her confused glances. 'We met in town before. I know where she lives and you must be busy with the market, so let me do it.'

'Are you sure?'

'Absolutely. I can stop by the market and tell you how she is once I'm done if it will help put your mind at rest.'

'That's very kind of you, Naomi. Thank you.'

After breakfast, the men departed, and Naomi and Mia began decorating the trees.

'So what was all that about?' she asked a few minutes after they left.

'I could ask you the same thing.'

'Okay, what was your top-secret discussion about?'

'Oh, just an idea I had. There's no point in telling you because it might not even happen. Honestly, put it out of your mind. But why do you want to go and see Alina?'

'She seemed really nice and she mentioned about her son being a lawyer. I was going to head into town tomorrow anyway. I don't mind calling in, seeing if she needs anything.'

'Well, that's nice of you. Right, what happened with Levi? Tell me everything.'

Naomi kept her eyes on her friend and though she laughed along as Naomi described her date with Levi, something was definitely off, and it had started when Noah had mentioned her father.

'Okay,' Naomi said when they took a break. 'Enough's enough. What exactly is going on?' Both were sat on the sofa opposite the roaring log fire, sipping cups of coffee.

'With me? Nothing.' Mia was all wide-eyed astonishment, but her voice was just a little too high, a little too brittle.

'Come on, I've bared by soul to you today. I can tell something's going on with you too. It was the mention of your father.'

Mia seemed to crumple. 'You spotted that, huh?'

Naomi nodded.

'Everyone keeps saying that he should be proud of me, but I'm really not sure he is. He's never been very forthcoming when it comes to emotions, and, don't feel bad for this, but I think you telling me about Gabriel, it just got me thinking about him and my father not talking. It has literally been years.'

'Why *has* it been so long?'

'They're both too stubborn to make the first move. I gave up talking to Father about it a long time ago.'

'But you're still in the middle.' Mia nodded sadly. She'd hit the nail on the head.

'That's it exactly. Gabriel doesn't mean to put me in the middle, but the whole situation is difficult. Especially at Christmas.'

Naomi placed an arm around her friend's shoulders.

'At least I'm here. We'll have a wonderful time no matter what.'

'We will, we can go skiing and then have a delicious dinner.'

Naomi grimaced. 'I'll agree to skiing as long as I can get straight into my pyjamas afterwards. I'm still not that good.'

'Deal.'

They chinked their mugs together and Naomi marvelled at how different she felt inside. Pain still rung through her body at her argument with Gabriel last night but knowing there were no more secrets between her and Mia had lifted her mood.

Her thoughts also kept running to Alina and the advice she'd given. When she returned to her room later that day, she would do some more reading about community care law. The idea of it, of doing something more in line with her values, something that meant something to her, hadn't left her. It kept growing stronger and after today she felt there was nothing she couldn't do if she dug deep enough. She just hoped that feeling would last and not be overtaken by the pain that surged through her every time she thought about Gabriel and the way things had ended between them. Ended, she was sure, for good.

Chapter 17

The sights and smells of the market filled her senses just as they had the first time she'd visited. Only this time, having got to know her a little, people smiled and waved as she went past and she greeted them in return. She even saw Kaylee from the restaurant, clearly enjoying a day off, and they shared a hot chocolate before she made her way to Alina's house.

'Are you going home for Christmas?' Naomi asked the young woman.

Kaylee nodded. 'I fly back at the end of next week.'

'Will you come back here?'

'Definitely.' She sipped her hot chocolate. 'I love it here. And there are other places I want to see too, but there's something special about the mountains, the snow.'

Naomi smiled thinking about snow and stars, but those thoughts led her to Gabriel, the shooting star, their near kiss and everything that had come after.

'Have you seen Levi again?' she asked, changing the subject before her feelings grew too strong.

'He brought another woman to the restaurant the other night.'

'What?' Naomi's eyes widened in shock. 'The day after he took me?'

'Sorry to tell you but it seems he's a bit of a player.'

'Wow.' She laughed to herself. It was sad really. She wondered what he felt he had to prove to behave in such a way. She knew now that every behaviour started somewhere. 'I bet he thinks he's really cool.'

'So cool,' Kaylee joked.

They talked more about her family, and Naomi's, though she didn't mention being adopted. She was happy she'd opened up to Mia, but she wasn't about to start blurting it out to near strangers.

Kaylee left to go skiing and Naomi strolled through the streets, admiring the mixture of buildings, the strange combination of both French and German architecture, both of which she loved. As she left the centre of town, she found more shops to visit, more food to sample. She really loved the mix of French and German food here too. She could definitely see herself coming back to visit Mia at least once a year. She might even get better at skiing if she kept practising.

Alina's house was set a few streets back from the main thoroughfare and the sounds of the market diminished as she grew closer. It was a typical Swiss house with white walls, punctuated by dark timber beams. The windows were small, and snow gathered on the roof. She knocked on the door and stepped back.

It was impossible to hear movement inside and as she was about to knock again, the door opened. Alina's aged face peered at her, her dark eyes widening when she saw who it was.

'You.'

Naomi couldn't tell if it was a question or a statement. 'Me. Noah mentioned you'd been unwell, and I thought I'd stop by, see if you needed anything.'

'That's kind. But I'm all right. I think it was only something I ate. I was just going to go shopping.'

'Why don't I come with you? I can carry your bags for you.'

'I don't need any help,' she said tersely. Alina had been so kind the other day and so chatty, Naomi knew it was the remnants of being unwell that were making her tetchy.

'I know you don't, but I've got some shopping to do too, so we could go together.'

'That is a pathetic excuse.' A slight smile pulled at her mouth, the wrinkles deepening.

Naomi laughed. 'Oh all right, it is.' It seemed honesty was going to be the best policy when it came to this wily old woman. 'You were so lovely to me the other day and you gave me a lot to think about so when I heard you were poorly, I just wanted to check you were okay. I can see you are so if you'd prefer to go shopping alone, I completely understand. I hate it when people fuss about me as well.'

208

'No, no,' Alina replied, waving her hand in the air. 'Now you're here we might as well go together. Let me get my things.'

Naomi waited as Alina gathered her coat and bag, and together they walked to the first shop Alina needed. Naomi pulled Alina's small shopping trolley bag behind her, not caring about how incredibly uncool she looked. She hoped Gabriel didn't see her but then brushed him swiftly from her mind.

'So you've been sick?' Naomi asked.

'No.'

'No? But Noah said—'

'That's what I told everyone who kept coming round.'

'Oh. Why?'

'Because I was embarrassed. I slipped when I was getting out of the bath and hurt my back. I didn't want everyone knowing I'd nearly fallen over. They'd only fuss more and be checking on me every day. Calling me all the time and interrupting my programmes.'

Naomi couldn't help but laugh. 'Why didn't you just tell them? Everyone here seems really friendly.'

'They are friendly, but they'd tell my son, Roger, and then he'd worry, so I told them I'd eaten something that had disagreed with me.'

'I see. Is this the first time you've fallen?' she asked, knowing she might get both barrels but she couldn't go along with lie if the truth was that she did need checking on.

'Yes,' she replied indignantly. 'And that is the truth.'

'In that case,' Naomi declared, her worries subsiding, 'I won't say a word.'

'Good. Roger arrives tonight but not till late otherwise he would've helped me with the shopping.'

'You must be looking forward to seeing him.'

'And his husband and my wonderful grandchildren. They all love me because I spoil them, giving them everything they want.'

'That's what grandparents are for,' she replied without thinking. The only thing was, she didn't know that because she had no idea who her grandparents were. Her adoptive parents didn't have any extended family at the time of her adoption, and of course, she had no idea about where her birth parents had come from. She focused her mind on something else. 'I've been thinking more about what you said the other day.'

They entered the first shop and Naomi carried a basket for Alina as she loaded everything she needed inside.

'Oh, yes?'

'I've been looking at switching to community care law. It's a branch of law that deals with children in foster care. I've even found some opportunities I might apply for.'

They strolled up and down the aisles of the little supermarket.

'So, what's holding you back?'

'I don't know.' *Fear at earning less money*. She hated that it was the truth. Hated how materialistic it made her sound. But she didn't want the money to spend on fancy handbags and designer clothes. She only ever wanted that money in the bank, for a rainy day. As a security blanket.

'Money isn't everything,' Alina replied.

Naomi came to a standstill. 'How did you know?' A wry smile battled with the confusion widening her eyes.

'Money or love are always the reasons.'

'Isn't that what people say about murder?' Naomi joked.

They started moving again, the basket cutting into Naomi's palms it was so weighed down.

Alina chuckled. 'Well, it's true for jobs as well. Does money make you happy?'

'Not especially.' She stopped once more. 'Alina, how much more food do you actually need?' The basket was full, overflowing with more than the whole town could eat.

'I like to make sure I have everything the grandchildren could want. This is the last item.' She put it in and they made their way to the checkout.

The cashier and other customers nearby bombarded Alina with questions about her illness, offering their assistance and expressing joy at seeing her back on her feet. Naomi bit her lip, keeping her smile down, though Alina gave her a mischievous grin.

'You should talk to Roger,' she declared as they left the shop. 'When you see how happy he is because he's helping people, you'll see that money doesn't matter.'

'I think I knew that already.'

'Then stop wasting time and make a change. No one can do it but you.'

211

She knew that well enough from her discussion with Mia this morning. Naomi thought of the shooting star she'd seen the other night. She'd wished then it could make her brave. Was it the wish coming true or was it her own determination? She didn't know, but whatever it was, she wasn't going to lose the momentum the last twenty-four hours had given her. Though she hated thinking about him, she was proud that Gabriel had been brave enough to forge his own path even against his father's wishes. But she wouldn't think about him again. Not today. That was the last time.

Once she'd walked Alina home, she'd head back to Le Petit Chateau and ensure those job vacancies were still open. One had looked particularly exciting, and her holiday here wouldn't last forever. As soon as Christmas was over, she'd be back to London, picking up her life again. Only this time, she'd be picking up the reins and driving in another, more satisfying direction.

'Now, come on,' Alina said bossily, shaking her out of her thoughts. 'I have to buy lots and lots of wine for tonight.'

'Alina,' Naomi declared, lugging the already fit to busting trolley behind her. 'You're an absolute legend.'

'I know, I know,' she replied with the same dismissive wave of her hand. 'That's what everyone says.'

Chapter 18

The Christmas tree for the front of Le Petit Chateau arrived on the biggest lorry Naomi had ever laid eyes on. It reminded her of the one she'd seen in Covent Garden during past Christmases. But concern pulled at her as she realised she'd forgotten to arrange outdoor-friendly decorations. Yet, when she raised her concerns with Mia, she simply laughed them off and told her it was all in hand.

'How do we get it upright?' Naomi asked.

'Wait and see,' Mia replied teasingly.

Naomi did as she was told, shoving her hands deeper into her coat pockets to keep out the cold. The wind was particularly biting today and snowflakes drifted in the air around them. More snow had been forecast but it wasn't supposed to arrive till later. Gabriel strolled past her. They'd exchanged civilities about the weather and wished each other good morning, that was it. He'd then disappeared to assist with the tree. Naomi couldn't help but notice a slightly frostier atmosphere between Gabriel and Mia too and she hoped she hadn't caused another family feud by being honest about the past.

As if sensing her unease, Mia said, 'Last night I told Gabriel off for the way he treated you.'

'Ah,' she replied. 'I thought something was a bit off between you two. Don't make things difficult between you and your brother for something that happened years ago.'

'I won't. It won't. But he needs to know what an idiot he's been. And I like telling him off. When we were younger it used to be the other way around so this is payback.'

'Okay.' She laughed. 'Just don't fall out over me, please.'

They fell into silence, staring into the horizon. After a few minutes, Naomi spotted people from the town marching towards Le Petit Chateau. She recognised Noah and Elias, and many of the stallholders she'd seen at the Christmas market plus lots of other families and children. They were all carrying boxes or bags and Naomi's brow furrowed as Mia's smile grew wider and wider. She gripped Naomi's arm in excitement.

'Look, they're here.'

'What's going on?'

'You'll see.'

Boxes and bags were placed on the ground and the men began to lift off the massive tree, manoeuvring it carefully and with such brilliant teamwork, Naomi laughed as she imagined it as a team-building exercise at work.

Finally, the tree, which wasn't actually as big as she had at first thought – though it was definitely at least ten feet tall – was in place. Soon ladders were put up, braced at the bottom by friends and neighbours, and lights were wrapped around the bare branches. The bundles of wires were so big and the tree so wide, the lights were passed from person to person like they were playing pass the parcel. The men laughed and joked, the women cheered and teased, ordering the lights up or down or across. All the while the children were jumping up and down catching the flakes of snow falling from the heavy clouds overhead.

Once the lights were wrapped around the tree, Gabriel flicked the switch and the gloomy day was lit with a twinkling orange glow. It was magical. The snow was falling heavier now but no one could be deterred from decorating as they gathered the bags and boxes they had brought with them, taking out decorations and hanging them on every available branch.

'What's all this?' Naomi asked Mia.

'Your trip to the market to find decorations for the inside of Le Petit Chateau inspired me. So when Noah came up to the chateau to deliver the decorations, I asked him if he thought people would like to hang something on the outside tree too. It's been put up every year since my father started the business, but we've always decorated it ourselves and the town has joined us for the lights to be switched on. But I thought this year it was time for a change. Thankfully, he thought it would be a good idea and everyone has brought something to hang. The local school are making some decorations too and they're coming to hang them later.'

'What a wonderful idea, Mia.' Naomi turned to the crowd. 'And they all look so happy to be taking part.'

'They've always been supportive of our plans for the resort and it's about time we acknowledged that more. We've always brought in a lot of business which helps the town but they could easily have objected many times when we've looked at expanding. They deserve thanks for that but it's something my father sometimes forgets. Don't get me wrong, he's generous and well liked but it's the little things like supporting small businesses that show just how much we appreciate them.'

'You're very inspiring,' Naomi told her friend.

'Me? It's down to you, really.'

Naomi smiled warmly at her friend. 'Speaking of inspiration, I need to go and speak to someone.' She made her way to Alina who was standing back, watching a man hang decorations on the tree with his two small children. He stepped back and slipped his hand into the man's beside him. 'Alina, it's lovely to see you. You look well today.'

Her eyes glinted. 'And you. Are you enjoying the tree?'

'I am very much, thank you.' She hesitated unsure how to start the conversation. 'I wanted to say how grateful I am for your words of encouragement yesterday. Last night, I decided to apply for some jobs.'

'That's wonderful. I was going to say you look happier already.'

'Do I?'

Her mind flew back to Gabriel and their argument. She didn't feel happier, not exactly. She felt lighter, freer, but not quite happier. Though that night had been unpleasant, something had changed within her. A weight had shifted. That night, their past, was out in the open. He knew how he'd affected her, and Mia now knew about it too. There were no more secrets pressing on her and it was like a weight had been removed from her chest. An invisible, heavy weight she'd grown so used to carrying she hadn't even known it was there.

'Is that your son?' Naomi asked, nodding to the taller of the two men she'd seen holding hands. He was older than she'd been expecting. In his fifties. But she could see the similarity already.

'Yes. He's looking forward to meeting you. I told him all about you. Here, you should hang one of these.' Alina held out an ornament for Naomi to take.

'I couldn't. You or your son should do it. I know how worried you were he might not be able to make it.'

She looked at the sky at the snow falling heavily now. 'I'm glad he came yesterday. Any later and he might not have made it at all.'

'Do you think this'll continue?'

'I do. So we better head back soon. Please, take one. We have more than enough.' She held the decoration out again and Naomi took it, taking tentative steps forwards.

She ended up next to Gabriel who was lifting up small children to hang baubles on the higher branches. They giggled excitedly and the sweet sound filled the air. He glanced at her, gauging her reaction, and she dropped her eyes away. The children were making her laugh and she didn't want him to see her smiling and think things were okay between them. They weren't. Not yet. Not until he actually apologised for walking away the other night and that night all those years ago. Even if he didn't know why he'd done it, she still wanted an apology or explanation. Some ownership of his actions.

As she reached out and hung the bauble on the tree – the glittering fairy lights giving off dazzling prisms of light – she remembered how much she had loved Christmas as a child. The sense of joy here reminded her of her family and the exciting build-up to Christmas her parents always managed to create. Remembering what Mia had said yesterday about her family, Naomi was more grateful than ever for the memories of love and happiness her adoptive parents had given her. She hadn't had the best start in life but thanks to them things had only got better and better. They would decorate the tree with baubles they'd made together or ones she'd made at school, and it was those times she needed to remember when life became hard, when the fear of abandonment or not being good enough reared its head. She didn't think it would ever go away completely, but if she stood up to the horrible voice that whispered those words in her ear, she might be able to silence it somewhat.

Alina came to her side and handed her another ornament

to hang. 'My son, Roger, is happy to talk to you about his work if you ever need any advice. He told me to give you his card, or you can pop in to speak to him anytime while he's here.'

She handed over the small square of paper and Naomi tucked it in her pocket before turning and waving thanks to Roger. He waved back. 'Thank you, Alina. I might take him up on that.'

Gabriel glanced over, clearly wondering what was going on, but she never met his eye. After hanging the ornament, she went back to Mia.

'Does it look awful?' Mia whispered. 'Father always likes things elegant and matching. I'm not sure how he'll feel about this.'

'It looks beautiful. The decorations here are always so gorgeous there's no way it wouldn't look nice. Is your father coming here for Christmas?'

'No, but he wants a photo when I send him my next progress report.'

'He'll be blown away. I'm sure.'

Mia drew her eyes away from the tree, surveying the scene with concern. 'We might have to close the slopes if this snow continues.'

'Really?' Naomi thought this sort of thing must happen all the time.

'We have to when it comes down too heavily and causes a hazard. The visibility is low and it can cause accidents. People fly down those slopes and if they can't see where they're going . . .'

'I get it. What will you do?'

'I'll give it half an hour and talk to the site managers but I'm not convinced this will ease up.'

Naomi stared at the clouds and dropped her eyes to the scenery before her. The snow had begun to pile on the branches of the trees and the roofs of the chalets. It was beautiful. Perfect if you were sitting inside with a hot chocolate and roaring fire, but her nose was frozen and her fingers – even in the thick gloves she was wearing – were chilled to the bone. She'd be happy to get inside, and it seemed everyone else had the same idea too. Before long, everyone returned to the town, the children having snowball fights as they left.

Mia and Naomi waved them off as Gabriel came to join them.

'That was a great idea, Mia,' he said.

'I told you Naomi inspired it. She's the one we should thank.'

'Right.' He caught her eye and she waited for him to speak.

When he didn't, disappointment filled Naomi, and she walked ahead of them. 'We should go inside,' she said coldly. 'It's freezing.'

Chapter 19

The next morning just as Naomi was tucking into another delicious breakfast made by Gabriel, the entrance door swung open, and Mia burst in.

'Disaster! It's a complete disaster. I have no idea what I'm going to do and I need some coffee. Perhaps something stronger. Right now.'

Naomi hastily swallowed her mouthful. 'Whoa, okay, let's take a minute.'

'I don't have a minute. I need to get this sorted now.' Mia's calm and in-control attitude had once again disintegrated, which told Naomi her stress levels were at maximum given that it wasn't taking much to push her over the edge.

'Take a seat, take a breath and whatever it is we can sort it.' She rose from her seat and poured coffee from the percolator into a cup, taking it back to the table where Mia had flopped into the vacant chair. 'Here, drink this and tell me what's happened. Is it the snow?'

It had continued to snow heavily through the day and all that night. Mia had braved the short journey to Le Petit Chateau for them to have dinner together, but after that she'd gone home and Naomi had been content to have some time alone, taking herself off to her room and checking out more job vacancies in community care law just in case something new had come in. She hadn't realised that it was such an under-valued area of law. Opportunities were rich and varied and reading about the subject had made her heart race with excitement. There was so much she could do to help the children who were in care or being adopted and the caregivers who needed support in figuring everything out.

This morning, the world was covered in a thick blanket of white. The trees were heavy with snow, the branches bending under its weight. Eager skiers had been on the slopes as soon as they were able and the resort hummed with activity. The sky above was blue and cloudless as if the clouds had given everything they'd had and had simply disappeared when they were spent. Vanishing as the last drop of snow left them. The mountains were covered once again with only the rock-iest of outcrops visible.

Mia added milk and sugar to her coffee. 'It's not the snow. It's the caterer.'

'The caterer for the gala?'

'Yes, he's double-booked so I need to find someone else.'

'Okay,' Naomi replied calmly. 'Give me a list and I'll start calling people for you.'

She pushed her unbrushed dark hair back from her face. Her fingers caught in a tangle and she wrenched them out. 'It's what I've been doing for the last half an hour since I got his email telling me he wasn't coming. An email! He didn't even have the guts to call me.'

'That's a bit low. But there must be someone who can help.'

Mia shook her head sadly. 'A party of this size on Christmas Eve? No. Everyone is booked.'

Naomi stood up and filled a plate with tiny pastries and fresh fruit. She placed it in front of Mia. 'Drink your coffee, eat something and then we'll handle this. Let's pull together a list of caterers within a twenty-mile radius and I'm sure we'll find someone.'

'Okay,' she replied, calming a little as she bit down hard on a piece of melon. 'Let's go through my database.'

Naomi made notes of names and numbers as Mia read them out, then they split the list. 'See, we've got lots of names here. How hard can this be?'

The answer was very. They both called a dozen caterers, and no one was able to help. If the numbers weren't a problem, the date was and if the date didn't immediately scare them off, the sheer number of people made them virtually hang up as soon as Naomi had finished speaking. Mia had been right.

'I better go and tell my father,' she said sadly. 'He'll want to know what's happening and I'll have to try some caterers from further afield. I hate using people I haven't had time to research and try out. You never know what the quality will be like.'

'I'm sure he'll understand you haven't got much choice and you're a good judge of character. You'll get an idea as soon as you speak to them.'

'I hope so. I'll be back soon.'

Naomi hugged her friend and watched her disappear out the front door. She was normally so bouncy and ready for anything it was painful to see her stressed and slouched. Just as she left, Gabriel entered from a door at the back of the dining room, checking if anything on the breakfast buffet needed refilling.

'How was it today?' he asked over his shoulder.

Hearing his voice, seeing him in his chef whites, an idea sprung into her brain. Naomi stared at him open-mouthed before turning to the door Mia had just left through. She pointed at him. 'You!'

Gabriel's eye's widened in surprise and his forehead creased in worry. 'What?'

'Nothing,' she replied. As she was only speaking to him when it was absolutely necessary, she decided to speak to Mia about her brother – the chef! – and get her to ask him to cater for the gala party. Surely he'd be able to help with the catering. How had Mia not thought of it herself? Naomi could only think she was so panicked and stressed she wasn't thinking clearly. 'Breakfast was great, as usual,' she said, watching his face change as he wondered why she'd acted like such a weirdo.

'Right. Thanks.'

It was the first kind thing they'd said to one another since the argument. She'd expected him to disappear back to the kitchen, which she now knew was in the basement of the chateau, but still, he lingered.

'Do you want more coffee?'

'Umm, yeah. Sure.' She didn't have any plans for the day so another coffee and some more job hunting were in order. Perhaps a stroll in the freshly laid snow. She loved watching her footprints imprint in the sheet of white, even though it was childish. She might even go skiing again. She'd been out a few times now and was definitely getting better. As long as she stuck to the beginners' slope, she'd be fine.

'Naomi,' he said, finally turning to face her. His eyes were sparkling in the lights from the Christmas tree, and he rubbed a hand over his jaw. 'Can we talk? I need to explain myself, but not right now. Could we talk . . . over dinner, maybe? Please?'

So now he wanted to talk?

Her first instinct was to say no. To say it was all too late. If he'd wanted to speak to her, he should have done it the other night when she was finally brave enough to talk about it all. To make it clear how much his actions had affected her. What could he even have to say that would make it better? She didn't want to sit and rehash everything they'd gone through the other night to end up at exactly the same place: no apology from him. Had it taken him a few days to think of excuses for his actions?

'Please?' he asked again, his voice imploring. 'There's a lot to say.'

'Is there?' She met his gaze. His jaw was set but something about him urged her to give him this chance. 'Fine. But on one condition,' she said, standing her ground. 'That you help Mia with the catering for the gala party.'

'The gala?' His eyebrows shot up, his eyes widening in surprise.

'The caterer's double-booked and cancelled on us. Mia's in a panic trying to find a replacement. We called quite a few this morning but no one's available.'

'Me?' He pointed to his chest. 'You want me to do it?'

'Yes. You're a chef and from what I've tasted a pretty good one.'

'But I'm not—' A moment's vulnerability flashed over his face. 'I cannot.'

'Why? It's just picky bits. Surely that's easier than working at a restaurant.'

He began tidying the plates of food on the breakfast table. 'I'm not sure what I make will be good enough.'

Her stomach lurched at the vulnerability in his voice. 'Of course it will.'

'No, you don't understand.' He began pacing. 'The food for the gala, it's important. It has always been the most inventive. It showcases the area, the traditions, the local produce. It is the most—'

'Gabriel, I don't think you're scared the food won't be good enough, I think you're scared that *you* won't be

226

good enough.' It was a feeling she knew all too well and her voice softened. 'But I know you are good enough.'

He ran a hand through his hair and though she didn't want it to, her heart went out to him. The connection that had always existed between them since that first night together seemed to pulse with life once more. It had always been there, somewhere inside her, somewhere in her heart, despite everything that had happened.

'I just don't want to let Mia down.'

'Well, if you want to have dinner with me you don't have much choice. And for what it's worth, I think you'll be fine. I've tasted your food, remember. The home-cooked stuff and the fancy restaurant stuff.'

Relief relaxed his features. Did her belief in him mean that much? She shook the thought away.

'Fine,' he said. 'If you promise to have dinner with me, tonight, here at Le Petit Chateau, I will help Mia.'

'Deal.' She held out her hand for him to shake. When he slid his hand into hers, electricity bolted up her arm. She stared into his eyes, feeling warmth light her body. It was a look they'd shared before when she'd been swept up in his arms. Remembering his soft lips on hers, the way his body had made her feel, heat rose in her cheeks forcing her to look away.

'I'd better find Mia and tell her,' she said, stepping backwards.

He retreated too, heading back to the kitchen, and she exhaled a long deep breath.

Dinner with Gabriel.

Though she'd sorted one problem for Mia, she'd lined herself up with another. She stiffened, her body reminding her to be on guard around him. What would he say? Could anything he said change things between them? Her eyes flicked to the large clock on the wall, ticking down like a time bomb to a moment she wanted yet dreaded at the same time.

Chapter 20

Later that evening, Naomi came down to the dining room of Le Petit Chateau. Assuming they'd be eating there, she was shocked to find the room empty, lit only by tea lights. Her eyes roved over the festively decorated space, her heart skipping a little. The hanging Christmas decorations spun, catching the light, and the Christmas tree twinkled with a warm golden glow in the corner, the glass ornaments bright in the darkness, as she called out.

'Gabriel?' Her voice echoed around the empty space, and she took a few more steps into the room. A moment later he emerged from a door at the back that led to the kitchen. He smiled nervously.

'You look beautiful.'

Unsure what to expect tonight she'd worn her normal jeans and a jumper but had curled her hair and added a smoky eye. Feeling good about herself had always been her armour at work and she knew she'd need it tonight if they were raking over the past.

'Thank you,' she replied, nervously tucking a stray hair behind her ear. He was wearing normal clothes too though he had a black apron tied around his waist.

'It's this way.' He motioned to the door that led outside to the terrace at the back of the dining room. 'Do you have your coat?'

'Yes, it's just over there.'

She'd hung it on a coat rack in the corner of the living room earlier and she retrieved it, slipping it on.

The night was clear and crisp, perfumed with pine from the tall trees surrounding them. The snow had stopped and though tufts of cloud littered the sky, the stars were shining through, the full moon silvery and bright. The terrace area was also lit by tea lights, but still she couldn't see where they'd be eating. She followed him down a set of steps that led to a path. His hand brushed her back as he walked beside her, guiding her down the track towards a dense copse of trees. He pushed an overhanging branch out of her way, some of the snow falling to the ground, revealing a clearing. A table and two chairs had been set out with more tea lights and lanterns dotted around. He'd even hung fairy lights around the space, and they glittered in the breeze. Her breath hitched. It was enchanting. Like something from a fairy tale. She might even say sweepingly romantic . . . just as she had after her date with Levi when she'd admitted to Gabriel she'd hoped her first date after her divorce would have been something better.

Yet, she told herself to be wary. Under any other circumstance this would be the most romantic thing anyone had ever done for her, but she had to remind herself of why they were here. They weren't here to get swept up in the emotion of it all; they were here for him to explain. She hoped for him to apologise. Something that would bring this painful part of her life to an end. With the chapter closed, she might be able to quiet the evil voice in her head a little more. The one that told her she'd never be good enough to be loved completely. She edged forwards, grateful to see a couple of heaters next to the chairs along with thick woollen blankets. He'd thought of everything.

'Do you like it?' he asked, shuffling his feet.

'Very much,' she replied in barely more than a whisper, cursing herself for speaking without thinking. He pulled out a chair for her and she sat down. Then he took the bottle of wine from the ice bucket and poured her a glass. It was the wine she'd enjoyed at the restaurant. Another nice touch.

'I'll just get some snacks.' He left the clearing and through the branches she watched as he took the stairs two at a time and came back a few minutes later with a wooden board loaded with delicious-looking food. 'This is roasted mushroom and Swiss chard dip.'

She took one of the small crackers and dipped it in. The nutty scent of Swiss cheese reached her immediately and her taste buds rejoiced as soon as she put it in her mouth. 'It's wonderful.' He relaxed at her compliment, his posture changing as his shoulders dropped down. Next to it were tiny tartiflettes, the tops golden and dotted with crunchy bacon pieces. They too were delicious and she wondered what the rest of the meal would be like given it had started off so wonderfully. She wasn't sure it could get any more delicious.

An expected silence engulfed them as they ate but Naomi wasn't going to be the one to start the conversation. She'd leave that to him and felt it was only fair to give him time after he'd invited her here. She couldn't believe they were still so close to Le Petit Chateau. The clearing felt so secluded. The world far, far away.

'You shouldn't have gone to all this trouble.'

'It's no trouble.' He sipped his wine and loaded his own plate. After a second, he said, 'What did Mia say when you told her I would cater for the party?'

'She face-palmed and moaned because she hadn't thought of it first.' He laughed. 'Then she started beating herself up for getting more and more stressed and not thinking clearly. I told her this evening she's to have a long hot bath then read a good book and not think about work at all. She needs a break.'

'She does,' he replied, eating some of the dip. 'But that's good advice. She's always worked too hard. My father puts a lot of pressure on her, but she also puts pressure on herself.'

The mention of his father caused a pained look to pass over his face and she wondered if it was worse to have never met your birth father or to have him in your life

232

and then have something tear that relationship apart.

'I wish things could be different with my father but . . .'

'Maybe one day they will be.'

'I don't think so.' The pain in his voice lingered in the quiet night but Naomi was sure she heard regret there too.

After that, the conversation died, and the atmosphere grew thick once again with expectation. She hadn't wanted him to go through all this trouble to discuss something so painful. He'd said he wanted to explain but she knew they couldn't just launch straight into the nitty-gritty of it. She wasn't going to ask again why he'd upped and left without a word all those years ago over the first course but there were no social rules to follow for this situation and it confused her. Instead of talking about what they were really here for, they were playing a game, dancing around each other and the difficult subject that sat like a giant elephant next to her, watching them eat. They continued to make awkward small talk until Gabriel disappeared to bring out the main course.

'Fondue,' he declared after he'd laid the table with everything they needed. A plate of breads, meats, pickles and small roasted potatoes sat beside it. Naomi's mouth watered. The cheese bubbled and hints of white wine and garlic lifted into the air, lacing the night with the scent of their dinner. She wanted to dive straight in, it all looked so delicious, and for a moment she forgot why she was there. The night had grown colder, and a chill passed over her skin. She shivered and gathered her coat closer around her but before she could do anything else, Gabriel had darted up and put his blanket over her lap.

'Thank you,' she said quietly. 'Don't you need a blanket too?'

'I'm more used to the cold I think.' His attentiveness was unnerving. She'd grown used to her and Ollie hardly seeing each other. To have someone pay so much attention to her was surprising. 'We can go inside if you want.'

'No.' She'd said it a little too loudly, too quickly. The setting was so beautiful, so romantic she really didn't want to and she couldn't face the possibility of leaving the food even for a second.

She loaded a piece of bread into the caquelon with the long fondue fork set out by her plate, and dipped it into the melted sauce. She swirled it around and placed it on her plate, then used the normal fork to transfer it to her mouth. It tasted divine. Comfortingly cheesy, rich and velvety, but far more flavourful than she could have ever imagined. She added a small potato to her caquelon. 'I'm happy to stay out here and we might see another shooting star.'

Thoughts of their near kiss crossed her mind. Mia's words about love being a matter of the right time, the right place, the right moment, flooded into her brain and she distracted herself with another delicious mouthful of fondue. Still, it seemed the memory had stirred something in Gabriel too because he suddenly lifted his head and met her eye.

'Naomi, I asked you to dinner because I wanted to talk about that night. And you've been very patient with me, not pushing me to speak as soon as we sat down but—' He'd done the mind-reading thing again and she studied the bubbling cheese fondue to stop herself from smiling. Could he really know her so well even now? It had felt like he'd known her better than anyone that night, but it had been years since they'd seen each other. Years since they'd talked. And so far, things hadn't exactly been easy between them. They'd had an instant connection then, but they were different people now. 'I know it's time I told you what happened. Why I left. Why I made the decisions I made. Even if they were stupid ones.'

His last words gave her a flash of hope and pierced her heart, but she pushed the warm feeling growing inside her aside. She'd learned from her career that there were two sides to every argument and though it hurt her, she'd hear him out and try to see his point of view. She wasn't unreasonable, just hurt. She placed her fork down, giving him her attention. He shifted his chair and swallowed. Naomi wondered if he'd feel more comfortable if she didn't watch him. Sometimes it was easier to speak if something else was going on, and as she was hungry and he'd gone to all this trouble, she continued to eat, but flicked her eyes up to his whenever possible.

'When you and Mia were at university, my father was pressuring me to become a part of the business. He pressured us both. Only, Mia was great at it. She loved it and didn't see it as pressure. Didn't feel it the same way. But he wanted me to do what Mia does now and though he knew I was terrible at that sort of thing, he wouldn't take no for an answer.'

'I remember,' she said gently. 'We talked about it.'

'We did.' He smiled at her, though his jaw was tight. 'You remember I wanted to be a chef but didn't know if I could be strong enough to disobey my father?' She nodded. 'I knew the argument it would cause. The pressure it would put on Mia. We wouldn't be sharing the burden – she'd carry it all and I was conflicted about what I should do. It was the hardest decision of my life. I'd been struggling with it before we met, then, that night, when we talked, you were so certain of what you wanted. You had everything mapped out and it made me feel even more lost. That wasn't your fault,' he added quickly. 'I'm just explaining how I felt, so you understand. After I talked to you, I felt suddenly brave enough to stand up to my father. I was going to tell him I wanted to be a chef and that he had to ease off Mia too. That he was putting too much pressure on us both and it was hurting us. I don't think I would have been brave enough if we hadn't met that day.'

'So you left to tell him?' She hoped more than anything that was the reason. If she'd spurred him into action that would make it easier somehow. But his next words pushed any comfort she might have felt away.

'Partly. I—' He shook his head as he thought. 'I have to be truly honest with you, Naomi. This whole thing has been going on for far too long. For too many years

236

and I won't lie now we have this chance to put everything right. I also left because . . . because I freaked out.'

She paused, placing her knife and fork down, her appetite rapidly diminishing. Her eyes were glued to his face, watching the different emotions pass over him.

'You were so open and honest. So vulnerable. I hadn't encountered anything like that with a woman before. With you there was no pretence, no pretending and I wanted to be like that. I wanted to be that type of man. Not the coward I was, afraid of my father's disapproval, thinking about spending my life in a job – in a life – I would hate, just to make him happy.'

He fell silent.

'I don't understand. Why did that make you freak out?'

'After the night we spent together I realised I had feelings – real feelings – for you. For someone I had only just met and at such a young age it frightened me. I thought maybe I'd just got caught up in the moment.'

Her heart pounded, beating a fast, unpredictable rhythm in her chest. So she hadn't imagined the instant connection between them? He'd felt it too.

'I panicked. I was young and stupid. I thought that on top of everything that was to come with my father, falling for you . . . it was all too much. I know it's a pathetic excuse—'

'Wait, what? You were falling for me?' It had taken all her effort to get the words out. Emotion rose inside her like a giant wave crashing against the shore. He nodded and her heart jumped into her throat.

'I knew I was and that it would only get stronger the longer I stayed with you. You could call it love at first sight if you like, but it was more than simple physical attraction. There was just something about you.'

In all the years she and Ollie had been together he'd never spoken about her in such passionate terms and her thoughts and feelings about her marriage began to crystallise into a deep self-realisation. Perhaps baring herself to someone was worthwhile after all. It had been painful when Gabriel had left but it allowed him to fall in love with her. The real her. The whole her. Not the pieces of herself she'd shared with Ollie. And she realised too, that even if she had shared everything about herself with Ollie, deep down, they'd never been suited. There'd never been the same connection she'd felt with Gabriel.

'I feel ashamed of myself for leaving without a word,' he continued. 'Without trying to contact you. All I can say is that I was in my early twenties and had a lot of growing up to do. I always knew I was lucky to have the life I had, the money my father had earned, the job lined up for me, but I never fully appreciated my privilege. I'm still glad I walked my own path, but I should have been more grown up about it. I was immature in many ways.' This confession brought colour to his cheeks, but he continued. 'After I spoke to my father his reaction was worse than I'd ever imagined it could be. He called me so many things. Said I had broken his heart. I'd never seen him that angry.' He brushed a hand through his hair. He too had stopped eating, the emotion driving all thoughts of food from his mind. 'I know how lucky I was to have a father with such a successful business with a job lined up for me. I was very grateful for that, and I didn't expect him to support me while I trained but . . . he told me I was dead to him. Told me if I wanted to take my own path, I had to do it totally alone. He made me move out of the house; told me he wouldn't support me in any way. It was horrible for everyone. Especially Mia.'

'And that was soon after that night?' she asked, giving him a second to compose himself.

'Yes. I was such a mess. I thought about you all the time, but I had no idea what the right thing to do was. I didn't know if you'd felt the same way, if you'd want to speak to me as I hadn't said goodbye. I hated that you might think I'd used you—'

'I did think that sometimes,' she admitted. At first the thought had crossed her mind, but deep down she'd never been able to square it with the man she'd known. Somewhere inside she'd known he hadn't just used her for sex like some young men do. There'd seemed so much more to Gabriel. She just hadn't known what that 'more' was.

'After I left home, everything went from bad to worse. I was working whatever jobs I could while I applied to culinary school and even when I got in, I was working all the hours I could to pay the rent. By the time I started to get my life back together, Mia mentioned you'd met someone.'

Ollie.

'I couldn't just crash back into your life. It wouldn't have been fair. And then a year or two later you were married.'

Naomi sipped her wine, hoping the hit of cold liquid on her throat would distract her from the emotions jumbling around inside. After that night, Naomi hadn't ever mentioned Gabriel to Mia, and had never imagined Mia mentioning her to him. To think that he'd thought of her and that he'd considered getting in touch, shocked her.

'Instead of talking to you, I ran away. I tried to avoid it all. I was a coward.' Shame rang through his voice. 'I'm sorry I hurt you, but you must know that – for me at least – there was a connection. I realise now how special it was. Perhaps if the timing had been better things would have been different, but, really, me leaving was nothing to do with you. It was all to do with me and I'm sorry if what I did hurt you.' His voice cracked a little.

Naomi needed a moment before responding. He'd been so open, honest and vulnerable, just how she'd been that night. She couldn't walk away and treat him the same way he'd treated her, especially now she knew what had driven him away and how deeply he regretted his actions.

'Perhaps,' she began, pausing to reassure herself she could say what was on her mind. 'I always thought you broke something in me that night—' He looked up, panic in his eyes. But maybe it was more that the events of that night broke me, rather than you on your own. It didn't help,' she said with a slight smile. 'But if I'm honest, they were insecurities I'd had for a long time. I know why I

240

have them, and I've tried to reason them away so many times, but I've never quite managed it. My adoptive parents have loved me for years and given me a home life most people dream of. But still, it creeps up on me in the middle of the night. I don't know if they'll ever go away. I might be destined to carry them forever, but that's down to me, not you. I let what happened make me a certain way and I need to accept that. I let my walls build up so high no one's ever been able to get in, but you didn't make me do that.'

She wished now she'd tried to contact him. That she'd spoken to Mia about him. Things could have been so different if she had, but at the time it had seemed impossible. Something she just couldn't do.

Her hand rested on the table, twisting the stem of her wine glass. Suddenly, he reached out and gently unfurled her fingers from the glass, taking her hand. The contact woke up every fibre in her body. His skin was warm against hers, comforting but sending her pulse racing. Gabriel leaned across the table as he spoke to her.

'You have to stop being ashamed of the fact you were in care and adopted. I'm not saying forget about your past, no one can do that, but don't be ashamed of it. It's what makes you special. The way you saw the world back then, it made you different to anyone else I'd ever met. It was something I loved about you. Something I've never forgotten. You shouldn't be ashamed about who you are. You have nothing to prove to anyone.'

Heat was rising in her chest. Her heart beating faster.

She felt physically uncomfortable, her body acting in a way her mind couldn't control. She had to move and release the feelings building inside her. She stood up, stepping away from the table. Gabriel did the same, watching her as she began to pace around. She took deep breaths of the cool, crisp night air.

She wanted to get that part of her back again: the young woman who was going to change the world. The one who hadn't built walls so high she couldn't see out and no one could get in.

Finding Ollie, marrying him. That had been about security. Not just material comfort but emotional too. They'd never had a very passionate relationship, but it had been safe and sheltered. The life they'd built had protected her from her feelings of inadequacy, or so she'd always pretended. She'd been able to bury them deep inside under a successful life, but they'd always poked through. And she'd been lonely. So, so lonely inside her defences. She focused on the mountains in the distance, feeling for the first time in years the sting of tears. But she wouldn't let herself cry. She studied the snowy mountain peaks, closed her eyes and felt the cold air prickling her skin. Perhaps it was time to find that younger version of herself again. The version that wanted to fight for the underdog knowing just how it felt to be one.

'You're right,' she conceded, turning to face him. Without realising it with her mindless pacing, she'd rounded the table and ended up next to him. He must have expected another of her lawyerly arguments as his eyes widened in surprise. 'I rushed into marriage with Ollie because I thought he was the sort of person I should marry. And I got caught up in corporate law rather than pursue something more fulfilling because it paid well and the offer came along just when I needed to start repaying my student debt. But since then, I've been stuck. Too scared to change.'

'You should do what makes you happy.'

'I stayed with Ollie, even though I didn't love him, and he didn't love me, all because I didn't want to let go of the things I thought would make me happy. I couldn't bear the thought of not having the safety blanket he and our life provided.'

'You didn't love him?' Gabriel asked, moving closer to her.

'At first maybe, but not for a long time, I think.' She turned to him, gathering courage to bare her soul one more time. Fear held her back. What if he left again? What if she said what was on her mind and he judged her harshly? Then a length of steel penetrated her spine, sending courage through her. She'd always feared other people's judgements and knew now that was no way to live her life. She tried again. 'I was a terrible wife to Ollie, Gabriel. When I look back now, I was cold towards him, and I always held something of myself back. I never told him the whole truth about being in care and being adopted. Our marriage was doomed to fail because of me.'

'It wasn't doomed to fail,' he replied comfortingly. 'I'm sorry it didn't work out, but that isn't your fault. He was lucky to have you. You're perfect in your own special way.'

Gabriel stepped even closer to her.

She could see the rise and fall of his chest. His breathing had quickened. She stared into his eyes and before she knew what was happening, his hand was hooked around her neck drawing her towards him. His lips met hers, soft and gentle, and she melted into the warmth of his body. She wanted the moment to last forever and wrapped her arms around him, encouraging him to continue. The cold of the night melted away as heat rose from both their bodies.

She pressed herself into him, wanting him to feel how much she needed him, and his hands slid under her coat, pressing into her back as he held her close. Their kisses became steamy, passionate, and without giving herself time to think or second-guess, she broke away and took his hand, leading him inside.

Chapter 21

Naomi awoke with her head on Gabriel's chest. This time they were secluded by the pillows and duvet rather than the trees and snow, and she snuggled down enjoying the warmth of his body as it flooded through hers.

Their night had been more passionate than anything she'd experienced before. Certainly better than anything she'd had with Ollie and she was beginning to see how watered down her life had become. How settling for the safety and security she thought would make her happy had meant forgoing the adventure of real, powerful emotions. She listened to his breathing, the gentle steady rhythm almost lulling her back to sleep.

'*Morgen*,' he said a few minutes later his voice thick with sleep, and she looked up through her lashes to see him rubbing his eyes.

'Hey.'

He kissed her again, rubbing the bare skin of the arm she'd draped over his chest. Her fingers toyed with the smattering of hair on his chest, down the length of his torso, ending just above the duvet.

'Are you holding me down so I don't run away again?' he joked. 'I promise I have no intention of going anywhere.'

She laughed and returned his smile with one of her own. 'No, I'm just sleepy.' She stretched.

'Not too sleepy I hope.' He rolled onto his side and began kissing her again. She gave herself to him once more and they fell back asleep again, waking again unsure what the time was.

'Are you hungry?' he asked.

'Starving. We never had dessert last night.'

'Chocolate pancakes coming right up. And then, we should go skiing.'

'I'd love to.' She'd been practising and had begun to enjoy it, though she still wasn't ready for anything too scary yet.

She watched him dress, admiring the width of his back and the tone of his shoulders. Knowing she couldn't put it off any longer, she slid out of bed and threw on her clothes. Though she offered to help, Gabriel dismissed her to the lounge with a coffee while he rustled up something for them to eat.

'I won't bother with the buffet I normally lay out for you, if that's okay?' he asked.

'That's fine. Chocolate pancakes will be delicious.'

She settled herself in the lounge, her legs curled under

her, her hands wrapped around her cup. She hadn't felt this happy in a long time. She felt reborn. Like a caterpillar coming out of its chrysalis, she'd shaken off something of her old self. She wasn't naïve to think it would never come back. She knew the voice would always be with her telling her she wasn't good enough, but if she changed the things in her life she had power to, she knew she could fight its negative effects.

She checked her phone and saw that an email had come in from one of the jobs she'd applied for. It was the position she'd wanted most. They were offering her an interview and had commented on how impressive her résumé was. Right now, she didn't think the day could get any better. She was just typing a response, confirming the time and date of interview when Mia appeared, charging through the entrance in her customary manner and plonking into the chair next to Naomi. Hans came straight to Naomi for a fuss.

'I don't suppose you know where Gabriel is do you? I've been looking everywhere for him.'

Naomi felt heat build in her cheeks and kept her eyes on the dog. 'He's just in the kitchen, I think,' she replied nonchalantly.

Mia looked towards the dining room and the door down to the kitchen. 'What's going on?' she asked, pointing at the tea lights still dotted everywhere.

'Nothing.' Naomi concentrated on her screen, avoiding her eye. She'd forgotten they were there and could feel her cheeks burning.

'Put your phone down and look at me,' Mia ordered and, reluctantly, Naomi did as she was told. Her friend gasped, covering her mouth with her hands. 'Oh my God! Did something happen with Gabriel last night? I know you were having dinner with him so he could explain about what happened. Did you two . . .'

Before she could finish the sentence, the kitchen door flew open and Gabriel appeared, smiling, his hair ruffled, a plate in each hand and a napkin over his arm. 'I decided against the chocolate pancakes and have made an omelette with Tomme Vaudoise: a traditional cheese made from raw cow's milk and I've added onion, ham and green peppers. It will be – oh, Mia! I didn't see you there.' A vibrant red began creeping above the neckline of his jumper.

'Hello, brother.' Mia grinned widely, enjoying the advantage of seeing her sibling squirm. As children, Naomi knew it had always been the other way around with Gabriel mercilessly teasing Mia. She was clearly enjoying her revenge. Hans trotted over to his owner, sniffing at the plates as Gabriel lifted them higher into the air.

'*Morgen*, Hans. Have you been a good boy?'

'He's been fine,' Mia replied. 'A very good boy. He deserves a treat.'

'No people food,' Gabriel scolded, his eyes darting between Mia and Naomi.

He placed the plate in front of Naomi, who used the side of her fork to cut into the fluffy omelette. While she

248

wanted to help Gabriel, she wasn't getting in between the two of them.

'Did you want some breakfast?' Gabriel asked Mia. 'You can have mine and I'll go and make another.'

'No, it's fine. I've already eaten.' As Gabriel sat down near them both, Mia leaned over the arm of the chair and theatrically assessed the dining room. 'No buffet today? What happened? Weren't you up in time? Late night, was it?'

Gabriel choked on his food and Naomi felt her own cheeks warm. Still at least Mia was teasing her brother and not her, though she'd be in for it as soon as they were alone she was sure. 'I was a little later to the kitchen this morning and we decided an omelette would be nicer.'

'Really. Did you two get everything sorted then?'

'Yes,' Naomi replied, hoping this would ease Mia off Gabriel. 'We did.'

Mia gave her brother the side-eye, eventually turning her gaze to her friend. 'So what are you up to today?'

'Umm, I think Gabriel and I were going skiing.'

'Oh, really?' Her voice dripped with innuendo and implication.

Naomi ignored it. 'And I need to head back to the market. There's a couple more things I want to get to finish off Le Petit Chateau.'

This seemed to finally nudge Mia off the topic of Gabriel and the amazing night they'd just spent together.

'It's looking fantastic,' Mia replied. 'But I can't think what more you'd want to do; it looks perfect to me.'

'You'll see.'

She'd been thinking of adding a few finishing touches so the place was as festive as possible and so there'd be a little bit extra to see when she did the big reveal to Mia before the gala party on Christmas Eve.

'It seems Mrs Scrooge has finally disappeared,' Gabriel commented between mouthfuls. 'Does that mean I've won our bet?'

Mia quirked an eyebrow. 'What bet?'

Naomi pretended to be shocked. 'We made a bet that visiting the Christmas tree farm would make me feel festive and it didn't completely so no, Gabriel, you haven't won the bet.' He grinned at her and the air danced between them.

'I thought this evening,' Mia said overly loudly, 'we could spend some time together. I know I've been super busy, but I've missed you.'

Naomi put her plate to one side and smiled. 'I'd love that. You can help me prepare for my interview.'

'Interview?' Gabriel asked, looking up from his nearly empty plate. He moved it away from Hans who watched with the saddest eyes Naomi had ever seen.

'I applied for some jobs in community care law. It was a bit impromptu. I wouldn't normally do something like that without thinking it through for six months and making sure it's exactly what I want but I was inspired and couldn't help myself. Now I have an interview for a position.'

'That's amazing!' Gabriel and Mia both declared,

jumping up in excitement. Naomi stood as well, only to be engulfed in their hugs.

'When is it?' Mia asked as they let go.

'Next week. The nineteenth. It's a video call so I can do it from here.'

'I'm so proud of you.'

Naomi flopped back into the chair and had to rapidly adjust her plate to stop the last few mouthfuls of omelette falling to the floor for Hans to eat.

'Yes, congratulations, Naomi,' Gabriel said. She wasn't sure but there seemed to be a tiny hint of sadness in his voice. Naomi couldn't read anything from his expression and decided she'd wait until they were alone before asking him what was wrong.

After a few more teasing looks, Mia headed out to her first meeting and Naomi and Gabriel agreed to meet on one of the beginner slopes. She'd dressed appropriately in some ski gear and she was looking forward to showing Gabriel how much she'd improved since that first disastrous lesson he'd tried to give her.

As she waited in the snow, she wondered what could have caused the slight turn in his mood. Was it something she'd said or something his sister had done? Was he simply as tired as she was from the wonderful, yet emotional night they'd shared?

'Are you ready?' he asked, skiing to a stop at her side.

'Definitely. You?'

He nodded. 'I feel much better now I've eaten. I'm ready to go. I thought we could start over here.' He led her to one of the beginner slopes that was less crowded.

'You read my mind,' Naomi replied, smiling. 'I can't wait to show you my skills.'

'Let's go then.'

His mood seemed different and putting it down to her own tiredness and imagination, she forgot all about it.

The next hour was spent laughing and joking as they skied sedately. Him teasing her or testing her balance by trying to make her fall over but always catching her as soon as she wobbled. The sky was vivid in colour, seemingly brighter against the pale white snow, and the dark green pine trees stood like legions on guard on the gentle slopes of the hillsides. Out of breath, from the activity and from laughing, they finally stopped.

'So? Are you impressed?' she asked, taking off her helmet and smiling proudly.

'Very. We can probably try the intermediate slopes tomorrow.'

'I don't know about that. I think I'd like to build my confidence a little more here. But I bet you didn't think I'd be able to ski this well before I left, did you?'

The change of tone she'd noted earlier returned again now.

'You have got there quickly.'

'Gabriel, what's wrong?' She laid her helmet on the ground and reached out for him. 'You sound annoyed or upset. You did the same thing this morning when I mentioned my job interview. Is everything okay?'

He removed his helmet too, flattening his hair. 'It's fine. Everything's fine.'

But she could tell that it wasn't and wasn't prepared to wait to find out what it was. 'Gabriel, it's taken us over ten years to put right the first misunderstanding between us, I don't really fancy another ten years over this one. Please just tell me what's going on. Have I said something wrong? Are you embarrassed Mia found us this morning?'

'What? No. I mean – I was a little, at first, but only because I wasn't expecting to see her until I'd had a chance to shower and change.'

Pictures of him in the shower buzzed into her mind and though she would have liked to keep imagining them, she pushed them aside. 'Then what is it?'

'I don't know exactly how to say it without sounding stupid.' She waited, able to see in his eyes that he was arranging his thoughts. 'The job interview – you talking about leaving – it feels like we're over before we've even begun.'

She hadn't dared to hope that he'd thought last night was the start of something and had worried it was just a one night thing. Her heart swelled.

'We can work something out. Can't we?'

He held her face, kissing her again. 'No one else has ever come close to you and I don't want to let this go when it's taken us so long to get this far.'

She smiled, brushing her hands down his jacket. 'It has taken a while, hasn't it?' She reached her head up and gave him a long, lingering kiss, and though the wind whipped her hair into her face she didn't care, because right now she felt on cloud nine. 'I have to go back to the market for some finishing touches. Want to come with me?'

'I'd love to. I'm not working until later and Hans needs a walk.'

'Great. You can drive.'

They'd taken a few steps towards the chateau when Gabriel paused. 'Before I get in a car with you and Hans again, promise me you didn't feed him anything you shouldn't have?'

Naomi giggled. 'I haven't I promise. Come on, I could do with a hot chocolate before we go.'

She picked up her helmet and as he carried all their paraphernalia, she leaned in to him. It felt like what they'd had had existed on some level inside her for more than ten years. Perhaps Mia had been right and it was about meeting someone at the right time in your life and, for her, the right time for them to start again was now.

Chapter 22

Naomi waved hello to the now-familiar faces of the market as she and Gabriel walked through. Clouds were gathering in the sky, darker and heavier with snow, and the temperature was dropping as they blocked out the sun. Gabriel was also greeted with smiles as they thanked him and his sister for sourcing local produce and items for the gala that was now only ten days away.

'I can't take any credit for that, I'm afraid,' he said. 'That's all down to Naomi.'

'And Mia,' she added quickly, eager for her friend to get her share of the credit. 'She loves how Le Petit Chateau is looking.'

'Mr Mathis will be pleased, I think,' Noah said, and she was aware of Gabriel stiffening beside her, though his smile stayed in place.

They carried on their way, weaving through the crowds that had grown heavier as Christmas approached, pausing at a glühwein stall. The heady aroma of warm red wine mixed with cloves and cinnamon filled the air.

'Have you tried any yet?' asked Gabriel.

'No, I was driving the last time I came.'

'Then you should have one now.' He ordered one before Naomi could object and handed it over. Not that she was going to protest anyway. 'Try this. It's delicious.'

'It smells it.'

Though she'd tried mulled wine at home, the contents of the tiny cup in her hand were out of this world. Ollie's parents had always heated an expensive bottle of mulled wine, adding a sliced orange and dishing it out in small glass coffee cups every Christmas when they went round for dinner. Naomi had never really liked it but she'd tried every year to enjoy it, making the appropriate noises in front of her mother-in-law. This mulled wine, though, was on a totally different level. It tasted nothing like the horrendous warm wine she'd been forced to drink at home. The spices were well balanced and they enhanced rather than over-powered the subtle flavours of the wine. No garish embellishments were needed.

'This is amazing! What's in it?'

The stallholder's English wasn't as good as some of the others and Gabriel translated for her. 'Red wine – a good red wine that you'd want to drink on its own – brandy, cinnamon, orange, cloves, star anise, freshly grated ginger and lots of sugar.'

'Wow this—'

Gabriel leaned away from her as the stallholder told him something else, then he threw his head back and laughed. 'And more brandy, she says, so you better be careful.'

'Don't worry, Hans will look after me, won't you, boy?' Naomi stroked his head and he leaned into her legs.

'What is it you wanted to get?'

Naomi told him about the Christmas scenes she'd seen at one of the stalls and after walking around they found it. Swearing Gabriel to secrecy, she ordered the three she wanted. Two for the entrance of Le Petit Chateau and one – a tall, four-tiered one with a star on top – for the largest table in the lounge.

'Why can't I tell Mia?'

'Because I want there to be something she hasn't seen on the night of the gala party.'

'Okay. That makes sense. Where to now?'

'I don't know, really,' Naomi replied. 'Shall we have a wander around? There must be lots of little roads and places I haven't explored yet.'

They continued to stroll in and out of the stalls, admiring the festive displays of Christmas decorations and gifts, the appetising food and beautiful surroundings.

'Have you been to a chocolate shop yet?' Gabriel asked, slipping his hand into hers while the other kept hold of Hans's lead.

'No, I haven't!'

'What? I can't believe you haven't been to a Swiss chocolate shop yet. No one does chocolate like we do.'

'I know, and I'm annoyed with myself for not going yet, so please take me there now.'

Gabriel laughed. 'You are very bossy, but okay. We'll go to the best one in town. The one Mia and I have always gone to.'

He led her through side streets and alleyways, the shop windows lit up with the familiar glow of Christmas lights.

'Oh, a bookshop,' Naomi declared as they passed a bay window stacked full of books. She saw some English titles mixed in with French and German ones. 'Let's go in here quickly.'

Gabriel opened the door and asked the owner if Hans was allowed in too. The owner was delighted and came out from behind the counter to greet him, which Hans thoroughly enjoyed. The shop smelled of old paper, just how a second-hand bookstore should smell, and Naomi began to browse some books to read in her downtime.

'You have *Larousse Gastronomique*,' Gabriel said, pointing to a large book in a glass cabinet behind the counter.

'I do.' The shopkeeper beamed with pride, his face crinkling as he smiled. He was wearing a thick plaid shirt and a bow tie with casual corduroy trousers and also smelled faintly of aged paper. 'It is a very special edition.'

Naomi turned to see what they were pointing at. 'What's *Larousse Gastronomique*?'

'It's one of the most important books on French cooking ever written.'

'And this one,' the shopkeeper said, 'is a first edition from 1938.'

'A first edition?' Gabriel's eyes lit up.

Naomi laughed. 'Why don't you get it for yourself?' she asked.

Gabriel shook his head. 'Because I wouldn't be able to afford it. They are very rare and very expensive.'

'I'm afraid so,' the shopkeeper said sadly.

'How much is it?' she asked.

'One hundred and fifty euros.'

'More than I can afford,' Gabriel looked down at Hans and stroked his head. 'Shall we go?'

'I'd just like to take these, please.' She handed over the paperbacks to the owner and after a few minutes they'd left the shop. Gabriel smiled but she could tell he was a little sad he hadn't been able to buy the book. It was clearly special to him.

'Why is *Larousse Gastronomique* so special to you?

Gabriel gave a wry grin. 'Ah, you know me so well. I always said I would buy myself a copy when I made it as a chef. I have later editions, but I've always dreamed of having a first edition. The trouble is, I haven't made it yet.'

'You will,' she replied, threading her arm through his. 'It'll happen. The right job will come along at just the right time.' She was beginning to think Mia's idea of fate applied to more than just men and dating. And in her opinion, Gabriel didn't need to wait. In her eyes, he was already successful – his food was absolutely delicious. He could cook simple traditional meals as well as fancy fine dining. She still needed to get him a Christmas present. Had she just found the perfect one?

Within seconds he'd shaken off any residual disappointment and they made their way to a small, red-painted shop. Gold lettering above the door proclaimed the legend: *Müller's* and the same name was etched into the glass panelling of the front door. Naomi paused at the window, captivated by the traditional Christmas ornaments filling the display alongside every conceivable type of chocolate. Row upon row of milk, dark and white chocolate treats were neatly stacked in the window. They were mixed with all the fillings and flavours you could imagine and just running her eye over the list available made her mouth water.

'Shall we go inside?'

She nodded eagerly. Gabriel tied Hans's lead to the lamppost next to the shop and the dog settled down for a few minutes' rest. 'I won't bring him in,' he said, 'as it's a food shop.'

Inside, the array of chocolate was even more impressive. A circular glass display in the centre was full of treats wrapped in bright wrappers of green, gold, pink and orange. Along one wall were slabs of chocolate bark scattered with fruit and nuts and everywhere she turned the delicious smell filled her nostrils. She couldn't quite believe such a small shop could contain so much chocolate.

'It's all made here,' Gabriel said. 'In the kitchen out the back. Nikolas is an expert chocolatier.'

'Everything looks amazing,' she directed to Nikolas who was smiling at them from behind the counter. His face was covered in deep wrinkles that moved like the ocean when he grinned. 'I don't know what to buy.'

'What do you like?' Nikolas asked from behind the counter, and Gabriel stepped back. 'Do you like light or dark chocolate?'

'Dark normally. I don't really like chocolate bars you can buy in shops. I find them too sweet.'

'Have you tried a good quality milk chocolate? It isn't sugary sweet like mass-produced chocolate. Come.' She followed him to the counter, and he brought out a chopping board and a knife. Then he fluttered around the shop, grabbing different chocolates and laying them out in front of them. Naomi watched with wide eyes, enthralled as he cut her pieces to try. 'Taste this.'

Over the course of the next fifteen minutes, she tasted different strengths of milk and dark chocolate to find out which she liked best, all the while guided by Nikolas's knowledge. At one point, when he gave her a piece of rich milk chocolate – nicer than anything she'd ever tasted in England – she couldn't help but close her eyes as the flavours washed over her mouth. They discussed flavourings and textures until Nikolas had tempted her into buying far more chocolate than she could ever eat alone. She'd even got her mum a special box of truffles that she knew she would adore. She couldn't help but think it was a good thing Mia was coming round that night, so that together they could eat some of the chocolate before she was faced with getting it all in her suitcase home.

Then Alina came in and Gabriel excused himself, taking the chance to go outside and check on Hans.

'Naomi, you look well,' she said, as the door shut behind him.

'You too, Alina. Are you after some chocolate as well? I've got enough for the whole town I think.'

'I always buy Nikolas's chocolates. They're the best. No one is as talented as he is.'

'Stop,' Nikolas protested. 'You will make me blush.'

Alina smiled and turned back to Naomi. 'Gabriel seems happy.' The comment filled Naomi's chest with warmth. 'Has he made up with his father?'

The question took her by surprise but then, the town and the Mathis family were closely entwined. She panicked, worried how to answer but was relieved to see the question was directed at Nikolas and turned her attention to some chocolates as they talked.

'I don't think so,' Nikolas replied sadly. 'Renard asks me about him all the time. Have I seen him? Is he well? What is he doing? Does he seem happy?' He waved his hand. 'I always tell him to speak to him himself instead of asking me. I only see Gabriel sometimes when he comes in here or when we supply something special to the restaurant.'

'Sounds like he regrets being such a tyrant. As he should,' Alina commented drily.

'Alina,' Nikolas scolded. 'You cannot say that.'

'I can and I will. I know he is your friend, Nikolas; he was and is a friend to many of us, but he was horrible to that boy. I hope he knows what a bully he was.'

Nikolas shot a glance at Naomi who smiled nervously as she paid for her mountain of chocolate.

'Perhaps it is you who've made him so happy?' Alina said, suddenly turning to Naomi.

'He's my friend,' she replied calmly, unwilling to gossip about her relationship with Gabriel but happy that the old lady thought that. 'Does Mr Mathis regret how difficult things have been between them?'

Nikolas answered. 'Very much so. But I think he's scared of reaching out to him. He's scared Gabriel hasn't forgiven him.'

Naomi wasn't sure that he had, but the conversation had put an idea in her mind. Nikolas handed her a receipt and placed the last few items into another bag. She bid Alina and Nikolas goodbye and stepped outside. The cold air hit her and she shivered. She knew how horrible it was to have a fractured relationship with your parents. Her adoptive parents had given her everything but there was still a gap where her birth parents should have been.

'It has definitely got colder,' she said, as Gabriel smiled at her. 'We should head back to Le Petit Chateau.'

Gabriel nodded as he stroked a happy-looking Hans. 'Could you have bought any more chocolate?'

'I don't think so.' She laughed, struggling to put her gloves on and hold the handles of the various bags.

'Ready?'

'Yes, I think so. Do you think it'll snow tonight?'

He looked at the sky, at the clouds gathering overhead.

'Definitely. There's even a chance it could hit sooner. Let's go. I'd like to give Hans a decent walk before it starts. When this does hit, I'd rather be indoors than driving through it.'

She looked around the town, taking in the Christmassy lights, the festive atmosphere, and the choppy yet snow-softened views around her, and felt her heart twinge.

'It's my turn to ask if you're okay?' Gabriel said gently as they walked together back to his car. She loved the sense of calm the place had given her. She didn't want to lose that when she returned to London. Was that possible? She wanted to return home to kick-start the change in her career, but the thought of being away from Gabriel and possibly losing what they were only now discovering made her mood drop.

'I think I've eaten too much chocolate,' she joked, eager to keep the mood light.

She'd had such a lovely day she didn't want to ruin it. She couldn't deny the niggles starting to plague her mind. She'd never had a long-distance relationship and could only imagine how difficult that was. Most of all, she didn't want to lose Gabriel now they'd found each other again. The exchange in the shop had brought other thoughts to her mind too. She hated knowing Gabriel and his father hadn't spoken in such a long time. It seemed such a waste. She wanted him to be happy and something told her he never really would be as long as this rift lasted in his family.

Chapter 23

'So, I don't want all the details but what exactly is going on between you and Gabriel?' Mia asked as they snuggled on the sofa in the lounge. The snow had come down as Gabriel had predicted, not long after they'd arrived back at Le Petit Chateau. And now the fire was burning and the flames dancing, the heat warmed Naomi right through after her day skiing and shopping. She and Mia had recently changed the cushions for a stack of vibrant red ones and along with deep burgundy curtains, the living room was the epitome of Christmas class. The chocolates Naomi had bought for Mia sat between them, half empty, and the Christmas tree they'd decorated together glittered in the corner.

'Well—' She didn't really know what to say. With Mia being Gabriel's sister, Naomi didn't want to gross her friend out, but she did want to talk about him. His name stayed in her head whenever she wasn't with him.

She wanted to be near him and most of all she wanted him in her bed, his body wrapped around hers. She pushed those thoughts away knowing Mia was waiting for a reply. 'I guess you could say we've managed to put the past behind us. We talked everything through, and I understand now why he left. He's apologised for it and though what happened still hurts, now I know his side of the story I can at least deal with it. Time to move on I think, and finally put the past behind us.'

'And you're moving on together?'

'I don't know.' She sipped her wine. 'I – is this too weird for you?' she asked her friend and Mia laughed.

'A bit, but not too bad. Go on and stop trying to avoid the question.'

Naomi smiled. 'The truth is, we haven't really discussed anything yet, but we both want to see where this can go. I really like him; I always have. I thought back then we had something special, and he said the same the other night, but if we try again now with me in London and him here—'

'That brings its own problems.'

Naomi nodded. 'I don't know what to do. I can't just move here, and he can't just upend his life and come to London.'

'Why not?'

Naomi frowned. 'Because his life's here, isn't it?'

'No, it isn't. He's got a job here, but he's moved around a lot for different opportunities and he's only here temporarily. Didn't he tell you that?'

Naomi shook her head. 'Like I said we haven't really talked about the future. Not in any detail. I don't think he hasn't told me on purpose; it's more that it hasn't come up yet.' She stared at the flames trying to figure out if this changed anything. The warm glow was mesmerising. Naomi didn't want to think about Gabriel moving to London. Even if he could, there were so many complexities, so many things to sort through and decide.

Mia spoke gently. 'You should talk to him about coming to London with you.'

'Move in with me?' Naomi exclaimed. 'No! That seems way too presumptuous. Too soon. We've slept together once since—'

Mia slapped her hands over her ears. 'No! La, la, la, la, la.'

'All right.' Naomi laughed. She reached out and pulled her friend's hands away from her ears. 'But my point is, we haven't really been on any dates or done any of the traditional things people do before they move in to together. Most people see each other for months even years before they make a commitment like that.'

'So? That doesn't matter. You should both do what feels right and what makes you happy. Isn't it at least worth a try? I haven't seen him this happy in a long time. You either. And he could always get a place of his own. He doesn't have to move in with you.' She reached out and took her friend's hand. Mia was right. She hadn't been this happy in years – if ever – and it wasn't just because of Gabriel. It was because there were no secrets between her and Mia. She was opening up to people. Who knew maybe one day she'd even cry. And she was reassessing her life, thinking about what was important to her and what wasn't. Naomi's thoughts turned to Gabriel's happiness and inevitably to his father, Renard Mathis.

'Mia,' she began cautiously. 'When I was in the chocolate shop today, Alina and the owner Nikolas were talking about your father.'

Her friend stiffened. 'What did they say?'

'That Renard asks about Gabriel a lot and that he regrets how things have been between them.'

She seemed surprised. 'Does Gabriel know?'

'No, I didn't tell him. I don't think they meant anything unkindly. If anything, they were on Gabriel's side. But is that right? Does he ask you about Gabriel?'

She sighed. 'Unfortunately, it is. He mentions him more and more lately.'

'Why do you say unfortunately?'

'Because although my father's beginning to wish he'd done things differently, Gabriel is still so angry. No, that's not quite right. He's not angry exactly, he's bitter. Hurt, still.' She took a sip of her wine, watching the deep red liquid move in the glass. 'He doesn't want to see my father again until he can look him in the eye and show that the sacrifice was worth it.'

'But if your father wants to make up then—'

'I know, but you know how Gabriel is. He's stubborn. He doesn't always make the right decisions. After the row, he's always felt like he has something to prove, and according to him, he hasn't quite got there yet.'

'That's silly,' Naomi declared. 'He's a very talented chef.'

'And he qualified from one of the most prestigious culinary schools in Paris but because he isn't working in a fancy kitchen, he thinks our father will still be angry with him.'

'But you don't think so?'

'No.'

'Have you told Gabriel your dad wants to make up?'

'I've hinted but as you know, I hate being put in the middle, so I try and keep out of it. They're both grown men; they can contact each other anytime they like to end all this. I have too much else to think about with running the business.' She scratched her forehead and Naomi saw again the dark circles under her eyes, deeper than they'd been before.

'Are you sleeping?' she asked.

'Barely. I've just got a lot of work on at the moment. The business expansion is happening at such a rapid pace.'

'You need an assistant.'

'If I ask for one, he'll think I can't cope.'

'Will he? If he's changing his mind about Gabriel, could he not realise that you needing some help isn't a bad thing?'

'I don't need help,' she snapped, then softened. 'I'm sorry.'

'It's okay. I only meant that being overworked doesn't always mean someone's not coping, especially if the business has been expanded.' She took Mia's hand. 'I'm worried about you, that's all. You deserve a life, too.'

'A life? What's that?'

'My point exactly. Are you all ready for the gala party?'

'Now you've decorated – beautifully, I might add – and Gabriel's doing the food, we're ready to go, but there are other things going on across the other chalets and ski lodges. It's a busy time of year.'

'You need to make sure you get a break. You can't keep pushing yourself until you burn out.'

'I'm fine, really,' she replied, her lips lifting into a smile that didn't reach her eyes.

'Liar.'

'Okay, maybe I could do with a break. I admit it. It's been busy with the renovation of this place. I could do with a little time off.' Mia rubbed her eyes.

Though Mia was overworked, Naomi was sure part of her exhaustion also came from being stuck in the middle between Gabriel and her father. This rift in the Mathis family was affecting her best friend as much as it was Gabriel. Mia had always been ambitious and worked hard to achieve everything she wanted, but there seemed to be an emotional weight on her too. Naomi could see it now, knowing how she had always carried one herself.

The vague thought that had started earlier began to solidify into a plan. It was a risk, but she was good at calculating risks. She did it in her job all the time and she was sure this was a risk worth taking. A plan began to take shape in her mind. Silently, as they talked of other things, she worked through the possible outcomes and could only see the end result as being positive for everyone concerned. This was it; she was certain. She'd decided what to do, and tomorrow she would put her plan into action.

Chapter 24

Snow crunched under Naomi's feet as she made her way to Mia's car. She'd let her borrow it under the pretence of shopping for some more decorations at the market, which at least was partly true. While sitting in front of the fire with Mia last night, she'd decided to buy some long garlands made from the local trees. A stall at the market sold them, tied with giant red-ribboned bows that would make the lounge and entranceway look stunning. And with only five days to go to the gala party, she really needed to do it as soon as possible.

She was just climbing into her car when Gabriel called her name. She paused as he ran over to her. 'Where are you going? I thought we could go skiing again, or maybe for a nice long walk. Hans has been driving me crazy. He needs a good run around somewhere so he calms down a bit.'

'I'd love a walk later, but right now I'm nipping into town.'

'Shall I come with you?'

'No,' she replied a little too quickly and Gabriel's eyebrows rose. 'It's fine. I'd quite like to have a wander around and I don't know how long I'll be, but I'd definitely like to take Hans for a walk with you later.'

'Excellent. I have some prep I can do for the gala anyway, which will make Mia happy. She keeps asking me what more needs doing and when.'

'She is very good at her job.'

'So shall I meet you here at, say' – he checked his watch – 'three?'

'That sounds perfect.'

He leaned forwards and kissed her mouth, taking her a little by surprise, but she soon sank into the feel of it as his arms curled around her. 'Have fun,' he said as they parted. 'And drive carefully.'

She enjoyed the drive into town. The mountain roads were clear of snow, yet everywhere around her it blanketed the trees and hillsides. The lights of the town came into view and nerves began to grow in her stomach. Was she doing the right thing after all? She adjusted her hands on the wheel and decided she was. She'd thought everything through and couldn't see how, under the circumstances, the result could be anything other than good. She drove past the market, parking as near as possible.

Before buying the garlands or putting her secret plan – conceived last night – into action, there was one important thing she needed to do. Retracing her steps, she found the bookshop and nipped in.

The door closed behind her, leaving the cold wind outside, and the shopkeeper smiled.

'Hello again.'

'Hello.'

'Did you forget something yesterday?'

'No, no. Well not exactly.' She looked behind him to see the copy of *Larousse Gastronomique* was still there. 'I'm after that, please.' She pointed at it and his eyes widened.

'A Christmas present perhaps?'

'A secret one.'

He nodded his understanding. 'Perfect.'

'Can you gift-wrap it for me please?'

'Of course. It will make a wonderful Christmas present. Gabriel is very lucky.'

And so was she.

With one task accomplished, Naomi's nerves began to rise as she entered phase one of her secret plan. She approached the chocolate shop and glanced around. There was no reason why Gabriel should be there – she knew for a fact he was staying up at Le Petit Chateau to begin preparations for the gala – but something in her needed to check just in case. Neither he nor Mia knew what she was doing and she didn't want them to. Not yet, anyway.

'Hello again,' Nikolas called from behind the counter. 'You can't have eaten all that chocolate already?'

'No, I haven't, I promise. I was just—' She looked around again and edged towards him. 'I'm sorry, but I heard you talking with Alina yesterday about Renard Mathis.'

'Yes, that's right.'

'Is it true that he's sorry for the way things have been between him and Gabriel?'

'Very much so. He's always been one to fly off the handle. He has a temper. But he is getting older – like we all are – and his temper is mellowing. I think he realises how much time has passed and all he has missed out on.'

'Do you have a contact number for him at all?'

'I do.' Nikolas's eyebrows rose in surprise. 'And an email address. Does Gabriel want it?'

'Not exactly.'

'Oh. Right.'

'It's for me. For something I'm trying to do.'

'I see. Well, let me get it for you.' He shuffled off to the back of the shop and Naomi's eyes roved over the delicious display. The smell was making her hungry. She didn't think it was possible for her to want any more chocolate. She stared at the candy canes poking out of a glass jar on the counter hoping they'd stem the urge. She'd never liked candy canes. 'Here we are,' he said, handing her a piece of paper with the email address and telephone number clearly written.

'Thank you so much. Do you mind if we keep this between ourselves though? I just need to ask him some-thing. Something important. It might be better if we don't mention this to Gabriel or Mia yet. I'd actually like to tell them myself later. Is that okay?'

'Of course. My lips are sealed. Renard will just be happy to hear from Gabriel's girlfriend.'

Girlfriend? News travelled fast here, she thought with a smile. The idea of being referred to as Gabriel's girlfriend warmed her heart, and she bounced out of the shop feeling light as air that everything was going to plan.

She went to the Christmas market, breathing in the heavenly smells as she made her way to the stall she wanted. She ordered four of the garlands and arranged a delivery date before returning to her car. But on the way back her stomach rumbled loudly and she realised how hungry she was. She took a moment to look around at all the food on offer before deciding what to have. There was *Grittibänz*, a dense Swiss Christmas bread, all the things she had tried before as well as *Basler Mehlsuppe*, known as flour soup. She hadn't tried that yet and it sounded ideal for a cold day. She'd follow it with a type of cookie called a *biber*: almond paste sandwiched between two pieces of gingerbread. She could practically taste it already.

After eating, she returned to the car. Back in the driver's seat with the heater on she removed her gloves and took her phone from her pocket. She checked the number on the piece of paper and dialled it carefully. Nerves built in her stomach as it rang, each beep forcing them higher and higher into her throat. Finally, someone answered.

'*Ja? Hallo? Wer ist das?*'

The voice was clipped, harsh. He sounded younger than she'd thought he would. Hearing he'd softened towards Gabriel had led her to assume his whole demeanour would be soft and she had to remind herself he had cut his own son off, and he was a businessman – a very successful one – which meant he could be difficult when he needed to be. She'd met lots of people like that as part of her job and, luckily, they no longer intimidated her. She cleared her throat.

'*Morgen*, Mr Mathis. Umm, do you speak English?'

'*Ja*. Who is this?'

'My name's Naomi Winters and I'm a friend of Mia's. I'm a friend of your son Gabriel too.'

'Gabriel? Is everything all right?'

'Yes, yes,' she said quickly, hearing the panic in his voice. She couldn't help but think that level of concern was a good thing, though she hadn't intended on worrying him unnecessarily. 'I'm staying at Le Petit Chateau and there's something I'd like to talk to you about.'

He hesitated for a moment and Naomi held her breath. Eventually he said, 'Go on,' and closing her eyes as relief flooded her, she laid out the plan she'd concocted. A plan she was sure would mend the Mathis family rift for good.

Chapter 25

Naomi spent the next few days anxiously preparing for her interview and staring at her phone in case Renard Mathis called back to cancel their plan. The interview was only days away and though she'd researched everything to do with the company, the type of law she wanted to move into, and practising possible questions, she still felt woefully under-prepared. The little voice in her head was back telling her she wasn't good enough, asking who did she think she was trying to change, and scariest of all, she felt the pull of material comfort. The safety blanket of wealth was calling to her. Yet, for the first time ever, she knew it was fear – an unfounded fear that she'd allowed to dictate her life for far too long. She wouldn't cancel the interview; she'd apply for another job if she didn't get this one. She was ready for change.

She and Gabriel had been spending as much time together as possible. There'd been long romantic walks in the snow, candlelit dinners and nights spent together in the luxury and comfort of Le Petit Chateau. She hadn't been ignoring her best friend either. With Naomi's urging, they'd had trips to the Christmas market, evenings doing face masks and pedicures and generally being together talking about all the things they'd missed out on since the last time they saw each other.

The day of her interview had finally arrived, and Naomi was full of nervous energy. The video interview was at three o'clock and she'd been up bright and early unable to go back to sleep once her eyes had opened. Now, sat in the lounge of Le Petit Chateau, she couldn't stop her leg jiggling up and down with nervous antici-pation. She should have planned an activity to do today. Something to keep her busy and distract her mind from the mounting anxiety that was tying her stomach in knots. When she'd applied, she'd thought she'd just see how it went, but as time had moved on and she'd real-ised a few things about herself, it meant more to her than she'd imagined.

Gabriel exited the kitchen having made them another delicious breakfast. She could get used to having a chef as a boyfriend. She'd never been that great in the kitchen and since Ollie had left and they hadn't been going out for dinner every night, she'd lived off the few meals she'd learned to cook at university.

He came to a stop in front of her, his hands on his hips. 'We are going out.' He held out his hands and pulled her up to standing. As soon as she was upright and in front of him, he held her waist, drawing her closer and kissing her.

'Where are we going?' she asked a second later.

'We're going to St Gallen.'

'And where's that?'

'It's a town not far from here. Come on, it won't take us long to drive there.'

She looked down at Hans who was curled up in front of the fire. 'What about him?'

'He's coming too. He likes St Gallen and the lazy dog can sleep in the car.' He whistled. 'Hans, come, boy.' The dog stood up slowly and stretched.

'Are you sure he wants to come?'

'Definitely. I'll take his ball and we can stop on the way back to give him a run. Hans, ball.' Hearing the word, the dog spun in a circle and began charging around the room. 'On second thoughts, I shouldn't have said that yet.'

'No, I don't think you should.'

As soon as the three of them were in Gabriel's car, Hans spread out on the back seat, Naomi felt her nerves receding. They were still there in the back of her mind but having something more immediate to think about, something else to focus on, was helping her control them. Gabriel had banned her from googling St Gallen, telling her she had to wait and see it all for herself. She was both excited and nervous.

The journey to town took about an hour and she loved watching the scenery as they drove by. How could she ever have thought mountains and snow could be boring? At one point they passed a beautiful lake, the waters as calm and reflective as a mirror. She'd fallen a little bit in love with Switzerland and, she was surprised to admit it, skiing too.

Soon they were in the middle of the town and Naomi's mouth fell open in wonder. It was like something out of a fairy tale. The market square was full of medieval buildings and German architecture. Dark wooden beams criss-crossed the tops of houses, shutters were open either side of windows and doors were framed by stone archways. Strolling by the half-timbered houses, she felt as though she'd walked onto a Disney set. Some of the houses had been painted with medieval scenes and had richly carved oriels: bay windows corbelled out from a wall decorated with gargoyle-like heads and ornate woodwork.

They passed a shop selling *biber*: the famous gingerbread spiced pastry. Except these were as big as car wheels, decorated in Christmas motifs. The smells emanating from the shop made her stomach growl – though thankfully Gabriel hadn't heard. He might have thought he wasn't feeding her enough.

Under the layer of snow, she could feel the cobbled streets beneath her feet. No matter which way she turned the baroque architecture captured her attention and the ever-present mountains and hills were always on the horizon. The different languages she'd grown used to were here, too.

'What is this place?' she asked Gabriel as he slipped his hand into hers.

'St Gallen is a World Heritage Site.'

'I can see why.' Her eyes were drawn to a Christmas market opening up before them, buzzing with visitors. But then Gabriel began to lead her away. 'Aren't we going in there?'

'Not yet. We're going to the monastery.'

'Oh. Right.' She tried to sound excited even though monasteries weren't top of her list of places to visit – not when there were vendors selling such delicious-smelling food and drink.

Gabriel once again read her mind and laughed. 'Don't worry. I promise it won't be boring and after we'll come back here to eat.'

'Good because I've been eyeing up that stall selling something cheesy and delicious.'

He led her through the streets to the Abbey of St Gall. She'd been expecting a ruin, maybe a few buildings with robed monks running in and out, but the sight that met her stole her breath again. The entrance reminded her of cathedrals she'd been to visit as a child when her parents had taken her on days out, except dialled up by a thousand. Inside, the white columns emphasised the painted ceilings and ornate ironwork.

'This way,' Gabriel whispered, taking her through to a library.

She could hardly believe her eyes. The vaulted ceiling was covered in frescoes and dark wooden cases filled with books lined the walls all the way up to the ceiling. The tomes inside had their own kind of beauty, especially as some of them were thousands of years old.

'Unbelievable,' she muttered.

'You like it?'

'It's wonderful.'

Ollie had liked to go and see the latest exhibition or attend gallery openings. He loved art and culture too, but Naomi had never been able to relax on such occasions. He'd take the chance to tell her about the piece, the find, the architecture. He was an incredibly clever man, and at first, she'd lapped up his words. But as time had gone on, they'd only served to make her feel more insecure. There was always so much she didn't know. Once, she'd promised herself she'd get some books on Renaissance art or Rococo architecture just so she could speak with him as an equal, but she'd never had the time.

'What do you know about this place?' she asked Gabriel.

'Only what the signs say. Let's read them together.'

She allowed herself to be led to a large interpretation panel detailing the history of the place and they stood side by side reading in silence. It was one of the most peaceful moments of her life. Ollie wouldn't have bothered reading, or he would have skim-read and agreed or disagreed with the panel, but here, she and Gabriel were equals in their ignorance. She didn't feel less than for not knowing; she felt happy.

'Why are you smiling?' he asked, cocking his head to one side in an adorable fashion.

'I'll tell you outside.'

They looked around the rest of the monastery and went back outside. Gabriel untied Hans who had been patiently waiting. As they explored the tiny medieval streets, where the buildings overhung the pavement on their way back to the main square, Gabriel prompted her again.

'So, what were you smiling at?'

'Our stupidity.'

'What?' Gabriel laughed.

'Not stupidity exactly. Ignorance, I suppose.' Seeing Gabriel's bemused expression, she explained. 'Whenever I went anywhere with Ollie he was just such a . . . such a know-it-all! He'd always overexplain things to me like I was stupid.'

'Sounds like mansplaining to me.'

'To be fair to him it wasn't quite like that. He was just very knowledgeable about these sorts of things and liked to share it. When we first got together, I used to drink it up. I felt so unworldly because we'd never had fancy holidays when I was younger. We never went anywhere. I thought he was educating me in a good way but as time went on, it just made me feel less-than. It played into my insecurities, and I wish now I'd had the strength to tell him how it made me feel.' She was aware of Gabriel watching her. 'It was just nice to stand there with you and learn something together.'

'I don't know if that's a compliment,' he joked.

'It is, I promise. I was truly myself. I didn't feel the need to pretend to be something I wasn't. I felt like I could say that I didn't know something, and you wouldn't think badly of me for it.'

'Of course I wouldn't. No one can know everything. There's nothing wrong with not having learned or experienced something.'

If only she'd known that as a twenty-something-year-old, maybe her fears and insecurities wouldn't have taken such a hold of her.

They made their way back to the market square but before she dived in, she had to take some photographs to show her parents. Perhaps she'd even bring them here one year for a Christmas holiday. In the centre of the market square was an enormous Christmas tree, bigger than any she'd seen. It twinkled with the glow of thousands of lights, illuminating the snow-laden sky. All around them, giant lights in the shape of stars filled the streets, some hanging from wires, so they looked like they were floating, others stuck to the medieval buildings. It was enchanting and wildly romantic. The smaller Christmas market near Le Petit Chateau was wonderful for its sense of community and its links with the town. It felt calmer there, but there was a palpable excitement in the air here. Children danced and played, staring at the lights with wide-eyed wonder.

Down one of the small side streets, they found a shop selling stationery and beautifully crafted fountain pens. She'd been wondering what to get Mia for Christmas for ages and now she'd finally decided.

'Can we just nip in here?'

'Of course. I'll wait here with Hans.'

Naomi dived in, awed by the stacks of beautiful paper. She deciding on a set with a rosy glow as she thought it would suit Mia. She purchased writing paper, envelopes, and larger sheets too in case she wanted them for work. Then she saw an elegant ink pen in a beautiful gift box and added that too. The kind woman behind the counter even gift-wrapped it all for her and she took the bag she offered with a wide, happy smile.

After she left the shop and rejoined Gabriel and Hans, they strolled around for a while until they came to the stall she'd seen when she first arrived. She couldn't help bobbing up and down a little as they approached. She ordered a *kartoffelpuffer* – a potato pancake filled with cheese – and couldn't contain her excitement as she began to eat. It was as delicious as she'd hoped and hot enough to warm her up. The air was cold and though they'd been walking, her toes were frozen.

'Can I have some?' Gabriel asked and she frowned, making him laugh. 'Just a little bit.'

'I'm going to order a bratwurst from the stall over there and I promise I'll share it with you.'

'Okay then. But not too much. I'm starving.'

After eating they continued walking. She admired the stalls selling candles, lace and embroidery, and locally made food. She had to refrain from looking too closely knowing that she'd buy everything here if she didn't keep control of herself.

'There is one more dish you must try,' Gabriel said, racing off leaving her with Hans. He came back a moment later. 'This is a *gipfel*. It's like a cross between a croissant and baklava.'

She took a piece and popped it into her mouth, the sweetness of it ideal after the savoury pancake. It was heavenly, a perfect mix of a doughy croissant and syrupy baklava.

'I could happily eat here for the rest of my life and not get bored.'

'Me too. Many of the recipes are traditional and like I said before, this is home food that should nurture the soul.'

Her soul did feel nurtured. For the first time someone had been able to reach the real her and it felt good. She didn't want to leave St Gallen, but remembering her interview, she checked her watch. 'You've done a wonderful job of distracting me all day but we should probably head back soon. I'll need to sort my hair out before I go on camera.'

'You look beautiful.' He kissed her and she wrapped her arms around his neck. Hans nudged his way between them and they broke apart laughing. 'We should probably take him to a park before we get back in the car.'

'Good idea.'

They found one nearby and Gabriel unclipped Hans's lead, allowing him to wander off and sniff the ground. Gabriel followed, and without thinking, Naomi reached down, cupped two handfuls of snow forming a ball, and threw it at Gabriel.

It hit his back and he stopped before slowly turning around. 'Did you just throw a snowball at me?' He looked over his shoulder, checking for snow.

'I might have done. What are you going to do about it?'

'Nothing. Nothing at all.' After glancing at Hans, he scooped up some snow and threw it at Naomi. A direct hit on her leg. She squealed and fired back. Before long, they were in the middle of a giant snowball fight. Children who were playing in the park suddenly joined in too and snow flew through the air, hitting them and the trees. Hans ran around between them thoroughly enjoying the activity. With the help of the children who had all seemed to congregate on Naomi's team, they were declared the victors to the cheers of the watching parents.

'I admit defeat,' Gabriel said, hand on heart. 'You're the winner.'

'And what do I win?'

'How about a kiss?'

'Hmm.' She held a finger to her lips. 'I'd prefer a trophy but—'

Before she could say any more, he pulled her towards him, pressing his lips against hers. Her body filled with excitement sending waves of heat through every nerve.

'Was that a good enough prize?' he asked breathlessly.

'I guess if I can't have an actual trophy it'll do.'

Gabriel laughed. He let her go and brushed snow from his hair, shoulders and jacket. 'I always knew you were trouble.'

'Me! You encouraged everyone else to join in.'

'I didn't! It was Hans. Children always love Hans, and he loves a snowball fight.'

They looked down at the dog, his tongue once more lolling out as he panted. Naomi knelt down and fussed him. She was going to miss him when she left. She was going to miss everyone here. Nerves flew up as she realised how much closer the interview was.

Gabriel seemed to sense her emotions. 'Come on. Let's get you back for your interview.'

'Yes. Thanks.' This job would allow for a certain amount of remote working. But was it possible to hope Mia was right that Gabriel might come to London with her? The only way to know would be to ask him, but she didn't want to jump the gun before she'd even got the job. She also didn't want to face the rejection if he said no – that would definitely put a dampener on the rest of her time here, not to mention Christmas.

Chapter 26

Ready and waiting in her room, Naomi paced the carpet. She'd already tried sitting still but that didn't really work out, and staring out of the window at the snow had made her think of the snowball fight and Gabriel's kiss. She needed to focus; this job interview was important to her.

She'd changed into clothes she'd borrowed from Mia: a smart black jumper and tailored black trousers. Her feet were encased in thick fluffy socks but as long as she didn't drop her laptop, no one was going to see those.

Her phone buzzed and she panicked they were calling to cancel the interview but instead it was a WhatsApp message from her parents wishing her luck for the interview. They'd sent a picture of them smiling cheesily into the camera, a wide expanse of ocean behind them. The message underneath read: *Stay calm, you've got this!* She smiled, typing a quick thank you in reply and promising to let them know how it went.

Her mouth was dry, and Naomi grabbed the glass of water next to the small desk she'd set herself up on and drank. Then she worried she'd need a wee mid interview and nipped off to the toilet again just to make sure. She hadn't been this nervous about an interview before. Even when she'd joined the firm she was working with now she'd felt confident enough walking into the room and sitting in front of the panel. Why was she in such a state? The only conclusion she could come to was that this meant more to her than she had allowed herself to admit.

Within seconds of returning from the bathroom, the monitor flicked to life as the interview began. A panel of three men and women stared at the monitor. Some of them were scowling before she'd even said a word. Others were giving bland smiles that didn't even get close to their eyes. Naomi suddenly wondered how many people they'd interviewed today, and a wave of nausea rolled over her.

The friendly-looking woman in the centre wearing a smart dress and a string of pearls smiled.

'Hi, Naomi, I'm Ingrid.'

The middle-aged woman had a kind face and warm smile. She tucked a greying hair behind her ear as she thanked Naomi for applying and joining her for the interview. Naomi introduced herself already feeling at ease thanks to Ingrid's smiling and happy demeanour.

The interview began with Ingrid explaining how they specialised in helping children in foster care get adopted and helping caregivers establish legal guardianship so they could do things like enrol children at school, register them with doctors and obtain any financial assistance they needed. As she spoke, Naomi felt the nerves give way to a kind of excitement. Something was firing within her. It was the same ambition she'd felt at university, when she'd been so sure she was going to change the world and help people. People like her. And even though the remaining members of the panel continued to scowl, she felt confident.

'Your résumé is very impressive. You've worked with some amazing clients and I've no doubt they'd give you excellent references. The speed of your promotions speaks for itself, so I guess my only real question is . . . why do you want to switch to community care law? I get the feeling this is going to be quite a reduction in salary for you.'

'Well, I . . . umm—'

When Naomi had practised this question in the past, she'd stuck to unoriginal explanations like, she wanted to take her career in a new direction, she wanted a different challenge, she wanted to widen her law experience. Even as she sat there, she contemplated those answers along with the flattering responses that she was impressed by their company and really wanted to work with them. But then something in her mind clicked, like a light bulb being switched on.

'Can I be honest with you, Ingrid?'

She laughed nervously. 'Yes, please.'

The rest of the panel glanced at one another. One even tapped his pen against his lips like this was a trap.

'I don't normally talk about this. In fact, it's something that I've hidden from people – even the people I love – for a very long time.' She scratched her temple, unable to believe that she was actually doing this. 'I was adopted. I spent the first few years of my life in foster care, but I was lucky enough to find parents who wanted me.'

Ingrid's face had gone from surprised to rapt. One older gentleman on the panel had raised a single bushy eyebrow.

'I know from my own personal experience how difficult things can be for the children and for the adoptive parents. There's a lot of paperwork that goes with the care system, not to mention being adopted, and the process is slow. I've spent a long time in corporate law because I thought it would make me feel better about myself, better about the fact I was adopted and the shame I felt that it brought. But now, I've realised that I want to do something far more worthwhile with my life. I think my experience will enable me to deal with people going through these difficult situations with empathy. Basically, I'd like to use my experience of having gone through the same process to help others.'

Naomi let out a breath. Her chest had tightened. She felt hot and clammy. She'd laid herself bare and exposed the wounded parts of herself again. It was exhausting but healing and there was a sense of exhilaration, too. It hadn't been as difficult this time around and she wondered if the more she spoke about it, the easier it would become. Before she left London, she would never have thought she could tell all this to the man who'd broken her heart all those years ago and now to a stranger during what seemed like the most important interview she'd ever had.

'Sorry,' she said with a half-laugh. 'I know that's a lot.'

'It is,' Ingrid replied, glancing at her colleagues. They were scribbling furiously on notepads. 'But thank you for telling me. I was expecting something more formal. You know the "I love your company's work ethic" or "I want to branch out in my career" type of replies. But I much prefer your answer. You certainly sound like you have the passion we desperately need and a real understanding of what the people we help are going through. Can I ask – if it's not too personal a question – have you traced your birth parents?'

She shook her head. 'No. I've never traced them, though I have thought about it. My adoptive parents gave me everything I could wish for – a stable, loving home where I felt loved and listened to – and though I've always had a sense of security from them, in the back of my mind I have been curious as to why my birth parents gave me up. There could be a hundred and one different reasons, and I think, because I don't know the exact reason, I've always been scared it could happen in my other relationships. I realise now that if I've felt like that, then other children will too. When I was offered my first job I was won over by the salary. I thought the security of financial comfort would fill the hole inside me, but I've realised now it won't.

Only facing it and working in a field that makes me proud of myself and that I'm passionate about will.' Feeling she should say something more professional and less personal, she blurted, 'I noticed that your company also suggests family therapy, which I was very impressed by.'

'Yes, and it's for one of the reasons you've just mentioned. Although we're a law firm we don't want to just process things and send people on their way; we want to help them build their lives and therapy can help work through feelings like the ones you've described.'

'I think it's a wonderful idea. I wish I'd done something like that years ago. If I'm honest again, it's only recently that I've realised just how much my feelings of abandonment have affected my adult life.'

What on earth was she doing? Where was all this coming from? Yet, saying the words out loud helped them sink in. They explained so much about the way she'd always been with the people around her, the walls she'd built up to defend herself. Ingrid's voice brought her out of her thoughts. She asked more questions about Naomi's employment history and the experience she'd gained. Some of the other panel members spoke and they discussed more about the role. All the while, she crossed her fingers below the desk, out of sight of the camera, hoping that being so honest hadn't made her seem vulnerable or as though her own experience would stop her being objective. Something she'd need to handle cases.

'Well,' Ingrid said. 'That's all our questions. Did you have any for me?'

'Only that the advertisement mentioned there could be compressed hours. I was hoping to take on some pro-bono work too.'

Ingrid's smile widened. 'I'm happy to hear it and the answer is yes. Most of our staff do pro-bono work and it gives them a huge sense of satisfaction. It's basically why we allow you to manage your own working arrangements.'

'That's fantastic. And that's everything from me. Thank you for your time.' She was just about to end the call when Ingrid spoke.

'Great. Can you just give me two minutes before you leave? I'm going to turn the camera off and mute myself, but I won't be long.'

'Sure.' Naomi smiled, though nerves were biting hard. Had she done such a terrible job or scared them off they were going to say no right away? Couldn't they have sent her an email with a standard thanks, but no thanks? She took the chance to drink some water. Her throat was dry, and her head was pounding due to both fear and adrenalin. She'd need a nap after this or maybe a walk in the cold, something to push the remnants of stress and anxiety from her mind.

She tried to be patient, but time was dragging. Two minutes turned into five and just as she was about to stand and stretch, the camera came back on.

'Thank you for bearing with me, Naomi. I just wanted to discuss something with the panel and thankfully we're all in agreement. We'd like to offer you the job.'

'Really?' Her hands shot to her mouth. She couldn't believe it. She'd anticipated an anxious wait over Christmas while they considered her against all the other applicants. 'Thank you so much! I can't tell you how much this means to me.'

'We're sure you'll be an amazing asset to the team. You've really impressed us today. I'll send you an email with all the details and outlining next steps, but we really hope you'll accept.'

'I will, definitely.' She told herself to calm down and cleared her throat. 'This opportunity means a lot to me. I'd be delighted to accept. Thank you.'

'Great, we can't wait for you to join!' Ingrid signed off and Naomi closed down her computer.

As she stepped away, she jumped up and down and waved her hands in the air. She grabbed her phone and immediately called her parents.

'So?' her mum asked, getting straight to the point.

'I got the job!'

She heard her father whooping in the background as her mum shouted 'Yes!' so loudly Naomi's eardrum quivered. 'We're so proud of you, darling, well done! Have you told Mia yet?'

'Not yet, I only just got off the call with them.'

'Then go and celebrate with your friend and we'll raise a glass to you here. Well done, darling!'

They chatted for a moment more before Naomi ended the call. Pulling open the door, she ran downstairs to find Gabriel and Mia sitting in the lounge. She should have known they'd be waiting for her. They both shot to standing as soon as she entered.

'So?' Mia asked. 'How did it go?'

'I got the job!' she squealed, unable to contain her excitement. Gabriel and Mia pounced on her, hugging her close.

'I knew you could do it,' Mia said.

'How do you feel?' Gabriel asked.

'Shocked. Happy. It's all so crazy. I had no idea when I left London to come out here for Christmas I'd change jobs too, but this feels right. I really want this.'

A flash of something passed over Gabriel's face but he hid it behind a smile and a kiss. 'I'm very proud of you.'

Was he worried that it would affect their burgeoning relationship? She wanted to reassure him that her feelings for him hadn't changed, but she couldn't with Mia there. They could sit down and discuss it properly later. Right now, she wanted to revel in her bravery. It had been a long time since she'd felt truly proud of herself, since the self-deprecating voice in her head had been silenced. Tonight, she was going to eat and drink with her two favourite people: her best friend and the man she was falling in love with.

The words had flown unbidden into her head, and they shocked her.

'What's wrong?' Mia asked, suddenly concerned.

'Nothing,' she replied quickly. 'I've got a bit of a headache from the interview that's all. They're always so intense, aren't they.'

Gabriel slipped an arm around her shoulder. 'Why don't we all take Hans for a walk and then I'll cook us some dinner. Something cheesy and filling to give you some energy and if you still don't have any, at least you can go to bed early on a full stomach.'

'That sounds wonderful,' she replied, trying her best to shake the words from her brain. Was she brave enough to tell Gabriel she was falling in love with him? If she was, she'd have to do it soon. There was going to be enough happening at the gala party if her plans worked out. Perhaps after, when she knew he'd be at his happiest, she'd say it then.

'Come on,' she said, grabbing her coat. 'Let's go for a walk.'

'Umm, Naomi,' Gabriel replied with a smile. 'You might want to put some shoes on first.'

He pointed to the fluffy socks on her feet. She'd been so frazzled after the interview she'd forgotten to think about putting shoes on.

'Good idea,' she replied with a grin. Seeing his smile, the words she had unintentionally thought to herself earlier resurfaced, and they loomed, ready to spill out unless she kept her composure.

Chapter 27

The final few decorations, including the gorgeous garlands she'd ordered, arrived Christmas Eve morning and Naomi hastily put them in place. Mia had seen the chateau come together in all its festive glory, but she wanted to add a few last-minute touches to make the reveal even more special.

'Are you ready?' Naomi asked, her hands shielding Mia's eyes so she couldn't peek. She couldn't believe it was finally Christmas Eve.

'Just let me see,' she exclaimed, and Naomi and Gabriel chuckled.

'Ta-da!' Naomi whipped her hands away from her eyes as they stood outside the entrance to Le Petit Chateau.

The enormous Christmas tree had been decorated by the local people and it looked exactly how a community Christmas tree should. It wasn't as perfect as the one that stands outside the Rockefeller Center in New York but none of them wanted it to be. Everyone had been thrilled to get involved and the eclectic assortment of baubles and decorations only made the tree more appealing. Naomi and Gabriel had also added giant bows to the tree stand and a ring of hand-carved reindeer circling the bottom, lit by individual lights.

Mia gasped. 'Oh, it's wonderful.'

'I wanted to add some special decorations so today would be a surprise for you as well as everyone else.'

'There's more?'

'Much more.' Naomi took hold of her friend's shoulders and turned her around to face the chateau.

One of the garlands had been hung over the hotel's name sign and two more were wrapped around each of the entrance columns. Strings of lights had been hung around the trees surrounding the area adding to the hotel's festive look. Naomi hadn't thought that would be possible. The whole place already looked Christmassy with its piles of snow and banks of pine trees, but she supposed nothing said festive like fairy lights.

'It looks even more beautiful, Naomi. I can't thank you enough for doing this for me. There's no way I'd have been able to do it without you.'

'Don't thank me yet, you might not like what I've done inside.' Secretly, she knew Mia would, but it was fun teasing.

Hans followed Gabriel who opened the double doors for them, and they stepped into the warm. Hans gave a bark and a shake, removing the few light snowflakes that had settled on his fur. More garlands hung across the ceiling giving the impression they'd walked into a winter wonderland. The entrance was decorated with three poinsettias on each side, their deep red leaves giving a Santa's grotto vibe.

In the lounge, the mantelshelf over the fire had been draped in branches of pine tied with ribbon and decorated with sticks of cinnamon and the air was perfumed with Christmas spices. Either side of the fire were two of the large storm lamps that Gabriel had used outside the night they'd had dinner. Inside each one, a thick candle flickered, matching the dancing flames of the fire. The Christmas tree in the corner sparkled and underneath Naomi had wrapped some empty boxes in paper to give the impression of presents. On the tables were the Christmas scenes she'd ordered from the market, making beautiful centrepieces that everyone would be talking about.

In the dining room, the second tree twinkled and the stars, hanging from ribbons across the ceiling, spun in the air. On one side of the room, a row of tables had been set up for the buffet and the other was lined with drinks. At either end, the amaryllis she and Gabriel had bought gave the table some pizzazz. Staff were busy laying out glasses and bottles of wine and their hustle and bustle only added to the feeling of Christmas cheer.

'Oh, Naomi! It's wonderful.' She hugged her friend. 'I can't believe it. Everyone's going to love it.'

'As long as you do, that's what matters.'

'I do. I really can't thank you enough.'

'Well, I can't thank you enough for changing my life. If you hadn't forced me out here and given me the opportunity to clear my head and remember how to enjoy life, I'd never have realised what really matters to me.' Her eyes found Gabriel's and the intensity of his gaze sent a thrill through her. 'I owe you so much.'

'You don't – it's what friends are for.' After they shared a hug, Mia glanced over to the kitchen. 'Gabriel? How's the food coming along?'

He chuckled and ran a hand through his hair. 'I knew it wouldn't take you long to get back to business. It's fine. Don't worry. Everything is under control.' Hans barked as if confirming what his master had said was correct.

'You're sure?' Mia asked the dog and they all laughed.

'Yes,' Gabriel continued. 'We've been over the menu a hundred times and everything that can be prepared ahead already has been. After we've done this and the presents, I'll change and get back to the kitchen. Try to relax, Mia. Nothing more can be done now. Time for you to enjoy the day!'

'He's right,' Naomi added, resting her hand on her friend's arm. 'You've worked so hard for this. Time to enjoy everyone seeing it.'

'Okay,' Mia agreed with a nod. 'Let's do the presents then. I can't wait to give you yours, Naomi. I just need to run back to mine to get them. But thank you both again. You've done such a wonderful job I can't tell you how thrilled I am.'

Gabriel and Naomi were left alone, and he slid his

arm around her waist, turning her towards him. 'I think she's pleased.'

'Me too. Though I do wish she'd slow down and enjoy life for once.'

'My sister does everything at a million miles an hour. You won't change that.'

'No.'

'Are you excited about your new job?' Gabriel asked, taking Naomi by surprise. She could tell that something about it had been playing on his mind since she'd told him and she suddenly had a feeling she knew what it was.

'Very much. Did I tell you that I can do compressed hours?'

'For pro-bono work? Yes, you said.'

'Well yes, and I can also come out here for long week-ends.'

'To see Mia?' he said with a raised eyebrow. There was a shyness, a vulnerability to him that made her skin tingle. 'She'd like that.'

'And you if you're here. I was thinking more of you than Mia, but don't tell her I said so.'

His smile broadened, and he swung her into an embrace, holding her tightly and kissing her.

When they parted, she said, 'You make me happy, Gabriel Mathis, and I want to keep being happy for as long as possible.'

'That sounds like a very good plan.'

They were in the middle of a rather passionate kiss when Mia charged back in, making Hans bark in response. 'Will you two please stop that. Can't you sound some kind of alarm when you're kissing so I know not to come in?'

'I'll rig one up over the door,' Gabriel replied.

With the presents all gathered, they snuggled in front of the fire with coffees and hot chocolates, all a little nervous – all except for Hans who was now soundly asleep on the thick warm rug in front of the fireplace. The Christmas tree twinkled in the corner and the crackling warmth of the fire made the scene picture-perfect. It was a better Christmas than Naomi could ever have hoped for, and gratitude filled her chest.

The Swiss exchanged Christmas presents on Christmas Eve, which felt a little strange to Naomi, but she was happy to do it. She had a feeling they'd all be a bit worn out tomorrow and if nothing went wrong in the next few hours, their attention would be elsewhere.

'You go first,' Gabriel said to Naomi.

She handed him his present. 'I hope you like it. Merry Christmas, Gabriel.'

'I'm sure I will.' His smile was wide and affectionate. Then he turned his attention to the paper and began tearing it off to reveal the cookbook he'd wanted but had never let himself buy because he didn't think he was good enough. Naomi watched as his eyes widened and his mouth curved into a smile. 'It's *Larousse Gastronomique*! You went back and got it?'

'I did. I know you said you were going to buy it for yourself when you made it as a chef, but I think you should have it now. As far as I'm concerned, Mia too, you *have* made it and we're both really proud of you.'

He seemed almost shocked before standing and pulling her up into a firm embrace. 'Thank you, Naomi. I can't tell you how much this means to me.' He let her go but before she could sit down, he'd cupped the back of her head and pressed his lips to hers. She kissed him back until she heard a loud, clear cough from Mia.

'Sorry,' she said, feeling heat in her cheeks. 'Here's yours, Mia.'

She handed her the beautifully gift-wrapped box the stationers had given her. The gold bow stood out against the red paper and Naomi could see Mia was as impressed by the beautiful packaging.

'I'm not sure I want to ruin it by opening it. It's so beautiful.' Gabriel was busy thumbing through the pages of his book and Mia threw a cushion at him.

'Hey! This is a first edition! It's like, ninety years old,' he exclaimed protectively.

'I'm not opening my present unless you're paying attention.'

'Fine.' He closed the book and put it to one side, adding a log to the fire before Mia began.

She searched the package and found the perfect place to lift the paper, gently running her fingers underneath it so as not to tear it. Eventually, she unfolded the paper and lifted the lid of the box. 'Oh, Naomi, it's wonderful.' She examined the rose-coloured paper feeling its quality, then opened the lid of the pen box. 'And a pen too.'

Naomi giggled at her friend's enthusiasm. 'If you don't like any of it, we can take it back and change it.'

'Why wouldn't I like it? It's beautiful.' She began loading ink into the fountain pen and grabbed her notebook from her pocket to test it on. 'I'm not ruining this lovely paper with ink splodges. I think I'll use this for when I send thank you letters to our best clients.'

'Or you could use it for you. To write down your hopes and dreams, your plans. Don't forget your life matters too.'

Mia squealed, pressing the gift into her body and rushed up to hug Naomi again. 'I love it! Thank you!' After embracing Naomi again, she sat back down. 'Now, Gabriel, here's your present from me.'

The brother and sister swapped presents. Mia had bought him a new ski jacket he'd been eyeing up, and he'd bought Mia a pretty necklace that she'd apparently mentioned to him. Naomi watched on, smiling, but when he handed her the present he'd bought her, nerves suddenly filled her stomach, knotting it tightly. The box was small, the wrapping a little more haphazard and she couldn't help but wonder what was inside. After removing the paper, she took a deep breath before opening the box to reveal a beautiful silver necklace with her name on it.

'Is it all right?' he asked nervously. 'I wanted to get you something to remind you of who you are, and that you're enough,' he added, dropping his gaze.

'I—' Emotion stirred deep down inside her. She was overcome and pressed her hand to her chest. 'It's beautiful, Gabriel. Thank you.'

She kissed him again but giggled as Mia muttered, 'Oh not again.' The pair separated laughing. 'Here. Stop snogging and open my present.'

Mia handed Naomi a large box expertly wrapped with crisp paper corners. She sat with it on her lap and after trying to get in without tearing the paper gave up and ripped it open. She took the lid off the box to reveal an emerald green satin dress with a deep V-neck and floaty sleeves. Naomi took it out to look at its full length. It was almost to the floor, the satin cut on the bias so it would flatter and hug her body.

'Mia! This is the most beautiful dress I've ever seen.'

'You like it?'

'I love it. It's gorgeous.'

'I'm so relieved,' she said, pressing a hand to her chest. 'I knew you needed a dress for tonight, for the party, and I knew you hadn't had chance to get one what with decorating this place and preparing for your interview.'

'You make it sound like you've been working me to the bone. I've had loads of time to relax. I just kept forgetting to shop for a dress.'

'Well, there aren't that many shops here that sell this sort of thing. You have to try it on so I know if it fits. I also have some shoes you can borrow – I brought them with me.' She pulled out a pair of strappy silver high heels.

'You've thought of everything,' she replied.

'Of course I have! Would you expect anything else?' Everyone laughed and Mia instructed Naomi to run upstairs to put it on. 'I'll be up in a minute to see. Gabriel, you have to stay down here.'

'Hmm?' he said, finally looking up from his book.

'Oh, never mind. Come on, Naomi. Let's leave him to his reading and try on this dress. I'm bringing this plate of stollen with me though. I haven't had breakfast yet.'

'Wait. I got a little something for Hans too,' Naomi said. Gabriel's face lit up.

She pulled out a gift bag and as soon as she did, Hans's nose began to twitch. He stood up from the fire, stretching, and made his way to Gabriel who pulled out a giant bone. A ribbon was tied around it and he undid it, speaking to the dog.

'You are a very spoiled boy, Hans, you know that. Go and say thank you.' The dog cocked his head.

'I'm not sure he understands,' Naomi said.

'Here.' Gabriel handed Naomi the bone. 'You should give it to him.'

She made him sit and he planted his bottom to the floor, his eyes flicking between her and the bone. As soon as her hand moved towards him, he stood up, his tail wagging. He took it gently from her and regained his place by the fire, this time forgoing sleep in favour of chewing.

'That should keep him happy.'

'Hmm?' Gabriel said again, having retreated back into his book.

Naomi and Mia laughed.

'Come on,' Mia said. 'I need to see you in that dress.'

As they left, Naomi couldn't believe how happy she felt.

She'd anticipated a Christmas filled with loneliness and sadness and, instead, had had one of the most wonderful holidays of her life. She'd experienced things she'd never thought of doing before and had barely thought about Ollie or their house back in London. When she did think of him, it was with a sense of acceptance and peace she hadn't thought was possible a year ago. The last year had been tough, there was no doubt about it, but she'd come out the other side, stronger and happier. Her future was looking bright: her friendship with Mia better than ever, a new job to look forward to and the prospect of Gabriel being an integral part of her life.

A burst of nerves bubbled up as she thought about the plan she'd put in motion. She surreptitiously checked her phone. No, she didn't need to be nervous. She'd weighed up all the possible outcomes and the only one she could see was positive. She'd done the right thing, and, in a few hours, Gabriel would be the happiest he'd been for a long time and Mia would be too.

Chapter 28

It was finally time for the festive gala and grand opening of Le Petit Chateau. Snow fell as Naomi left her room, brushing her hands down the beautiful green dress that fitted like a glove. The shoes were a little higher than she was used to, but as soon as she'd slipped them on, she'd felt more glamorous than ever.

She'd attended functions at work and had always had to wear something that could go from a day in the office to night-time drinks. But the gala party called for something special, and she was eternally grateful to her friend that she'd had the foresight to buy her something.

Descending the stairs, she heard Mia and Gabriel's voices as they discussed with their teams everything that needed doing tonight. Mia was briefing the staff on their tasks for the evening and Gabriel was delegating various kitchen duties. As Naomi rounded the bottom of the stairs, they disappeared, leaving Gabriel wide-eyed with his mouth hanging open.

'Naomi!' Mia exclaimed. 'You look absolutely beautiful.'

'Thank you.' She'd pinned her hair into a classic bun at the nape of her neck and soft tendrils fell around her face. She felt beautiful and flicked her eyes to Gabriel to see what he thought.

'Gabriel.' Mia nudged her brother. 'Say something.'

'I – you – wow.'

Mia burst out laughing and Naomi couldn't help but join her. 'I think that means you look stunning,' his sister said.

'You do,' he said, blushing slightly but finding his voice. 'Absolutely stunning.' He kissed her cheek gently, and the soft brush of his lips sent her pulse racing.

'Thank you. So do you, Mia – you look amazing.'

Her friend had swept her hair into a smooth, high ponytail and she'd added a slash of daring red lipstick. She wore a long black dress with spaghetti straps and sequins. She looked like a movie star.

Mia moved to the window and looked out. 'People are arriving, and it's started to snow!'

'That shouldn't be a surprise here,' Gabriel teased.

'No, but it's Christmas Eve,' Naomi replied in defence of her friend. 'Snow on Christmas Eve is extra special.'

'See!' Mia stood shoulder to shoulder with Naomi. 'She might be your girlfriend, but she'll always be my bestie first.'

Her use of 'girlfriend' caused them both to smile as

Mia stepped forwards to begin greeting the guests. Classic Christmas carols played gently in the background, adding to the festive atmosphere.

'I'd better head to the kitchen,' Gabriel said. He really did look handsome in his chef's whites.

'Good luck,' she said, kissing his cheek.

'You too. Try and have fun. Mia, don't feel you need to work all evening.'

Within seconds of him disappearing to the kitchen, plates of food were being carried to the tables laid out in the dining room.

As the guests arrived, they shed their coats and took a glass of champagne, marvelling at the beautiful architecture and décor.

'Mia,' Alina said. 'You have done such a wonderful job. The renovation is beautiful. Your father should be very proud.'

'I hope so,' Mia replied, and only Naomi could see the trace of tension in her jaw.

'And of Gabriel too,' Alina added, looking over at the dining room filled with delicious-looking, fully loaded plates. Mia didn't speak but an uneasiness had settled. Alina quickly recovered. 'I love the way you have decorated it.'

'Naomi is responsible for all of the Christmas decorations,' she said, smiling at her friend.

'And we're very grateful. The whole town is grateful.'

'I should have done it a long time ago.'

'Don't worry,' Alina said, patting her arm. 'You can't think of everything all at once. You've had a lot on your shoulders, and no one was annoyed about it before. It is just an improvement,' she said, flinging her hands out to encompass everything around her.

Mia laughed and Naomi stepped forwards as Alina's son and his family arrived. 'Roger?' He came over as she called his name. 'I just wanted to let you know I got the job in community care law.'

'You did? Oh, I'm so happy for you.' He turned to his husband. 'Fynn, this is Naomi, the woman I was telling you about who is interested in community law. She got the job she went for!'

Fynn hugged her too. 'That's wonderful. I'm sure you'll be a lot happier doing something that speaks to your heart. When do you start?'

'The end of January. My current company were a little surprised about the change in direction, but when I explained my own situation of being adopted, they understood completely.'

'That's wonderful news,' Roger said again. 'Cheers!' He held his glass of champagne up and they all clinked glasses. 'What does Gabriel think?'

'He's happy for me. Mia too.'

'Of course they are, but they'll miss you being around I'm sure.'

Naomi took a sip of her drink as Nikolas from the chocolate shop bustled over. 'Excuse me,' he said and Roger and Fynn moved away, gathering their children and Alina, and stepping into the lounge. Naomi was happy to see them marvel at the decorations, especially the festive scenes that adorned each of the tables. 'Naomi, did you get hold of Renard?'

'I did, thank you.' She lowered her voice, ushering him into the corner of the room.

'Is it still a secret?'

'It is, so if you could keep it to yourself for now, everything will become clear soon enough.'

He gave an understanding smile and squeezed her hand. 'If it's what I think it is, then you've done a wonderful thing.'

He shuffled away and Naomi went to check on the food. Mia was busy greeting everyone and thanking them for coming but Naomi wanted to be as useful as possible to make sure her friend too got to enjoy the night. She straightened some of the trays and adjusted the baskets of bread, so everything looked lovely.

'Are you playing with my food?' Gabriel asked, appearing from the kitchen door.

'No. I'm just trying not to eat everything. It all looks incredible.' There were mini versions of all her favourite dishes, and she loved the mix of French, Swiss and German food that only seemed to occur here. A large fondue pot was the centrepiece surrounded by breads, meats and cheeses, pickles and potatoes. 'Can I just steal a tiny piece of something?'

'No, you cannot.' He playfully batted away her reaching hand.

'Spoilsport.'

'I'll save you something special for when everyone has gone home.'

'You'd better.'

With another quick kiss he raced off and Naomi went to help Mia who was surrounded by people. Naomi made her way into the throng and struck up conversation with as many people as she could, drawing them away from her friend. She showed the children all the different decorations and answered questions about which of the market vendors had supplied what. The stallholders puffed with pride as people admired their handiwork and commented how the tourists would be wanting them for their own homes.

With the initial rush over, Mia and Naomi were able to enjoy a rare moment together. Side by side in front of the fire, the logs crackling behind them, they surveyed all of their hard work. The carols were replaced with Christmas party songs and the children began to dance. Some of the other guests did too, laughing and smiling to each other. Naomi smiled to see Roger and Fynn dancing with their children and Alina clapping on. Nikolas shot her a nervous glance and Naomi did her best to nod without Mia noticing.

'Everything seems to be going very well,' Mia said.

'Yes, it does,' Naomi replied, glancing at her phone. Her nerves grew fiercer as time ticked on. It wouldn't be long now. In fact, if everything had gone to plan, it would be any second. She felt suddenly queasy and swallowed hard. She was beginning to doubt herself now. What if she'd done the wrong thing? She shook the thought away as Gabriel stopped at her elbow.

'That's all the food for a while. Can I have a glass of glühwein now, Mia? It's been non-stop downstairs.'

'I suppose,' his sister teased. Mia took one from the table and handed it to him. 'Why do you keep checking your phone, Naomi? Are you expecting a call from your parents or something?'

'Hmm? No, no,' she confirmed, shaking her head so violently she almost dislodged her bun. 'I was just wondering what the time was, that's all.' And she put her phone back into her tiny bag.

'But you've looked about ten times in the last two minutes. Are you sure everything's okay?'

'Absolutely.' She grinned widely, hoping Mia would believe her. 'Everything's perfect.'

I hope, she added to herself as a wave of nausea passed over her.

Mia gave her a strange look, Gabriel too, but she kept her eyes on the glass of champagne she held, her hands becoming clammy on the stem.

'I think Father would be proud of you,' Gabriel said to Mia. 'This is going to be the most sought-after resort in the whole of Switzerland.'

'I guess I'll find out what he thinks tomorrow when I update him on everything.'

'Remind me when you're making that call so I can be out of the way,' he joked and Naomi's stomach dropped, filling with dread.

She couldn't risk another glance at her phone and was in the wrong place to see the clock on the wall. She was only aware that the time had arrived when the noise in the room changed. Everyone fell momentarily silent and then chatter erupted as people began to welcome the unexpected visitor.

Mia and Gabriel glanced at one another, and Naomi's nerves grew so strong they closed her throat. She told herself to calm down. Reminding herself that only hours ago she'd been sure this was the right thing to do for the two people she loved most in the world.

'What's going on?' Mia said, stepping forwards. Gabriel followed. Then she gasped. 'Father?'

Gabriel's jaw tightened. His body stiffened and his eyes grew cold and hard. In that instant, Naomi knew she'd made a terrible error. This was not going to unfold as she had anticipated. In fact, she knew without any doubt in that moment she'd made one of the worst mistakes of her life.

Chapter 29

'What is he doing here?' Gabriel murmured through gritted teeth.

'I've no idea,' Mia replied. 'We were supposed to catch up tomorrow. A phone call. He didn't say anything about visiting.' She stared at her brother in panic, clearly worried what he was going to do. Naomi's throat had closed up.

She knew this was her cue to say something, but she couldn't get the words out. The party atmosphere had disappeared and in its place was a tense stand-off that everyone seemed to sense. The crowd parted as Renard moved towards his children. Everyone was watching to see how Gabriel reacted and from Gabriel's expression, he knew it too.

Renard's friends were greeting him saying how nice it was to see him and asking why he'd been away so long. He answered casually, smiling widely and thanking everyone for coming, shaking hands and giving kisses on cheeks.

He was a consummate professional: a schmoozing busi-nessman, but Naomi also felt there was something genuine about him. He looked people in the eye as he spoke and there was warmth to his voice. He did seem happy to be there and really did hope everyone was enjoying themselves. Gabriel's resemblance to his father was uncanny, though Renard's skin was more lined, his hair no longer blond but grey with strands of white. He was shorter than Gabriel, though his confidence made him seem taller. Renard inched closer to them.

'You didn't invite him then?' Gabriel murmured to his sister.

'Me? No. Why would I? I knew you didn't want to see him.'

Every muscle in Naomi's body tensed. She had to open her mouth and tell them. She gulped and tried to calm her breathing. Her chest rose and fell with ragged breaths, which she did her best to hide.

'I should go to the kitchen,' Gabriel said, trying to turn away but Mia stopped him.

'No. Everyone will talk if you just walk away now.'

'They're talking anyway.' He nodded to the guests who stood whispering, their heads bent together.

'If you leave, they'll talk more, and you'll look like the bad guy.'

'I don't care.'

'Please, Gabriel—' Mia's face was pleading. 'Don't leave me to deal with all of this on my own.'

What had she done? What the hell had she done?

Why had she ever thought this was a good idea? Nikolas might have said Renard Mathis regretted his actions and wanted to reconcile with his son, but it wasn't her place to force that to happen. A cold sweat had broken out on her forehead. She'd done it simply because she hated not having a relationship with her own birth parents. She'd projected her own fears and insecurities and now she'd created a situation none of them could get out of.

'Fine,' Gabriel replied, adjusting his stance so one hand went protectively around his sister. He planted his feet a little wider apart as if steadying himself for the knocks and blows that were inevitably going to come his way.

'Mia,' Renard said, after thanking someone else for coming. His arms were open wide and when he reached her, he wrapped them around her, kissing her on both cheeks. His affection for her was genuine – Naomi could see that – but Mia seemed surprised. 'You have done such a wonderful job with Le Petit Chateau. It is unrecognisable in the best way possible.'

'So you like it?' she asked a little nervously.

'I love it.' He turned to his son, and it was as though the whole room took a collective breath. 'Gabriel.' He held out his hand for Gabriel to shake.

Gabriel stood staring at it, his jaw twitching as he controlled himself.

'Gabriel,' Mia prompted.

Renard's face was unreadable, though his brow was furrowing the longer he was forced to wait. Eventually

Gabriel thrust his hand into his father's, his grip firm, but it wasn't the reunion Naomi had hoped to broker.

She hadn't expected Gabriel to respond in such a stand-offish manner and she hadn't expected Mia's panic. Had Renard Mathis always been harsher than she'd imagined? She'd imagined he would walk in; everyone would be surprised, but then Mia and Gabriel would speak to him and after a short discussion everything would be fine. Through the course of the evening Renard would have made it clear he wanted to reconcile, and Gabriel would have been swayed by his kind words. She'd pictured instant remorse and an agreement to put the hurts of the past behind them. It's what she would hope for if she ever met her birth parents. But the hurts of the Mathis family were well and truly in the present and the chances of putting them in the past looked slim to none. How could she have been so naïve?

'Son,' Renard said. 'It's been a long time.'

'And whose fault is that?'

While Naomi could understand Gabriel's response, she wished he'd soften just a little. With his answer, the mutters and whispers had started again. Renard ignored his son's response and turned to Naomi. Her stomach churned. The moment of reckoning was here.

'And you must be Naomi.'

'Naomi—' Gabriel spun to face her. 'How do you know Naomi?' he asked his father, though his eyes were still pinned on her.

She couldn't meet them, fearful of the pain and anger

she'd see there. She could feel Mia's eyes too boring into her.

'Naomi contacted me,' he replied calmly.

'You what?' Patches of red grew above the collar of Gabriel's white chef's jacket, reaching up his neck in a blotchy pattern. His pale eyes were wide, the colour brighter as he stared at her. 'You contacted my father? Why? Why would you do that?'

'Naomi?' Mia shook her head disbelievingly.

'I – I thought it might help you—'

'Help me what?' Gabriel fired back.

She was lost for words, panic stealing them from her. Where were her lawyer instincts now? Normally she could argue her way out of any situation, but this time, under the glowering faces of Gabriel and her best friend, she couldn't summon anything.

'She thought it'd help mend our relationship,' Renard said. 'Lower your voice, son; people are watching.'

'I stopped being your son a long time ago,' Gabriel spat. 'The day you kicked me out and said I was nothing to you anymore.'

'Gabriel, please,' Mia pleaded, blushing under the gaze of the crowd.

The two men locked eyes, Gabriel lifting his chin defiantly. Neither of them spoke, then he turned to Naomi. 'I cannot believe you did this to me. To Mia. On today of all days. The day she's worked so hard for.' Without waiting for a response he stalked away, the kitchen door swinging closed behind him.

Naomi remained where she was, her face flaming. That worrying, stinging sensation of threatening tears stabbed at the back of her nose and eyes and she drew in a breath, clenching her jaw as she pushed them away.

'Well,' Renard said, turning to her, his back to the crowd who were all looking anywhere but at them. 'It seems you were wrong, Miss Winters. My son isn't as ready as I am to forget the past.'

'I – I'm sorry,' she stuttered, but Renard had walked away into the crowd and was doing his best to get the party started once more.

Mia stepped past, pausing at Naomi's side. 'I can't believe you'd interfere like this, Naomi. After everything you've been through. After everything that's happened this Christmas. How could you do this?'

'I was thinking of you too. You've been so overworked. I thought it would help you both to speak to him. I thought if they – if you – just got together, you'd all speak and—'

'You shouldn't have interfered, Naomi. You had no right.' Mia glanced back at her father. 'And now I don't know if they'll ever make it up.'

Mia left too, heading to the kitchen and Naomi grabbed her coat from the rack in the hall and escaped through the crowd out onto the balcony at the back of the dining room. She saw the steps down and the path that led to the clearing where she and Gabriel had had dinner. Where they'd put the past firmly behind them through honesty and openness and yet, again, she'd kept secrets and done this to him all because she thought she was right. She should have known she couldn't force him to speak to his father, no more than anyone could force her to trace and meet with her birth parents. It was something that had to be done when the person was ready. How could she have forgotten that?

She glanced back through the window and saw that the party was recovering a little. She shouldn't have stuck her nose into other people's business. She never had before so why had she started now? She snuck back in, gently pushing open the kitchen door and making her way inside. The heat hit her instantly. Gabriel was working furiously and the tension in the air was heavy. The staff, clearly nervous of his unhappy mood, stayed well away. Mia was opposite him, leaning against a large silver fridge with her arms crossed over her chest. Everyone fell silent as Naomi entered. Gabriel glanced up but didn't stop working. He barked out another order and 'Yes, chef,' came back.

Mia looked at Naomi, and after glancing quickly at Gabriel walked towards her. 'Perhaps you should go back upstairs,' she said gently and Naomi's heart tore apart. 'I think Gabriel would prefer to work until the party is over, but you can still enjoy it.'

'Of course I can't enjoy it. Please, Mia. I'm sorry.'

'I know,' Mia replied. 'But it's not that easy, Naomi. Saying sorry doesn't undo what's just happened.'

'I know.' She stepped away from Mia and towards Gabriel. 'Please let me explain why I thought I could help.'

'Will you do this in your new job?' Gabriel snarled. 'Will you interfere and do what you want instead of what your clients want?'

'No. Of course not. It's just when I was in the chocolate shop, Nikolas and Alina were talking and they said that your father always asks after you and that he wanted to reconnect.'

Mia's hands shot to her mouth. 'I know you said you'd heard them speaking but I didn't know the town were gossiping about us like that. I'm so embarrassed.'

'No,' Naomi tried to reassure her. 'It was meant kindly. They agree that your father acted badly, but Nikolas said he was truly sorry for what had happened. I thought if you could just talk face to face . . . I've seen how much this has hurt you, Gabriel, and you, Mia.' Gabriel's head shot up. 'Yes,' Naomi said. 'It affects Mia too, though she tries to hide it.'

'Does it?' Gabriel asked his sister.

'Sometimes it is hard to be in the middle all the time. I feel like I'm walking a tightrope between you both. It's like a constant cloud hanging over me.'

He turned his eyes to his work. 'You should have said something.'

'Why? You wouldn't have changed your mind, and neither would Father. At least, I didn't think he had. He's never said anything to me because he knows I hate to be put in the middle, but if that is what he's told Nikolas . . .' She let the sentence trail away but Gabriel didn't pick it up. 'Where's my father staying?' she asked Naomi.

The room swum about her. This was supposed to be the icing on the cake. She'd hoped that the fact they didn't have to rush because he was going to be staying would be a good thing. 'I said he should bring some things in case you asked him to stay here at Le Petit Chateau.'

'He's going to stay here?' Gabriel exploded, ripping a tea towel from his waist and throwing it down onto the side. He stormed through a door that led outside.

'Oh, Naomi,' Mia said, running her hands over her face.

'Mia, I'm so sorry.' She ran after him. 'Gabriel? Gabriel, please wait.'

Even though she still had her coat on, the freezing air pierced the thin satin of the dress sending goose bumps over her skin. She pulled it tighter around her. 'Gabriel, please.'

He was pacing around the small deck, his hands on his hips. 'I don't know how you could do this to me, Naomi. Why? Why would you invite him here?'

'I thought it would help. I thought if you two could just talk . . . Nikolas said your father was sorry for what he'd done. Really sorry and he wanted to make up. And Mia had said you were both too stubborn to make the first move. I thought maybe if I did, you could put all the horribleness behind you and move on.'

'It wasn't your decision to make.'

'I know,' she conceded. 'I know. But please understand, I really thought that what I was doing was for the best. I thought if he saw what an amazing chef you were, he'd realise that you'd made the right decision all along.'

327

'I know I've made the right decision and I don't care if he recognises it or not.'

Though she was sorry for everything that had happened and knew she'd done wrong, something fierce stirred within her. She could appreciate Gabriel's feelings, but he had to let go of this hate, the same way she'd had to let go of her shame.

Calmly, she said, 'I understand, Gabriel, but don't you think it's time to let go of all this, especially if your father wants to? If you give him a chance, he might apologise.'

'I don't care if he does.'

'Oh, don't be so childish,' she fired back. He had to realise how much this was affecting Mia too. He glared at her.

'Childish? You have no idea what it's like—'

'To what? To not have supportive parents? My birth parents didn't want me. I know what it's like to have a fractured relationship with your family. I don't know if I'll ever have a relationship with my birth parents, but I was lucky my adoptive parents have always been incredibly supportive of everything I've wanted to do. I wouldn't be where I am without them and if your father's realised what a mistake he's made, you could have that support now if you'd just put your anger aside.'

'You think it's that easy?'

'I know it's not easy. It wasn't easy for me to let go of all the shame I've been carrying around, but you helped me do that and I wanted to do the same for you. I wanted to help you move on, like you had me.' He didn't say anything, just leaned on the railing staring out into the snowy landscape. 'If you can't forgive him, can you at least come to a truce? This is hurting Mia too and she deserves—'

'Mia understands better than you do.'

His words stung and it was becoming clear that the mistake she'd made was a grave one. Even if he could forgive her, she couldn't imagine them coming back from this. She'd driven a wedge between them and until he let go of his anger towards his father, that wedge would always be there. The mistake she'd made would always be fatal.

She'd lost him.

And though emotion swelled within her, hurt mixing with anger and frustration, she was determined to help her friend. Mia was the reason she was here and no matter what happened with Gabriel now she would always be grateful to her.

'Mia's been put in the middle for far too long and it's not fair. It's affecting her and you've been too wrapped up in your own anger to see it. The same can be said for your father – only when I told him, he wanted to make it right, but you don't want to. You'd rather let Mia carry on being miserable than accept a genuine apology from your own father. I'm not saying what he's done all these years is right, Gabriel, but he's finally realised it's not and is reaching out to make amends.'

'Would he have come if you hadn't invited him? Would he be here to apologise if you hadn't coaxed him into coming?'

'I didn't coax him—'

'I can just see you arguing him into it. Switching on your lawyer abilities and backing him into a corner so he had no choice.'

Anger overrode her pain at his words and the cold was instantly driven from her body as frustration flared red-hot. 'I didn't do anything like that.'

'Then what did you do?'

'I told him you were an amazing chef and that he should be proud of you. I told him you were a wonderful man and that he was missing out on connecting with this incredible person I'm in love with.'

Her voice had risen as she'd spoken, and the last few words echoed in the quiet night air. He stared at her, his eyes widening, and she felt naked. Once again, she'd bared her soul. She'd exposed her raw emotions and something in her pleaded for him to come to her, to calm down and see that though she'd made a mistake, she'd done it with the best of intentions. For him to hold her and tell her he loved her too.

'You blindsided me.'

'That's it?' She threw her hands in the air, shock and hurt overriding everything else. 'I tell you that I'm falling in love with you and all you can say is that I blindsided you?'

'You did.' She was about to try and explain again but the words died on her tongue. Without even looking at her, Gabriel glanced once more at the snow-covered mountains and said, 'I need to get back to the kitchen.'

'You're running away again?' She turned, following him as he edged towards the door. 'You are, aren't you? You're running away rather than facing what I've just said. Don't you have anything to say to me?'

'I have to get back to the kitchen,' he said again, opening the door and closing it behind him.

And then he was gone.

Chapter 30

Naomi paced the balcony. Her hands were in the pockets of her large coat, but her eyes darted around searching for an answer. The sense of space had vanished. The mountains seemed to loom over her, threatening and dangerous. Even the snow, which was still falling steadily, had lost its magic and was nothing more than the world doing its best to ice her out – to damage her. She took a breath, hoping to stop her heart from hammering against her ribs. She couldn't get enough oxygen in, and her teeth had started to chatter.

She had no choice but to walk through the kitchen to get back to her room and the idea filled her with dread. She scanned the chateau for another door, even a window so she wouldn't have to pass him, but there was no other way around it. She wrapped the coat across her, and keeping her head down, swung open the kitchen door. Pans clattered, voices sounded, and people moved around the kitchen hurriedly. She had no idea if Gabriel looked at her or not as she strode through, her head down, in the direction of the door.

Mia was no longer there. She'd clearly had to return to her hostess duties and had gone back to the party. Naomi spotted her from the corner of her eye as she hurried through the crowd. She was smiling and chatting but there was a tightness to her smile, a tiredness to her eyes that made Naomi feel incredibly guilty. The party was thankfully still in full swing. Renard Mathis, surrounded by people, was talking happily with a group of friends, the embarrassment of earlier forgotten. Only Naomi couldn't forget it. Nor could she forget the humiliation of the moments before when she'd told Gabriel she was falling in love with him only for him to walk away, leaving her heartbroken and alone.

She skirted around the edge of the crowd, exiting the lounge towards the spiralling staircase. 'Naomi?' Alina called, grabbing her hand as her foot touched the very first step. Reluctantly, Naomi stopped. She plastered on a smile and turned around. 'Are you all right?'

'Yes! Are you enjoying the party?'

The older woman studied her. 'Yes, but I can see you're not. What is it? Is it Gabriel? Is he being a big baby?' Naomi appreciated her attempt to make her laugh and though she lifted her mouth into a grin it didn't fool the older woman. 'Ah, he is sulking because his father is here. Renard told me you'd invited him to come. He's been wanting to make up for a long time but has been too scared to contact him. I think that was a very good idea.'

'Well, it didn't quite work out how I was hoping. I thought if Renard was sorry, Gabriel might be able to accept his apology but . . .' She let the sentence end there, Gabriel's words replayed in her mind.

'You were wrong?'

She shrugged. 'Not exactly. Renard hasn't even had the chance to make an apology yet. You saw what happened, didn't you? In hindsight, maybe doing this during the party wasn't a great idea. I didn't mean to embarrass anyone.'

'You haven't. Look—' She pointed at Renard. 'He has stayed away for so long, but everyone is happy to see him. He has done wonderful things for this community. We owe him a lot and he knows he has made mistakes. Who of us haven't? Give him and Gabriel time and you never know, things might work out how you'd hoped.'

If they did, she wouldn't be around to see it. She'd already made her mind up about that. 'Will you excuse me, Alina? I just need to nip up to my room.'

'Must you really? Will you not come and have a drink with me?'

The sweetness of her gesture tugged at her heart. 'That's really kind but I need to make a phone call.' She took her phone from the small purse she'd been carrying around all evening.

'Then of course. Merry Christmas, Naomi.' She kissed Naomi on the cheek. 'It will all be all right. You'll see.'

'Merry Christmas, Alina, and to Roger, Fynn and the children too. I hope you have a wonderful day tomorrow.'

She darted upstairs as fast as she could in the ridiculously high heels – stopping as soon as she was out of sight and ripping them from her feet. Naomi closed her bedroom door behind her, pressing her back against it to make sure it was shut. She could feel the cold wood through the satin of her dress and it made her shiver. But she needed peace and quiet, she needed time alone. Not to think – she'd already made her mind up as to what she needed to do – but she couldn't bear standing there feeling like everyone was talking about her. Nor could she risk Gabriel coming up from the kitchen and seeing him again. Her heart was already broken.

She took a deep breath and began to move around the room, gathering her belongings into piles to not leave anything behind. Then she sat on the edge of her bed. She had a plane ticket to book.

Naomi dropped the shoes to the floor but kept her coat on. She was cold through to her bones, her teeth chattering. She threw on a pair of fluffy socks and climbed under the duvet, hoping to warm her frozen toes. Finally, with her wallet in hand she began to search on her phone for flights back to London. As soon as that was booked, she'd pack. She found a flight, but her fingers hovered over the button. Should she go? She didn't want to leave Mia with all this mess but was there any point in staying? She wouldn't want to see her either. She tried to think clearly, calmly, but the only answer she could find was yes. She had to leave, and as soon as possible. Staying here would be worse.

At least she knew one thing. Staring around the plush surroundings of Le Petit Chateau, thinking about the comfortable life she and Ollie once had, she knew she didn't need those things, the material comforts, to be happy. They'd lost their hold on her and her life back in England would be full of things that mattered, not expensive handbags and designer shoes, or pretending she was something she wasn't. She clicked the button and began filling out her flight details.

Just as she'd entered her credit card details and confirmed her flight was booked, there was a knock at the door. Naomi paused, staring at her phone.

Was it Gabriel? Had he come to apologise? To declare his feelings for her? To wipe out the last half an hour and tell her he loved her too. That he'd just been too caught off guard by everything to tell her before. Though she hoped, she could tell from the knock it wasn't him. She went to the door and opened it to see Mia.

'Can I come in?'

'Yes, of course.' Naomi stepped back into the room.

'I brought you a drink. I thought you could use one.' She held out a glass of wine with a second glass in her other hand for herself. 'It'll help warm you up. You look freezing.'

'I look ridiculous,' she said with an attempt at a laugh, her arms outstretched, showing the full effect of the outfit: giant coat, emerald green satin dress and fluffy socks.

'You might want to change your shoes before you come back to the party, but you can probably keep the coat. We know it's important to dress for the cold here.'

Naomi tilted her head. Mia's gentle prodding wasn't going to work this time. 'I think it's probably better if I stay up here.'

'Why? Everyone loves you and they love the decorations. They're grateful and want to thank you. My father especially.'

'That's kind, but I'd really rather stay up here.' They walked into the bedroom and Naomi swapped the coat for a jumper, yanking it over her hair so that her bun was pulled loose. She let her hair down, removing the pins that had kept it in place and allowing it to fall down her back as if to illustrate to Mia there'd be no convincing her. She'd had enough humiliation for one day. She climbed into bed, pulling the duvet around her once more.

Mia sat on the edge of the bed. 'What did Gabriel say?'

Naomi felt her walls building again: her brain telling her to say nothing or that she didn't want to talk about it. But despite everything, she didn't want to go back to being that closed-off person no one could reach. Gabriel had hurt her this evening, but she wasn't about to undo all the work she'd done on herself over these last few weeks. She'd felt freer – her head less jumbled – and she didn't want to let that go.

'He was angry with me,' she said calmly. 'And rightly so – I know that. I made a mistake, Mia. I thought bringing your father here would help them to get over themselves and stop waiting for the other to make the

337

first move. I could see how it was affecting Gabriel, how it was affecting you and I wanted to help if I could.'

'Oh, my friend,' Mia said, taking her hand. 'I know you did it for the best, but Gabriel was right. You shouldn't have interfered, especially just because someone in town says something. Why do you think I haven't done anything all these years? Gabriel can only do it when *he's* ready. Not before. And because he's so like my father, the same can be said for him. My father will only do things when he's ready, and clearly he was. But we can't always make other people do what's best for them no matter how much we might want to.'

'I know. I was just really worried you were overworking yourself. I thought if they made up, he'd be more relaxed and you could talk to him about an assistant or something. I'm sorry I got it all wrong.' She dropped her eyes to her friend's hand that was covering her own. 'Do you hate me?' Naomi asked, glancing up at her friend.

'Me? Of course not.' She snuggled in next to Naomi and put her arm around her. 'I know you thought you were doing the right thing.'

'I ruined your wonderful party.'

'You didn't. Father is schmoozing everyone and he really is genuinely happy with Le Petit Chateau and the decorations. I do think he's changed, you know.' After a moment, she said, 'Gabriel will forgive you, in time. He just needs to get over the shock of seeing our father for the first time in years. You will be back making me feel sick with your lovers' antics before Christmas is over.'

'I don't think so,' Naomi said, feeling a stinging at the back of her nose. She was getting nearer to crying again, but she pressed the feeling down and gathered her strength. 'I told him I was falling in love with him.'

Mia sat up straighter, a grin playing on her lips. 'And what did he say?'

'That I'd blindsided him with your father. Then he left.'

'Left? What do you mean left?'

'He went back into the kitchen without saying another word.'

'What?' Mia turned her body so she could look at Naomi's face. She shook her head. 'He can't have. No, he wouldn't do that. He does love you. He must have—'

'He did. He's too angry with me and I don't think that anger will ever go away. I've made this giant problem between us, just like he did all those years ago and I can't see us ever moving past it.'

'But he loves you! I know he does. I've seen him with you.'

'Clearly not enough.' Her heart stung as if someone had ripped it apart. Could he love her and still respond the way he had? She wasn't sure. She knew she'd hurt him, and she regretted it with every ounce of her being. She tried to see things from his point of view but no matter how she played out the scenario, she still felt he should have said the words back to her if he'd felt them.

'No,' Mia said firmly. 'I know he loves you. He's being an idiot. Again. He just needs to speak to my father, which I think he will when he's calmed down, and then he'll see what a complete *dummkopf* he's been. Father said he'll try talking to him again in the morning, alone. He's going to stay here tonight, and I, for one, am glad. I do think he's changed, and I might have seen it sooner if we weren't always being so formal, making sure we didn't talk about Gabriel. Keeping everything strictly business. Though I was surprised and upset you did it without talking to me, I am glad to see him and for that I'm grateful.'

Naomi bit her lip. 'I'm glad things are better for you and your dad. But I've booked a flight for tomorrow to go back to London.'

'No! Naomi, please.' She gripped her friend's hand again, squeezing hard. 'You don't have to leave. Stay and spend Christmas with us. You can't go on Christmas Day.'

She shook her head. 'I can't stay here, Mia. If I did, I'd just hide here, in this room. I can't face Gabriel and he doesn't want to face me.'

'But—'

'It's over, Mia,' she said gently, catching her eye. 'It's over. It won't work with Gabriel. I've finally discovered on this trip what I want out of life and to be honest, I don't think he knows what he wants. I know he wants to be a chef, but I feel like he's trapped by this anger he has towards your father and he's only going to be ready for a new life when he's let that go. But I'm so grateful to you.' Still holding Mia's hand, she rubbed the skin with her thumb. 'You really are the best friend a girl could ever have. If you hadn't asked me here, I wouldn't have had the courage to tell you about being adopted. I wouldn't have changed jobs and I wouldn't be trying my best to communicate and be open with people. To the point that, when I get back, I'm going to see Ollie and apologise to him for always holding a part of me back. I never thought I was responsible for the breakdown of our marriage, but I realise now I was partly to blame too because I'd never really let him in. I wouldn't have known any of those things if you hadn't convinced me to come out here.'

'But with Gabriel, you could take it slowly. Do the long-distance thing for a while and—'

'Long distance won't ever work with Gabriel and if he doesn't love me—'

'Oh, Naomi, he does.' Her eyes were bright with certainty. 'He's just in shock. When the fight-or-flight instinct calms down, he'll realise he missed the opportunity to tell you how he feels, and he'll regret it. He'll want to see you and say it to you then. He'll be devastated if you leave.'

Naomi ignored her words because she so desperately wanted to believe them, but she couldn't. She'd meant what she said about Gabriel being ready for this and she really wasn't sure he was. 'Long distance is hard and I don't want things to be like they were with me and Ollie. We never saw each other. We were more like flatmates. I won't do that again. Before tonight I felt like I had a new lease of life, a new outlook on things. If I'm going to commit to someone, I'm going to commit with every part of me. No holding back. And Gabriel . . . I don't know if he can let go of this.'

'I wish you'd see him tomorrow. Then you'll see a difference, especially if my father has spoken to him. If I can see my father's changed, Gabriel will too. He'll know you were right.' Naomi refused to meet her eye, shaking her head. 'I can't persuade you, can I?'

'No. I'm sorry.'

'Can I at least drive you to the airport?'

'No, it's fine. I'll get a taxi. You should stay with your family, especially as it'll be Christmas Day.'

'You're my family too. Please, no matter what happens with my stupid brother, promise we will always be best friends.'

'Always.'

'Then as your best friend, I'd like to see you off.'

'Fine,' Naomi said, rolling her eyes in mock annoyance. 'If you must.'

'I must.' Mia snuggled in again and rested her head on Naomi's shoulder.

'Hadn't you better get back to the party?' she asked. 'Your guests will be missing you and if your brother and dad have run into each other again, they might be flinging bits of food at each other or something.'

'They won't. Gabriel wouldn't let anyone use his food like that. I'll go in a minute. If I'm losing you tomorrow, and you won't come back downstairs, I want to make the most of these last few minutes of quiet.'

Naomi's heart seared with pain as she stared out of

her bedroom window at the peaceful snow. Silver flakes drifted down in the dark night, dancing in the breeze, settling on the windowsill. She would miss her best friend as much as she'd miss the man she'd fallen in love with. Could she stay for Mia's sake? A part of her wanted to desperately, but she couldn't see Mia without the rest of the family and it was clear the Mathis family needed time alone together. Time to heal. Leaving was the best thing for everyone, especially for her.

Chapter 31

The next morning, Naomi checked the room for the final time, ensuring she hadn't left anything behind. Her passport was in her handbag, slung over her shoulder, and everything else was in the case pulled along at her heels. At least it was a short flight. She'd soon be back in her house and could focus on the future, her new job and the life she was going to build for herself. She had a lot to be grateful for, but her heart still stung knowing how she and Gabriel were parting. If this ended up being like the time at university, they'd probably never speak again. Her throat closed over, and she pressed her lips together, trying to quell the emotions inside.

She took the lift downstairs and spotted Mia waiting for her as the doors opened. She couldn't help glancing around for Gabriel but as she'd feared, he wasn't there. She peered at the dining room. The remnants of the party remained though the food had been cleared. A buffet breakfast had been laid out for her. Gabriel would have done it, but she couldn't bear to eat. She didn't have time anyway.

Mia approached her, sadness in her eyes. 'Are you sure about this, Naomi? You don't have to go. You could stay. We could go skiing and then have dinner and then watch the Christmas Day procession in town.'

On Christmas Day people took to the streets banging on drums and wearing giant cow bells called *trychlers* – their faces covered. It was an old tradition that was supposed to chase all the evil spirits away. She'd thought she'd watch it with her best friend by her side, her hand held by Gabriel. Another shot of pain pierced her heart.

'You wouldn't have to see Gabriel if you don't want to.'

The trouble was she did want to. She wanted him to come to her and apologise for not returning her words of love. She wanted him to recognise that she knew she'd made a mistake yesterday, but he hadn't come last night, he wasn't there this morning, and she knew she wouldn't see him again before she left. Mia would have told him of her plans. There was no way she wouldn't have. If he knew, he'd chosen not to be there to say goodbye and that hurt her even more.

'I think going home is best, Mia.' She checked her watch, though she knew exactly what time it was. It was merely to illustrate the point. 'In fact, we better get going. I don't know how busy the airport will be, or how long it'll take us to get there. It snowed all night, didn't it?'

'It did. The skiers are very happy and filling the slopes already.'

'I can still get a cab if you want to stay here, Mia. You've worked so hard; you deserve Christmas Day with your family.'

Mia crossed her arms over her chest, the car keys dangling from one finger. 'I'm driving you whether you like it or not.'

A moment's sad silence filled the room and after giving Mia a wan smile, Naomi moved towards the door.

She placed her suitcase in the back of Mia's car, taking deep breaths of the fresh mountain air. She'd miss how clean it felt in her lungs, how it refreshed her skin and dissolved the worries from her mind. Naomi climbed into the passenger seat and clipped on her seatbelt. She also hadn't had the chance to say goodbye to Hans. She'd miss the way he leaned on her legs when she was fussing him, the way he'd move the football around with his nose.

Mia started the car, and they left the ski resort, turning onto the roads that led towards the town and further on to the airport. She marvelled again at the way they wound down the mountainside and the tall heads of the pine trees grew level with the cars. She was going to miss it all: the ragged mountains, the snow crunching under her feet, the sense of endless space.

In silence, Mia continued through the centre of town. The bright lights of the Christmas market were on even though the stalls were empty. It must have been her imagination, but she was sure she could smell all the wonderful food and drink that had overloaded her senses when she'd first visited: the deep red wine scent of the glühwein, the potato fritters, the roasted chestnuts and the delicious hot chocolates. Her mind went to her and Gabriel sitting at the Christmas tree farm drinking the most delicious hot chocolate she'd ever had.

Naomi pressed her lips together remembering walking around the market and meeting Alina. She'd miss the people here too. She hadn't had chance to say goodbye to Alina and her family, or Nikolas and the stallholders who'd helped her turn Le Petit Chateau into a winter wonderland. The stinging returned to the back of her nose. She tried to ignore it, but it kept growing stronger. All these people had helped to give her a different outlook on life. Helped her to come to terms with her own history and lay the foundations for a better future for herself. Suddenly, the thought of leaving with so many things unfinished, so many goodbyes left unsaid, filled her with dread.

For so long she and Gabriel had left so much unsaid. There were things she'd finally told Mia that had made their friendship stronger and when she returned home she was going to contact Ollie and tell him all the things she should have said a long time ago. She didn't want to leave. Not yet. She wanted to find Gabriel and say goodbye to him no matter how painful a goodbye it would be.

'Naomi?' Mia said concerned, glancing at her nervously. 'Are you crying?'

Tears misted Naomi's vision and ran down her cheeks. She wiped them away, but it was as if a dam had burst in her chest, and now they were pouring out of her. She sniffed, trying to catch her breath, to make them stop. But this time, they wouldn't be held back or pushed down with sheer force of will. She was crying for the first time in years. It felt painful and hard but also strangely helpful, like she was ridding herself of all the old emotions she'd kept locked inside for so many years.

Mia pulled over and rammed on the handbrake. 'Naomi, what's happening? This is . . . well it's scary! What's going on?'

Her friend scrambled around for tissues, finding a pack in her coat pocket and handing one over to Naomi. She blew her nose and wiped her cheeks, but now the floodgates had opened, there was no going back. Her breathing became even more ragged as great, wracking sobs shook her body. Her face was wet, the tissue was wet, even her legs were getting wet where the tears were dripping onto her thighs. It was crazy. She opened her mouth to speak but couldn't get any words out. It felt like her whole body had entered a state of shock. She was shaking, as her body wrung itself out.

'Is it Gabriel?' Mia asked gently.

Naomi nodded, taking a deep breath and muttering, 'It's him and you and . . . everything.'

'Me? Why have I made you cry?'

Mia's startled expression and surprised tone was a lighter moment in the dark she was suddenly feeling. She managed to get the words out in one huge, garbled lump before falling back into soggy uneven breaths. 'Because you're my best friend and I, I-I . . . love you!'

'Oh, Naomi!' She reached over and wrapped an arm around her friend. 'I'm still freaked out about this whole crying business though. Talk to me. What's happening?'

Finally, Naomi was able to gain control of her emotions. She told herself to take even breaths in and out, and within a few minutes she was calmer and able to speak. 'The last few weeks have been brilliant, and I don't want them to end yet. I love how everyone here helps each other and looks out for each other. I've loved seeing you properly and – and – Gabriel. Decorating Le Petit Chateau for you, helping you, it's reminded me what it's like to help others and to be inspired. I've missed that so much.'

'It's been wonderful to have you here. But I don't understand. You're not wanting to stay permanently, are you? I mean obviously you can. We'd find somewhere for you but—'

Naomi shook her head. 'No, that's not it. Don't get me wrong, I love it here and I'd love to visit more often, especially as I'm getting much better at skiing—'

'Well . . .' Mia said teasingly, implying she wasn't getting *that* much better.

Naomi giggled and that too felt like a moment of relief. 'I've just changed so much and leaving like this, without saying a proper goodbye to anyone, it feels like I've not finished what I started. I've learned to let my walls down, to not be so defensive and to trust in a way I haven't been able to for a long time but—'

'But it's not quite done yet?' Naomi nodded. 'Then stay! I'll turn the car around and we'll go back to Le Petit

Chateau and have Christmas Day together. Then you can say thank you to everyone.'

Naomi considered it for a moment. Every cell of her being was screaming to say yes. To let Mia drive them back and for her to stay for the last week of her holidays as she'd intended. But then she'd have to see Gabriel and it would be awkward and painful. Their ruined relationship would ruin Christmas Day for Mia who deserved a good one. And she'd already gone out of her way to bring Naomi this far.

'It's time I went home,' Naomi said calmly. 'I've actually got a lot to look forward to. I'd like to do a bit more prep before I start my new job and—' She dried her eyes as another rogue tear escaped. 'I'm really looking forward to doing pro-bono work again and making a real difference to people's lives. Maybe it's just the timing. If it wasn't Christmas Day I probably wouldn't be this much of a mess.'

'You're allowed to be upset, Naomi,' Mia said, fishing out another tissue and handing it to her. 'I don't know why Gabriel wasn't there this morning. I told him you were leaving, and he genuinely looked devastated.'

Or relieved perhaps, Naomi thought but didn't say so. No, though she wanted to say goodbye to everyone properly, especially him, she didn't know if she could face it without breaking down. And as he'd had the opportunity to say that he loved her last night and hadn't, he clearly didn't feel the same way she did.

She wiped her face and took a deep breath in, then

out slowly. The soggy tissue was scrunched in her hand, and she looked down at it surprised that after all these years it would be Gabriel again, along with this beautiful place, that would make her cry. She flipped down the sun visor and checked her reflection in the tiny built-in mirror. 'Oh my God! Look at me! I look like something out of a horror movie.'

'You look fine,' Mia replied, laughing.

'I'm bright red, my nose is almost purple and my whole face has puffed up. You should have told me I'm an ugly crier.'

'Everyone is an ugly crier when the tears actually mean something. Are you sure we can't turn back?'

'Not this time. Come on. I'm sick of going back and forth now.' She wiped her eyes one more time and flipped the sun visor back up to hide her reflection. 'Time to move on.'

'Sure?'

Naomi nodded and, reluctantly, Mia put the car into gear and drove on. Naomi stared one last time out at the snow-peaked mountains; at the lanes and alleyways of the town filled with kind, helpful people; at the snow-flakes falling, settling on the car window and sliding down the glass.

She might say the words 'time to move on', but she wasn't sure she could. She'd go back to London and rebuild her life, but a piece of her heart would always belong here in Switzerland, with Gabriel.

Chapter 32

'Bye then,' Mia said, wiping her own tears away as they stood outside the airport at the drop-off point. She'd offered to park up and go in with her, but Naomi had refused. She wasn't the best company at the moment – despite trying to smile and act like she was fine.

Naomi wrapped her arms around her friend. Mia's dark hair – flecked with snowflakes – blew in her face as the wind picked up. The snow was falling heavier now, and Naomi worried it would delay her flight, or worse cancel it. She wasn't sure her bruised heart could take any more problems today.

'Go on,' she said, pulling away. 'Get back before this gets any worse.'

'I just wish—' Mia began. 'I wish it wasn't like this.'

'I wish things had ended differently too but at least you and your father are getting on better. And apart from this thing with Gabriel, as I said, this has been a truly transformational holiday. I'm forever grateful.'

'You don't need to be grateful to me – you've done all the hard work. Promise me something, though?'

'I'd like to know what it is first.'

A mischievous twinkle came into Mia's eye. 'That you'll try and cry at least once a month. It's good for you.'

Naomi laughed. 'I can't guarantee it'll be that often, but you never know.' She wiped at her eye, which was beginning to water again. 'Maybe now I've started I'll never stop.'

'You've got a few years of tears to get out of your system. Once a month at a minimum, I think.' Mia paused, smiling before launching herself at Naomi. 'I love you, bestie.'

'Love you too,' Naomi said, giving Mia one last huge hug. 'Let's not leave it so long till we see each other again. I'm thinking of selling the house and getting somewhere smaller, somewhere different.'

'Still in London?'

'Yeah, but somewhere that's mine, you know. If I've learned I don't need all the trappings of a "successful" life, I don't need a big house. I quite fancy a small flat somewhere pretty, but you'll have to come and visit.'

'I'll come and help you move. You'll need my organisation skills with starting your new job and all the pro-bono work you're going to be doing.'

Naomi laughed again. 'Okay. It's a deal.'

She stepped away, her heart lurching, but with a final wave she grabbed hold of her suitcase and walked through the large automatic doors of the airport. There was enough time for her to grab a coffee and Naomi was just on her way when a hand hit her shoulder and wrenched her around.

'Mia!' she shouted, sure it was her friend having forgotten something, and was surprised to see the man who held her heart standing in front of her. His jacket was open and sweat gathered at his temples. His pale eyes were pinned on her, bright with emotion, his blond hair decorated with melting snowflakes.

'Gabriel!' Naomi shook her head, in total disbelief. He didn't seem real.

Other people had heard her shout and were watching on. Passengers had paused, their cases held out behind them, trollies of luggage at a standstill.

'Don't go,' he said, through heavy breaths, still holding on to her coat. 'Please?'

Had he run all the way from Le Petit Chateau? He couldn't have, but she supposed he had followed them in his car. Hans was sitting at his feet, gazing at Naomi with his bright blue eyes. 'Don't go,' Gabriel repeated.

Having unleashed her emotions, she couldn't figure out how she felt. This was everything she'd wanted but she was still hurt. Despite her defences flying back up, she spoke with conviction. 'Why not? Last night you—'

'I know what I did. Or should I say, I know what I didn't do . . . or say.' His expression was imploring, and she had the feeling he was finally laying himself as bare and open as she had. 'And I am so sorry, Naomi. I'm an idiot.

A selfish idiot. A stupid selfish idiot. I should have told you last night that I loved you too, but I didn't – I couldn't. I was angry about my father showing up, and with you for inviting him and confused because everything inside me wanted me to shout out that I loved you but then I couldn't say it. I let my stupid anger at my father overwhelm me and I hurt you. I'm sorry.'

Hans barked to get her attention as she hadn't fussed him yet and despite everything, she laughed, stroking his head so he stood up and came to rest against her legs.

'I'm sorry too,' she said to Gabriel. 'I really didn't mean to blindside you. I just thought . . .' She couldn't go over it all again. 'But I'm sorry for interfering. I know now I did the wrong thing but it—'

'It was with the best intentions, I know. That's what my father and Mia said. And you didn't do the wrong thing.'

'What do you mean?'

He took a deep breath, his chest rising and falling. He pushed his hair back in that way that made her heart flip-flop around in her chest. 'You were right about everything. My father and I would never have made up if someone else hadn't made the first move. We're too alike, as Mia likes to remind me.' He looked up through his lashes towards the automatic doors and Naomi smiled to see Mia there watching them. 'I met with my father this morning and we talked everything through. I know that he's genuinely sorry for the way he acted but he was too scared to reach out. He said, he kept asking his friends in town about me and they all said I was still angry – too angry – and they were right. I was, and I don't know if I'd ever have let that anger go if it wasn't for you. You made us talk. You made us see each other differently. He said he was glad you got in touch because he had a reason to come – a reason to be brave. And you made me be brave, though I did my best to still be a coward. The day he told me I wasn't his son anymore, it broke something in me the way I broke something in you, but now you've helped me fix it, Naomi.'

He'd helped fix her too. She wasn't perfect and neither was he, but they were both works in progress.

'Naomi, I'm so, so sorry for last night. I should not have taken my fear out on you.'

'What were you afraid of?'

'That as a chef I wouldn't be good enough. That my father would be disappointed in my skills and think I'd wasted all this time. All my life. That I'd fail the test. But he said he loved the food, that it was exquisite and that he was proud of me. He was so sorry for all the things he'd said and done. The mistakes he'd made. I never thought I'd hear the words.' Gabriel dropped his eyes, clearly emotional at the reunion with his father. He gave a small chuckle. 'He even said that if I'd been the worst chef in the world, he would still have been proud of me because I wanted to be my own man and I've done it. But it's all thanks to you, Naomi.' He took her hands in his. 'There aren't many people who would do something like that for me. Who would think only of me, but you did.'

Naomi was pleased for him. Pleased for all of the Mathis family but what did it mean for them? His words were floating around her head as she tried to think logically about the situation.

'Naomi,' he continued. 'I love you. I love you with all my heart. In fact, I think I have loved you since that first day we met all those years ago. You've been a ghost in my mind, and I don't want to throw away our second chance at being together all because I'm an idiot and last night I was too scared to say I love you back.'

Brick by brick, the defences that had built over the last few hours fell away and a huge smile spread over Naomi's face. Tears sprung once more to her eyes and this time, she didn't try to hold them back. 'You do?'

'Yay!' Mia cheered and clapped from the corner. Naomi and Gabriel laughed as they turned to her. 'Sorry. Sorry! I'll just umm . . .' She pointed at the automatic doors. 'I'll wait in the car. Hans, come.' Begrudgingly, the dog followed the command, staring back at Gabriel and Naomi as if they'd betrayed him by allowing him to be taken away.

'Truly,' Gabriel said, turning back to her, his voice barely more than a whisper to begin with but gaining strength as he spoke. 'I let you go once, and I won't do it again. I love you and want to spend the rest of my life with you, if you'll let me.' Naomi watched, spellbound as he reached into his pocket and pulled out a sprig of mistletoe. 'You said you'd never been kissed under the mistletoe? Well, I think now's the time.'

He stepped forwards holding it over her head and without hesitation, Naomi moved towards him, allowing his lips to meet hers. Having cried out so much emotion, the kiss felt even better now. Every part of her body and soul connecting with him on a deeper level than she'd ever thought possible. She wrapped her arms around his neck, leaning into him, giving her spirit to his. Gabriel held her tightly and she knew those were the only arms she wanted around her for the rest of her life.

Though she hadn't heard it before, as they separated and she came back to real life, the sound of applause filled her ears. Everyone in the airport was clapping and whooping at the romantic scene before them. She had to admit, it was incredibly romantic – worthy of one of her favourite movies! She and Gabriel laughed, resting their foreheads together as they smiled.

'I'm glad Mia went back to the car,' Naomi said, glancing up and smiling her thanks at the crowd.

'Why?'

'She said our snogging made her feel sick.'

'Well, she'll have to get used to it, won't she? Here—' He handed her the small sprig of mistletoe complete with white berries. 'You have this. You should keep it. Somewhere safe, so you never forget the first time you were kissed under the mistletoe.'

'I don't think I'll ever forget it,' she replied.

It was the best Christmas present anyone could have given her.

Chapter 33

As the four of them drove back through the town, Naomi – who had been snuggled beside Gabriel in the back seat, an annoyed Hans thrust into a corner – shouted at Mia to stop.

'Why?' she asked, slowing the car down and pulling into a parking space. 'What's wrong? Did you leave something at the airport?'

'No, look.' She pointed out of the window at the streams of people all heading the same way, towards the Christmas market.

'Ah,' said Gabriel. 'The parade is starting.'

Mia turned from the driver's seat. 'We should go and watch. It's a wonderful thing to see.'

'It's a little bit crazy,' Gabriel added, holding his thumb and forefinger near each other to show how much. 'But just a little bit. It's quite fun.'

'I was hoping to see it but didn't think I'd get to. Will Hans be okay?'

'He'll be fine. He likes the noise, and everyone will give him attention. He'll be very happy.'

They exited the car and followed everyone else. Naomi's hand was in Gabriel's every step of the way as Mia held Hans's lead. As the procession approached, they found a spot at the front to watch.

The noise was unlike anything Naomi had ever heard. It was almost too much for her ears and though rhythmic, it wasn't exactly musical. Yet, watching row upon row of the townsmen walk along in a way that kept their giant cow bells, held by a band around their waists, ringing continually, was amazing. She recognised some of the stallholders and they smiled at her as they passed. She smiled back, waving. The bells were covered in beautiful dark blue cloths, all decorated with the same design, and behind them were men with bright old-fashioned torches.

In the crowd, they spotted Renard, and Gabriel waved his father over.

'It's been a long time since I saw this with you and your sister,' he said, his eyes glassy though he was doing his best to keep the tears at bay.

'Hopefully it will not take us as long to do this again,' Gabriel replied, and Naomi felt a glow of pride.

'So,' Renard said. 'You are not so much just a friend of Gabriel's, you are Gabriel's girlfriend.'

She beamed at him. 'That's right.'

'I am glad. As soon as I met you, I knew you would be good for him.'

'Did you?'

'Of course! He needs someone to point out when he's wrong.' Naomi worried this was heading into territory they had only just come out of, but Renard was smiling widely. 'Every man does.'

Gabriel relaxed, rolling his eyes playfully behind his father's back. He leaned in and whispered, 'Perhaps next year we will go somewhere hot and sunny for Christmas. Somewhere away from my family.'

'I don't think so. I think Christmas will always be at Le Petit Chateau from now on.'

The parade over, back at Le Petit Chateau, Gabriel, Mia and Renard were all busy reconnecting and Naomi took the chance to run back to her room and video-call her parents. She'd missed them and knowing now that material comfort would never measure up to real love and support – the love and support she'd always received from her parents – she wanted to see their faces and tell them how much she loved them.

'Hi, Mum and Dad,' she said as they answered the call.

They were on the cruise ship, heads covered with enormous sunhats, cocktail glasses in hand. It was evening there, almost nine o'clock, but the sun was still shining and from the pinkness of her parents' cheeks, it was hot too.

'Merry Christmas, darling!' her mum said. Her dad raised his glass in a toast and then fought with the straw poking out of the top.

'Merry Christmas! Have you had a nice day?'

'It's been lovely, darling. We've been having so much fun. Your dad's the king of shuffleboard.'

'Wow, that's quite a title.'

'Self-proclaimed,' he added, raising his glass again and once more trying to catch the straw before it went up his nose. 'What about you? What have you been up to today?'

How could she sum it all up succinctly? So much had happened. So much had changed. 'It's been great. I – I've met someone.'

Her mum gasped. 'How wonderful! Oh, darling, that's fabulous news. What's his name?'

'And when can I meet him?' her dad added.

Naomi smiled. 'His name's Gabriel and he's a chef. He's Mia's brother.'

'Oh, a chef. Wonderful. He's cooking dinner then.'

'I think he'd love that.' She took a breath. 'There's actually quite a lot I need to tell you. Have you got time?'

'For you, darling? Always.'

Obviously they already knew about her change of job, but she told them that she was planning on selling the house and moving somewhere new. She didn't speak about how she'd finally let her defences down. She didn't want to hurt them or for them to feel in any way to blame. They weren't. It had been her decision to live her life the way she had.

'It's wonderful to see you so happy, darling. I can't wait to hear all the details when we're home. Now, we have to go and get some dinner before they stop serving. Catch up tomorrow?'

'Of course. I love you both,' Naomi said, a tear springing to her eye. She covered it quickly by pretending it was an eyelash.

'We love you too, darling. Merry Christmas.'

'Merry Christmas, Mum and Dad.'

She signed off and went back downstairs.

After the drinks were refilled, Mia, Gabriel, their father, and Naomi gathered around the Christmas tree. After all the noise of earlier, Hans had settled in front of the fire and was happily fast asleep, his paws twitching as he dreamed of a chase. Having already exchanged gifts, they were relaxing – though Naomi was growing tense.

As happy as she was, there was one thing they hadn't yet discussed and that was how their relationship was going to work. She wasn't about to give up her new job and though she could visit here often, she needed to be in London. Gabriel had a job here, which meant the only option was a long-distance relationship and she worried they would drift apart not seeing each other.

Gabriel, who'd been chatting with his father, came over and sat beside her, taking her hand. 'You're very quiet.'

'I'm fine,' she replied. 'Just a bit worn out. It's been an emotional few days.'

'You're worried about returning to England and me staying here?'

Naomi gazed at him in wonder. 'How do you keep reading my mind? It's weird. Not to mention disturbing.'

'Because I know you, Naomi Winters. But you don't need to worry. I already have a plan.'

'Oh, and what's that?'

'Hans and I are going to move to London.'

Her jaw fell open and her eyes widened. 'You're what?'

'We're going to move to London. I've been looking at jobs there for a while now.'

'Have you?'

'As soon as we had that dinner, I began to think about it and I thought, I want to be with her all the time, not just every few weeks. I want to enhance my culinary skills, and do you know what I realised?'

'No, what's that?'

Gabriel gasped. 'There are restaurants in London too!' She batted his arm. 'Ow! That hurt. But truly, I've already started applying for jobs and have some interviews lined up in the new year. There is one restaurant in particular I'm very excited about.'

'Well, I was thinking of selling the house Ollie and I shared and buying something new. A flat with a garden or something.'

'That sounds nice.'

She could see he hadn't twigged what she was hinting at. 'A nice flat with a garden big enough for a dog to run around in . . . or near a park so we could take him out for walks whenever we wanted.'

'You mean . . .'

She waited, but he was unable to finish the sentence. 'Yes,' she replied, laughing. 'If you're moving to England, why don't you move in with me? Or we can rent somewhere together if that would make you feel more comfortable? Would you like to?'

Her voice rang with nerves, but Gabriel kissed her in reply. 'I'd love to. We've wasted too much time already.'

'I know it seems fast, but as long as we're both open and honest, I know we can make it work. Everything just feels right with you.'

'There is one thing,' Gabriel replied. 'I will have to practise my cooking skills so you'll have to be my guinea pig.'

'Oh, well, in that case, no. No absolutely not, that sounds terrible. Maybe it'd be best if you stayed here.'

'Hey!'

Before she could say anything else he silenced her with another kiss. This time she was aware of his sister and dad making a hasty exit out to the dining room balcony. And alone, in front of the roaring fire at Le Petit Chateau, surrounded by love and happiness, Naomi allowed herself to be swept away by the magic of Christmas. The walls she'd built had been torn down and she was no longer ashamed of who she was. In fact, she was ready to embrace the past as much as she was the future.

She glanced at Gabriel, enjoying another lingering kiss. Their future together was just beginning, surrounded by friends and family, filled with joy and love. She really couldn't wait.

Epilogue

23rd December

ONE YEAR LATER

Naomi and Gabriel stepped back through the door of Le Petit Chateau, Hans at their heels, eager to spend Christmas with Mia and Renard. Naomi's parents had arrived earlier that day and were already ensconced by the fire, chatting happily to Renard.

It was snowing again, and the giant Christmas tree outside glowed in the dim light, its glittering fairy lights twinkling. The beautiful ornaments Naomi had gathered last year were back on display as were two trees that stood in the place of where Naomi had left Tree-mothy and Tree-vor. The garlands were stretched over the crackling fire that filled the room with warmth, and the air was perfumed once more with winter spices.

The gala party was the next day, and Gabriel, of course, would be catering. Though this time he'd also organised a sous chef so he could spend some time out of the kitchen catching up with the people from town. Naomi couldn't wait to see Alina and hoped her son and his family would be there too. She had so much to tell them.

Naomi shook off her coat and Gabriel took it from her, kissing her cheek as he did so. They were so excited to have everyone together. Hans trotted over to Mia, leaning against her legs and enjoying the fuss she was giving him. She'd missed him and Naomi had missed her friend too.

She and Gabriel were now splitting their time between London and Le Petit Chateau. Gabriel would often come out to cater at events when he could fit them around his job at one of London's newest and most well-reviewed restaurants. He was finally making a name for himself, and his years of hard work were paying off.

Naomi's career was going from strength to strength in the new field she'd been working in. Even on her toughest days she woke up happy to be going to work, happy to be doing something worthwhile. The sense of achievement and fulfilment she got at the end of each day more than made up for the stress and heartache that often came with it. She didn't regret leaving corporate law and now they'd moved into their small but perfectly formed flat – in an up-and-coming area of London – she really couldn't be happier.

Lyn and Michael, her parents, came towards her as soon as they spotted her.

'Darling, you look frozen,' her mum said. 'Come and warm up by the fire.' She took her daughter's hand and led her into the lounge. Renard swiftly rose, placing kisses on each of her cheeks.

The Mathis family had healed the wounds of the last few years. Renard's relationship with Gabriel was going from strength to strength and he'd learned to let go of the business, so Mia was enjoying the additional responsibility. She now also had an assistant, so she didn't have to do absolutely everything. She was thriving and had even recently been featured on a 'watch list' of CEOs to look out for. On top of this, she looked radiant. The dark circles that had plagued her last year had disappeared as family and job harmony had returned.

After everyone chatted for a few minutes, Gabriel and Naomi's eyes met across the room.

'We should get a family photograph,' Gabriel said, giving Naomi a playful look.

'Yes, definitely,' her mum replied. She loved Gabriel, as did her father, and he'd seamlessly slotted into their family in a way Ollie never had. Not least because whenever they visited, Lyn could always get him to cook, giving her a night off and allowing Gabriel to try out new recipes, which were always delicious.

Gabriel began directing everyone to where they should stand or sit. He was to sit on the long sofa in between Mia and Naomi and the three parents would stand behind, Renard in the middle of Michael and Lyn. His phone camera set to a timer, he retook his seat and began counting down.

'Five, four, three, two, one . . .'

'I'm pregnant!' Naomi shouted a millisecond after he said the final number and everyone fell about, their mouths open in shock. All but Gabriel who had planned this moment with her. The camera hadn't been set to a single photograph but had been recording the whole thing and he and Naomi collapsed in giggles as Mia and Lyn began to cry and Michael declared he needed a stiff drink because he wasn't ready to be a grandpa.

'Oh, darling!' Lyn swept Naomi up in a hug. 'How far along are you? When did you find out? Oh, I have so many questions.' She let go and pressed her hands to her cheeks instead.

Naomi laughed, accepting a hug from Mia who had been waiting patiently but couldn't stop shifting from foot to foot. 'I'm twelve weeks. We wanted to wait until we'd had the first scan and I wanted to tell you all face to face rather than over the phone, so this seemed the perfect time.'

'You're a little minx,' her mum scolded. 'You nearly gave your dad a heart attack.'

He stepped forwards, finally taking his turn to hold his daughter. The sense of warmth and love he gave made her cry. She'd been crying a lot more over the last year and not just because of pregnancy hormones. Not quite once a month as Mia had instructed, but she certainly didn't bottle up her feelings or hide them deep down inside her anymore. She felt healthier both physically and emotionally.

'There's one more thing,' Gabriel said, after shaking his father's hand and accepting a hug. Naomi raised her eyebrows in surprise and then pressed her hands to her lips as he knelt down in front of her taking a small box from his pocket. 'Naomi Winters, you are the love of my life. The only woman in the world for me and I would like to spend the rest of my life with you. So, will you do me the honour of becoming my wife?'

'Yes!' She shouted so loudly Hans barked, thinking something terrible had happened. 'Yes, yes, yes! I will. I will.'

Gabriel stood, placing the beautiful diamond solitaire on her finger, and pulling her in for a kiss.

'Look away,' her dad said and she giggled as she and Gabriel separated.

Gabriel pulled her back for one more kiss. 'Now we have to decide where the wedding will be.'

'Well that's easy,' Lyn said, taking Mia's hand. 'The chateau of course.'

Naomi smiled, snuggling into Gabriel. She couldn't think of anywhere better to celebrate the love that had blossomed here and would continue to grow throughout their lives together.

Mia began to hand around glasses of champagne, giving Naomi an orange juice instead, and they raised a toast. 'To Le Petit Chateau and Gabriel and Naomi Mathis!'

Everyone echoed her words and Naomi silently thanked her friend for having persuaded her, almost a year earlier, to come out here. She could never express how much that short time had changed the course of her life, but she would be eternally grateful. She placed a hand on her stomach, telling the little bean growing inside her how lucky it was to be surrounded by such unconditional love. By such an amazing family.

Acknowledgements

This book is dedicated to romance readers everywhere and I'd like to begin by thanking each and every one of you for voraciously reading the utterly brilliant uplifting fiction our genre is known for. Your support for our genre means everything to authors like me and we wouldn't be anywhere without you!

I always pick up a romance by my favourite authors when I'm feeling low and I hope that if you read this book needing a lift, it gave you one. Romance rocks! As do romance readers! And I really do appreciate you spending time with my characters.

Thanks go to the wonderful team at Avon especially my talented editor and loveliest person, Elisha Lundin, and to everyone behind the scenes who worked so hard on this book. I may not be able to name you all, but please know your hard work is appreciated. Thank you for everything.

Thanks also go to my agent Kate Nash of the Kate Nash Literary Agency. She's incredibly supportive and knowledgeable and I can't wait to finally go out for those cocktails!

To my family and friends, thank you for being there whenever I need you. I couldn't do this without you. My particular thanks go to Ali Henderson who I'd only met via email before starting this book but has since become a firm friend I feel blessed to have in my life. Thank you for letting me talk your ear off on various train journeys and for helping me figure things out with your wonderful advice!

If you enjoyed *Christmas at the Chateau*, you'll love the first book in the series, *Summer at the Chateau*.

**A newly single woman.
A handsome stranger.
A chateau that keeps
bringing them together . . .**

The perfect feel-good romantic comedy that will leave you falling head over heels!

Available from all good bookshops now.

Two friends. One wedding.
A love that's long overdue . . .

A Wedding at the Chateau

The new heartwarming romance filled
with second chances, friendship,
and the irresistible magic of Italy.

Available to pre-order now!